Harvest Day

TAMAR SLOAN

HEIDI CATHERINE

SEQUEL HOUSE

CHAPTER
ONE
ECHO

"Get off me!" Echo swats at her face, only to find more tiny creatures swarming toward her. "Get away!"

She searches for Chase in the mass of onlookers behind the net but can't find him. Not that it would make any difference.

Chase can't help her.

Running is futile.

Death is inevitable.

The bees come at her in a shimmering cloud of black and gold and she collapses to the ground, burying her face in her hands. This isn't how she wanted to spend her last moments. She has to be brave.

Pulling herself to her knees, her hands fall away and she looks up at the sky, seeing a glimpse of blue before the swarm envelops her.

She tries to hold still. To accept her fate silently with whatever dignity she has left. But her skin burns as lethal venom is injected into her veins one tiny barb at a time and she lets out a scream.

With her heart pounding, Echo's eyes fly open and she

finds herself lying on her mat in the small home she shares with her father.

Two words pound at her temples.

It's today.

Her nightmares have become more and more vivid as her Confirmation has drawn closer. Maybe now it's finally here, she'll be left in peace.

Or maybe she won't be alive to dream.

She plants her feet on the dirt floor and stands. Pushing down the anxiety bubbling in her gut, she wipes the sweat from her forehead.

Her father is snoring softly and she tiptoes past his bed. The scurge is strong in him now, which means he needs his rest more than she needs to fulfill her promise of waking him. She can say goodbye later.

If everything goes to plan, maybe there'll be no need to say goodbye at all.

Picking up her backpack, Echo slips out the door, careful not to let it creak on its rusted hinges, and breathes in the early morning air. Soon, people will emerge onto the street, kicking up clouds of dust in their haste to get away from the desperation of their falling-down homes, and the air will taste like chalk.

A bird squawks in the distance and she looks up at the enormous net that domes their colony. If the bird is trapped, hopefully it hasn't caused too much damage. Maybe she could just—

No.

She doesn't have time to worry about either hunting a bird or fixing a net right now. Nola is counting on her. She can't possibly let her down. Especially not today.

The bird lets out a strangled cry and falls abruptly silent. Somebody will eat well today. Hopefully it was Chase. He could use a good feed. Actually, there's not a single Vulnerable in the Dead Zone who couldn't. They're all as hungry as they are sick.

She winds her way down the street, looking at the homes as if seeing them for the first time, which is ironic given it may be the last. Cobbled together from scraps of metal and timber, the Vulnerables make the best of whatever they can find. At least underneath the net, their colony is safe. Maybe not from starvation or the scurge, but from a far greater threat.

Turning the corner at the end of the street, Echo makes her first stop, bending to knock on a small door, about half the size of a regular one.

"Nola!" she calls. "It's Echo."

"Quickly!" the old woman calls back. "Check behind you before you come in."

Echo tucks her long dark plait over her shoulder and has a look around.

"Be quick!" Nola calls. "Hurry. Don't let them in."

Echo pushes hard on the door to dislodge the rags that have been jammed in to fill the gaps. It swings open and she crawls through and closes it, putting the rags back just the way Nola likes them.

"You didn't let any in, did you?" Nola's voice is laced with fear. "You weren't followed?"

Echo stands and separates the thick curtain that acts as a second door, entering the dimly lit room.

"It's okay." She spins around so Nola can inspect her from her battered armchair. "I'm alone."

Nola's eyes narrow through the netting she wears wrapped around her head, scanning Echo's compact body until she's satisfied she hasn't brought in any intruders.

"Did you sleep in your chair again?" Echo shakes her head as she moves forward. "You know it's not good for your back."

"Nothing's good for my back," Nola snaps. "Hurts lying down. Hurts sitting up. Hurts when I try to stand. The scurge is growing in me. I can feel it."

Echo leans forward. "Let's get you moving. I don't want you getting any sores."

"Already got plenty of them." Nola unwinds her netting and pulls back her lips to reveal her bleeding gums. "Lost another tooth last night."

"I'm so sorry." Echo puts a gentle hand on Nola's arm and helps her to stand. "I wish there was more I could do."

"You do more than anyone else." Nola leans heavily on Echo as she leads her to her wash bowl. "It's like they think they'll catch the scurge if they come near me. Bunch of scared bears."

Echo nods, knowing it's not the disease that's keeping everyone away, but rather Nola's sharp tongue. Lack of nutrition might be prolific in the Dead Zone but it's not contagious.

"Maybe if you didn't lock yourself up in here all day, people might think to help," Echo points out. "Stay outside when you collect your rations, instead of grabbing them straight off the doorstep."

"Not safe out there," Nola grumbles, pulling her dress over her head without a hint of shame. "They'll kill you. Gotta be quick. Can't let any in."

Trying not to stare at the bruises on her bony shins, Echo reaches into her bag to remove the flask of water she'd collected yesterday. Nola drinks half, then pours the rest into her washbowl while Echo picks up her bedpan and concentrates on not breathing through her nose. She opens a large hatch on the back wall and tips the contents into the gutter, being careful not to displace the cloth that's shielding the opening. She can feel Nola's keen eyes keeping guard, just in case she slips up.

This is a routine they've performed dozens of times.

"Nola," Echo says cautiously as she secures the hatch and places the pan back in its spot. "You know what today is, don't you?"

The old woman ignores her question, concentrating on rubbing herself with her washcloth instead.

"I might not be able to visit you again," says Echo, needing her to understand, just in case things don't go to plan. "It's my birthday. Seventeen. I just made it in. Are you listening to me?"

Nola flings her wash rag into the bowl and pulls on her dress, regardless of the dampness of her skin.

"It's today," Echo says gently. "I have to go to the B—"

"Betadome," snaps Nola, replacing her netting as she avoids Echo's gaze. "I know, I know. It's your Confirmation. I have the scurge, not dementia. I went there myself when I was your age."

"So, you realize there's a chance I might not be able to come back?" Echo blinks, unable to imagine Nola as anyone other than the old recluse she is now. "This could be my last visit."

Nola holds up three shaking fingers. "There are three possible outcomes for you today. One, you're proven to be a Vulnerable and returned here for a life destined for the scurge." She folds down one finger. "Two, you're an Immune and get to eat oranges for breakfast and roast pumpkin for dinner for the rest of your days." She folds down another finger until only her middle one remains upright. Slowly, she turns her hand so it becomes a rude gesture. "Three, the bastards kill you and you don't live at all."

Echo isn't sure if this bluntness makes her want to laugh or cry. At least she can be sure Nola understands.

"I want you to promise me something." Echo reaches for the old woman's hands. "If I don't come back, I want you to get out of that chair every day, okay? Chase has promised to check on you, but I want you to go outside. You can't spend all your time in here."

Nola squeezes her hands with surprising strength, an unusual softness seeping into her eyes. "Echo. If you don't come back, I die. You know that. I know that. Let's not pretend. You're the only one here who has any heart."

"Chase has heart." Echo blinks back a tear.

"Not if you don't return, he won't." Nola lets go of her and limps to her chair. "Anyway, what are you worried about? Almost everyone is a Vulnerable these days. What makes you think you're so special that you're an Immune?"

Echo shrugs, hoping this is true. "I suppose you're right. Besides, I have a plan."

Nola's eyes widen. "You know how to pass the test?"

Echo shakes her head slowly. "I know how not to pass."

"No, Echo!" Nola's voice is far louder and firmer than Echo's ever heard it. "No! If you have a chance to get out of this hellhole, you have to take it. Do you understand me? Don't you go staying here for me, or your dad, or some boy who's stolen your heart. This is your one chance. Don't mess it up."

Echo's pulse thuds. "My life is here."

"And my life used to be there," Nola spits out. "Trust me. Nobody would choose to be here when they could be there."

This revelation is a slap of shame across Echo's face. She should've known this about Nola. It's hard enough to imagine her as a young girl, let alone one who'd grown up in a life of protected privilege in the Green Zone.

"You didn't tell me," Echo whispers.

Nola waves a hand dismissively. "You never asked."

This is just another reason she can't leave. There's so much more she has to do. So much more she needs to find out.

"Go now. I'm tired. Leave me." Nola closes her eyes. "If you do whatever it is you're planning, you're a fool. I hope never to see you again."

"I'll see you tomorrow," Echo replies, her voice as empty as her name.

She crawls through the small door, doing her best to replace the rags as she closes it, unable to fight the feeling she's sealing her old friend in a tomb.

As she stands, a hand clamps over her eyes and her heart thumps as she tries to pry the fingers away. Then a familiar laugh tickles her ear and her panic turns to a feeling she can't define, but relentlessly teases her whenever Chase is near.

"It's only me," he says, releasing his hold on her. "Sorry if I scared you."

"You didn't," she lies, wanting to step away from him so she can see his face but also wanting to stay this close.

He's the one who takes a step back. He always is.

"Did you bring it for me?" she asks, dropping her voice to a whisper. "You know I need it today."

"First things first." He plucks a daisy from behind his ear and holds it out. She hadn't even noticed it underneath his blond curls. "Happy birthday."

"Where did you get this?" Echo takes the daisy and glances at the net above them, glad it's protecting her from any curious bees. She twirls the stem in her fingertips as she admires the delicate petals. She's never held a real flower before. And yet, her heart thuds, programmed to fear it. Flowers mean bees. Bees mean death. "You didn't go back there, did you?"

He looks to the ground. "I was fast."

"It's too dangerous, Chase. Don't go there," she pleads. "You know you're not an Immune."

"But you might be," he says, his voice laced with unwelcome hope.

She shakes her head, concerned he changed his mind about

what he'd promised to bring her for her birthday. "You have it, don't you? Tell me you brought it."

"I did." He pats his shirt pocket. "But listen, Echo, I'm not sure this whole idea of yours is a good plan. I want you to pass. Even if it means..."

She shakes her head, knowing exactly what passing her Confirmation will mean. That the kiss she's yearned for all her life will never happen. She can't be with Chase if her future is in the Green Zone. She may as well have a future on Planet Mars.

"You'd have a better life over there," he continues, sounding far more like Nola than she'd like. "I want that for you, even if I can't have it for myself."

Chase failed his Confirmation only a year before in spectacular form. He's lucky to be standing here. In the Dead Zone. But most definitely alive.

"Almost everyone is a Vulnerable," she says, repeating Nola's earlier words. "There's nothing special about me. But I need to be sure. That's why I need the pollen."

Chase groans as if she'd punched him. "Echo, there's plenty special about you. Who else do you see helping those with the scurge?" He spreads out his arms, indicating the empty streets.

"I see you," she says. "And if something goes wrong and I don't make it back, you have to keep your promise. Nola doesn't have long. It's not right for her to die alone."

"I'll help Nola," he says, taking the backpack she uses when taking supplies to anyone in need. "But nobody else."

"And my dad," she adds. "You have to help my dad."

He wraps an arm around her and that indescribable feeling punches her in the gut again. "Of course, I'll help your dad."

She leans in to rest her cheek on his chest. "I won't pass, Chase. I'm not an Immune. I can't be."

"But you might be." He closes her in a hug. "Why don't you just give it a shot? You don't need to cheat."

She sighs, feeling like every moment of her life has led up to exactly this one. How can she possibly choose a better life for herself over being able to improve the lives of everyone else? Living here is hard for Nola because she's a Green Born. She's seen what it's like on the other side. It's not like that for Echo. She can't possibly miss what she's never had.

"I have to be certain I don't pass, Chase," she says firmly. "And when they throw me out that black door, I want you to scoop me up in your arms and kiss me. I belong here. With you."

He shakes his head, disappointment etched into his dark eyes, and reaches into his pocket. She doesn't mind that she's letting him down. She has the rest of her life to make it up to him. When he sees how happy she's going to make him, he'll forgive her.

"Of course, I'll kiss you," he says, handing her a small package wrapped in cloth, and forcing a smile to his beautiful face.

"Promise?" She doesn't need him to smile. She needs him to mean it.

"Echo." He smooths back her hair, then trails his thumb down her cheek. "I promise."

For one crazy moment, she thinks he's going to kiss her then and there, but, of course, he doesn't. And he won't. Not until their Immunity is a match. It's both incredibly frustrating and ridiculously noble all at once. If it were up to her, she'd have kissed him when she was five.

"I have to go," she says reluctantly. "Dad wants to see me before I leave."

Chase nods. "I still wish you weren't coming back."

"I'm coming back." She pats her pocket in the same way he had earlier. "We know that for certain now."

"Go see your dad." He takes the daisy from her hand and tucks it behind her ear.

"You'll wait for me at the black door?" she asks, needing to be sure. It's the only thing that's going to give her the courage to enter that dome of death. Especially now. "I dreamed you weren't there. I couldn't find you in the crowd."

"You know I'll be there." He lopes off down the street with her bag on his back, leaving her shoulders light and heart heavy.

She's never wanted to fail a test more in her life. It's just a shame it's coming at such a difficult price.

The walk home feels longer than the one here, the contents of her pocket seeming to weigh more than the contents of her bag. She wishes she didn't have to cheat. She's always prided herself on her honesty. It's one of the things Chase says he likes about her most. But surely, he wouldn't have helped her if he didn't understand why this is so important?

She finds her father waiting for her on their doorstep looking paler than he did when she'd left him. She was too young to remember when her mom died but imagines it happened just like this, with the symptoms slowly creeping in before ending up like Nola. The fatigue. The bruises. The bleeding gums. The sores. The slow erosion of life. It's been difficult to watch her father following Nola down that painful road.

This only reaffirms her decision. No matter how desperate things are here, it's her life. This is her colony. These are her people.

Her father smiles, reaching out to stroke the flower behind her ear. He doesn't need to ask who gave it to her.

"You didn't wake me," he says.

"I'm here now." She takes his hand like she used to as a girl, noticing the bruises have crept down his arm to poke out the bottom of his sleeve.

"I have something for you." He opens his other hand to reveal a thin gold chain with a locket. "It's not worth much, but it was your mom's. I've been waiting until today to give it to you."

"But, Dad." She lets go of his hand. "You could have sold this. You should still sell this. It's too much."

He shakes his head. "Happy birthday, sweetheart."

Echo turns around as he fastens the chain around her neck, and she reaches for the locket. "Is there a photo in it?"

"Don't open it," he says. "What's inside is useless here. Wait until you get to the Green Zone. Open it there."

Guilt slams her in the chest as she wishes she could save him this pain and just tell him the truth. "I'm not going to the Green Zone, Dad."

He points to the sky and she turns, knowing what he's looking at.

The Sting—a giant tower with a glittering silver spike that soars toward the clouds. It's the centerpiece of the Green Zone. A symbol of pride to all the people who live there and a source of envy to all who don't.

"I want you to live there, Echo," her father says. "What's inside that locket will bring you luck. I want you to have a better life than this."

"What is it with everyone today?" Tears threaten at the back of her eyes, but she pushes them down with a smile. "First Nola, then Chase, and now you. You're all wishing me away."

"We love you," he says. "We just want what's best for you."

"This is best for me." She points at their home. "I'm happy, Dad. I don't need anything more than what I already have."

11

"That's not true." The tears that she refuses to shed spill down his cheeks instead. "I want you to have good food. Healthy children. Hope..."

"I have hope," she insists. "I hope not to be an Immune."

She tucks the locket into her shirt, glad she's taking matters into her own hands to ensure she fails her Confirmation. This conversation with her father would be so much more difficult if she thought it were the last one they might have.

"Come and watch," she says. "You'll see. I'll be exiting by the black door. I know it."

Her father shakes his head. "Chase will tell me what happened."

"Hey!" She plants her hands on her hips. "I'll come right back here and tell you myself."

He points once more to the giant Sting. "That's your future, Echo. I can feel it."

She throws her arms around his frail frame, giving him a fierce hug as the low sound of a siren wafts through the air, causing them both to flinch.

The Betadome is ready.

Echo's Confirmation has arrived.

It's time to get this over so she can move on with the rest of her life.

CHAPTER
TWO
RIVER

"What do you think you'll miss the most?"

River glances at his twin sister as they step into the elevator, trying not to scowl. "We decided we weren't going to ask those sorts of questions."

Flora shrugs, her gaze not quite meeting his. She tucks a short strand of dark hair behind her ear, only for it to spring straight back out again. "You're the one who decided that."

"I thought you agreed," he says, moving a little closer. "It's better this way."

She sighs. "Well, I thought so at the time, too."

River remains where he is in the center of the glass elevator. The metal doors slide closed, cutting off the hexagonal corridor they just walked down. Their rooms are down that corridor, rounded domes that have cocooned them the entirety of their seventeen years.

Flora must be worried she'll never see it again. That's why she's talking like this.

She shuffles a little. "I didn't realize this would be scarier than the Hive Stories."

His lips thin. The stories passed down from generation to generation of giant bees imprisoning humans in some fantastical giant hive used to scare him, too. But then he grew up and recognized them for what they were—tales told in hushed voices and darkened rooms to keep children on their best behavior.

He's about to press the button that will take them ten floors down when he pauses, unsure how to comfort her. Those had been nothing but stories.

This is very real.

"Both our parents are Immune," he says, keeping his voice strong. "Their parents were Immune." She knows they come from a long line of genes that will protect them. "It'll be fine."

Her green eyes, identical to his and so much like the verdant zone they live in, stare up at him, uncertainty shimmering through them. She goes to say something but must change her mind, because her lips clamp shut in a tight line.

River engulfs her in a hug, pulling her familiar form against his. "It'll be fine," he says again, this time more firmly.

"River," she sighs. "Just because you say it, doesn't mean it will come true."

He tugs a short lock of her hair. "Never underestimate the force of one person's will."

She squeezes his waist. "I love you, just remember that."

Despite the sweet words, River frowns. Flora is acting like the outcome has already been decided. He reaches out and presses the button that will take them to the ground floor. The only way she's going to find out her fears are unfounded is by getting this over and done with.

As if fate itself heard his thoughts, the second siren floats through the elevator. The first had them leaving their rooms. It's the same sound that will be echoing through every floor of the tower, the entirety of the Green Zone, and reaching the lifeless air of the Dead Zone itself.

It's time.

No, he thinks resolutely. It begins.

The glass bubble silently slips down the side of the Sting, and they progressively slide into the vista of the Green Zone. They both fall silent as they descend, the view familiar, but never losing its breathtaking punch to the gut.

"Viridescent," Flora murmurs, and River's heard the word enough times that he mouths it along with her.

It's her favorite term to describe the stunning greenscape they grew up surrounded by. Tall trees, lush with leaves and fruit, shade the understory below—shrubs and bushes and vines and herbs and grasses. Endless shades of green tumble over each other, competing for light and glory. Curved walkways dissect them, passing rounded houses and oval ponds of water. People serenely mill between it all, nodding and smiling at anyone they pass, their hands clasped close to their stomachs.

That will be Flora and River in a few hours.

Experiencing it themselves for the first time.

He almost reaches out and presses his hand on the glass like he has so many times before. He and his sister have spent the entirety of their seventeen years within the walls of the Sting, just like every other Green Born. Protected and cared for until their Immunity is confirmed, along with all teens in their seventeenth year.

The elevator comes to a smooth stop just as the siren ends, leaving them in silence that suddenly feels so much louder. The doors behind them whoosh open and River confidently steps out, bringing his sister with him.

The sirens will sound six times. By the sixth, they must be

standing at the green door of the Betadome, ready for their Confirmation.

Across the foyer, another set of elevator doors open, Cascade, Leif and Willow stepping out. Their gazes connect with River and Flora, flicker, then quickly slide away. Everyone's nervous.

Everyone knows their future is about to be decided.

The three teens they've shared classrooms and mealtimes and countless smiles with hurry to the single sliding door that will lead to the large glass doors beyond. They'll have to wait in the contained airlock that ensures bees can't slip through.

The very beings they honor. That their wonderful society depends on.

The deadly insects that kill with one sting...if you're unfortunate enough to be a Vulnerable.

"Be in peace," they murmur almost simultaneously as they pass.

"Be in peace," River and Flora murmur back.

River's about to follow them when Flora grabs his arm, stopping him. "I've been looking at the data."

"You spend too much time in the LaB," he chides. When he first suggested she have a look around, he hadn't expected it to be the place where she'd go more and more, rather than reading and learning about the history of their world, like they're supposed to. It probably hasn't helped this anxiety he's sensing.

Flora's only acknowledgement is a slight twitching of her brows. "The numbers of Immunes are falling each year."

River clenches his teeth. The trend is well known. And although Immunity has a genetic link, his sister is smart. Strong. An asset to the Green Zone. Of course, she's going to be Immune. "The odds are in our favor."

"Twenty-three teens will be entering the Betadome today,"

Flora says, an urgency creeping into her voice. "I've done the math. Following the trends of past years, two will be Immune. There will be even fewer out of the seven Dead Borns who'll be there."

Of course, there won't be any Dead Borns who pass. There hasn't been for years.

"Did you take into account the Year of Plenty?" asks River. "We had twenty Immunes pass that year."

Flora shakes her head. "That was an anomaly. An outlier. Those numbers don't get included."

"If it happened once, it could happen again," River says resolutely.

And if there will be only two, then it will be him and his sister. He refuses to lose his twin and best friend.

Another elevator arrives in the large hexagonal foyer, and River and Flora still when they see who exits.

Their father's footsteps falter when he registers his only children standing on the opposite side of the foyer. But he quickly recovers, crossing the smooth tiles patterned like honeycomb. His gray hair, once dark like theirs, is loose over his shoulders, his beard closely cropped. His sharp eyes assess them as he stops a few feet away, tucking his hands over his stomach. "Your suits fit well."

River glances down at the white, close-fitting outfits they're both wearing, their hoods resting on their backs. It will protect them when they exit the Sting for the duration of the journey to the Betadome. And removed just before they enter the great hive that is the foundation of everything they have.

River pulls back his shoulders. "And very soon, we won't need them."

His father grunts. "Of course, you won't."

Because they'll be Immune. Free to walk in the Green Zone, bees as harmless as flies.

River almost elbows Flora in an I-told-you-so gesture, but all he does is nod. Their father likes to see emotion as much as he likes to express it.

"Be in peace," he intones, his farewell nothing more than the standard words everyone in the Green Zone uses as he turns and exits the Sting.

"Be in peace," River returns.

Flora doesn't respond, and River realizes she didn't speak the whole time their father was here, as brief as it was.

She tilts her head, studying the door he just passed through. "Do you think the great Oren would miss us?"

"Of course, he would," River says automatically, although even he can hear the lack of conviction in his voice. "Not that he'll get the opportunity to."

"He didn't miss Mom," Flora says flatly.

He winces. Their father has always been aloof. But when their mom died five years ago, he built a fortress around himself as impenetrable as the Sting itself. "We don't know that. Everyone deals with grief differently."

Flora had cried for weeks, the tears still bursting out spontaneously for months afterward.

River had grown up overnight. He became the keeper of tears, the bringer of rare smiles, the reason for tomorrow.

And their father had retreated into the LaB.

In fact, it was River who encouraged Flora to join their father there after he saw the fracture in their relationship growing.

"He's not grieving," Flora spits bitterly.

Before River can ask what she means, the second siren sounds, longer than the first. They both tense, conscious time is counting down.

Pulling his hood over his head and indicating for Flora to

do the same, he draws in a deep breath. "Come on. We can talk about this after our Confirmation."

They walk through the first, smaller door then stand still as it closes behind them. Only once it's shut and the scan reveals they're the only ones in the airlock, do the much larger opaque glass doors slide open.

Progressively revealing the glory of the Green Zone.

From a distance, it's always been awe-inspiring. Humbling. Almost overwhelming in its beauty.

But when they take a single step outside, beyond the boundary they've never passed before, it's far more than that.

It's not just a magnificent sight that has River blinking rapidly, trying to assimilate it. The air is greener, heavy with the scent of foliage and blossom. There's the rustle of leaves in the breeze and the happy song of birds.

And there's the hum of bees.

River's never heard anything so fascinating and terrifying. His heart feels like a hummingbird in a panic, and an eagle soaring so high it makes his head spin.

One lands on his sleeve, making him freeze. Its wings flutter as its abdomen pumps, functioning as lungs. The stinger at the tip is obvious, larger on the superbees than it was ever on their ancestors. And far more deadly.

The bee lifts back into the air, flying off to perform its essential work—pollination. The tiny, dangerous insect is the foundation of the beauty they're now standing in. It's deeply humbling.

"Viridescent," Flora breathes, and this time River says it along with her.

She looks up, a brilliant smile lighting up her impish features. "I knew it would be beautiful, but..."

"I know," he beams back. "And this is about to become our home."

Flora will continue to work in the LaB. River will find a role somewhere in the gardens, just like he always dreamed. They could even start looking for a mate among their fellow Immunes. Someone to pledge themselves to.

His words must be a slap of ice water because Flora's dazzling smile falls away.

He's about to reassure her that everything will be fine when his throat constricts. He frowns as he draws in a breath, finding his lungs are tighter than he expected. Is he more emotional about this than he thought? But that would imply he's worried...

A pod slides to a stop to their right, the door rising as it waits for them to climb in. Flora tightens her hand around his. "Come on, let's go."

They've just taken a step when the fourth siren sounds and they instinctively move a little quicker. Flora climbs in first and River follows, sliding into the molded seat beside her. Like all the other pods whizzing around the Green Zone, the cream bubble can take four people comfortably. River marvels at the interior—as smooth as glass and the color of a cream eggshell, it curves around them like a cocoon. What's more, it becomes easier to breathe again.

River sits back, ignoring the small screen in the console that's announcing it's the day of their Confirmation, instead staring with wonder at the view beyond the window. He turns to his sister, expecting her to whisper *viridescent* all over again, only to find her staring at the clasped fingers in her lap.

He reaches over and covers them with his own. "Flora?"

But rather than look up at him, she looks out her own window and River sees what has her attention.

Ahead, the Betadome rises like a silvery apparition. A netted hive of monumental proportions. The breeding center of the fascinating insects they can't live without.

On the other side is the Dead Zone, an area that's been little more than a haze on the horizon all his life. But now, it slowly comes into focus.

And it's as lifeless and barren as he's been told.

River shudders at the thought of what life must be like there. It's a dusty, desolate cemetery. He wonders if Vulnerables ever pray for the admittedly painful, but quick death of a sting as opposed to the slow wasting away of the scurge.

The Betadome grows the closer they get, and River sees the crowd of white-suited teens already there. For the first time, he finally acknowledges what they're up against.

Only a few will be found Immune, although surely more than Flora's conservative calculations of two.

Some may even die.

The fifth siren sounds as the pod comes to a stop and the door opens automatically, waiting for them to exit. To discover the truth that has been dormant deep in their DNA.

River's throat tightens again, and he swallows. Hard.

Flora turns to him, tugging on his hand with urgency. "You need to be prepared, River. If this doesn't turn out the way you're determined it will—"

"It will," he snaps, the tightness in his throat propelling the words out harsher than he intended, but also wanting to convey this conversation is over.

He steps out of the pod, once more straightening his shoulders as he tugs Flora to his side.

He refuses to consider any other outcome.

CHAPTER

THREE

ECHO

E cho stands outside the giant netted hexagon known as the Betadome, reminding herself of the insurance she's carrying in her pocket. If in the unlikely scenario the bees aren't interested in her, she has a plan. She'll make sure she's classed as a Vulnerable, ejected back to the Dead Zone, and left to live out her days amongst the people she loves.

Then why is she so scared?

"Listen to the bees," says Avid, a boy who grew up only a few streets away from Echo. "Do they sound louder today? I'm sure they're louder."

"They're definitely louder," says Jupiter, who is neither a boy nor a girl, preferring to live very comfortably just as a person.

Echo has never been especially close to any of these people. But with only seven Dead Borns entering the Betadome this year, she's suddenly hyper aware of each of them, including the group of four huddled behind her. While they'll all enter via the same black door, the odds are that none of them will get to leave via the exit that's painted green. Those who are lucky will come straight back here. The unlucky ones will be carried out in a bag.

Echo exhales, accepting this is reason enough to be afraid.

"They're not louder," says Harsha, flicking her long blonde hair behind her shoulders as she breaks from the other three and steps forward. "They just sound like that because they're humming for us."

"Bees buzz," says Avid, pacing like a caged beast. "They don't hum."

"It sounds a little like a hum to me." Jupiter shoots Harsha a kind smile. "What do you think, Echo?"

Echo isn't sure she cares what the noise is called but knows Jupiter is trying to draw her out of herself. She steadies her shaking hands and tilts her head to listen. The sound comes in waves as the bees swarm from hives that hang from the tree branches, traveling through the wide spaces in the netting on the Green Zone's side of the Betadome and back again.

"It's what I imagine the ocean sounds like," she says, remembering her father once told her that oceans are supposed to make you feel calm. Perhaps if she holds onto that thought, it might help her now.

Before Jupiter can respond, the final siren floats through the air, causing them all to jump. Trailing her eyes up the net to where it connects with the much larger one that covers the entire Dead Zone, Echo braces herself to step outside its protection for the first time in her life. There are smaller holes on this side. Too small to allow even the tiniest bee to squeeze through. But once she steps into the Betadome, there'll be nothing but fresh air separating her from the deadly creatures that have taken over a planet once ruled by man.

How ironic that it was humans who created them. A solution that became just as deadly as the one they were originally trying to solve.

"Echo?" Jupiter touches her shoulder and she realizes they must have asked her something.

"Sorry." She pulls up a smile that has no hope of reaching her eyes. "What did you say?"

"I asked if you're okay?" Jupiter's hand falls away.

"I'm not who you need to worry about." Echo points to Avid whose pacing has come to an abrupt halt.

"Was that the final siren?" His voice is more highly strung than the net itself. He's going to attract a lot of attention with that kind of energy zinging through his veins. Perhaps Echo should try to stay near him.

"Stay calm," says Jupiter, fixing their attention on him.

"Calm?" Avid's voice rises another octave. "One sting and we're dead if we can't get the adrenacure in time. You know they always give it to the Green Borns first."

Echo shuffles her feet, unable to deny this is true. She's witnessed far too many people die behind these netted walls and almost all of them were from her colony. Getting stung isn't nearly as big a danger as not getting the adrenacure in time, and there are only so many vials that can be administered at once. The Green Zone denies it, but, of course, they favor their colony over the skinny street rats who never had the hope of a future in the first place.

It's no wonder her father couldn't bear to come and watch.

She scans the crowd for Chase, failing to find him even though he must be here somewhere. He promised. And he's never broken a promise to her. There's no reason why he'd start today. She pushes away thoughts of her dream, telling herself it means nothing.

Spectators are pressed up against the net, all keen to see how this plays out. It's without doubt, the most exciting day of the year. There's a crowd on the Green Zone's side as well, although the mood is different over there. Their children actually have something to lose, which means they treat this day with a little less excitement and a lot more dread.

The Betadome sits between the zones like a deceptively peaceful paradise. Originally set up as a safe place for the bees to breed, trees dot the hexagonal space, their branches hanging low from the weight of both their fruit and the hives. Echo can smell the sweet scent of honey in the air as the worker bees forage for pollen to keep their colony alive. It's hard to believe that soon this dome will be filled with frenzied movements, screams and the rattling throes of death.

"Maybe you'll be an Immune," Jupiter tells Avid. "Maybe the bees will pay you no attention."

"None of us are Immune," Harsha says on a groan. "We haven't had an Immune from the Dead Zone in ye—"

The black door swings open and thick smoke billows out.

Echo glances at the six anxious faces around her.

"Good luck, everyone," she whispers, a fine sheen of sweat breaking out on her forehead.

"I'm not doing it." Avid takes a step back. "I'm not going in."

"You have to." Echo fights to keep her voice steady. "We all have to."

He shakes his head. "We don't have to. They can't make us."

"True." Harsha rolls her eyes. "As long as you're okay with your food rations being cut off and starving to death. Then you totally don't have t—"

"He knows the penalty." Echo loops her hand through the crook of Avid's arm. Jupiter takes his other arm and they urge him toward the door. Somehow, together, they all feel safer and he allows himself to be led.

"Hold your breath," Jupiter warns as they step into the smoke.

Echo coughs, letting go of Avid to rub at her eyes. The other four join them, Harsha scowling as the door slides closed behind her and the smoke dissipates.

"It looks different on this side," says Echo, noticing how much larger the hexagonal space seems without the net obstructing her vision. The trees look greener. The fruit hanging from them brighter. The beehives more textured.

She blinks, trying to adjust to all the color. It's one thing to have seen this place from a distance, but to be surrounded by actual leaves and flowers is a whole new experience. After growing up in a world defined by shades of gray, it's like mother nature has tipped a rainbow over their heads. The scent of honey has intensified, and the noise of the bees no longer sounds like gentle waves, but a hurricane in her ears.

"It *feels* different," says Avid, seeming far calmer than he had a few moments ago. It's almost like the smoke designed to calm the bees and keep them from escaping had somehow settled him down as well.

Plucking an apple from the tree beside her and taking a large bite, Echo closes her eyes, wanting to block out the sensory overload so she can enjoy this moment. She's never had an apple all to herself, and she's unlikely ever to experience it again.

Her mouth waters with the sweetness and in four bites, the apple is gone. She tosses the scant remains of the core onto the fertile ground, noticing how the dark grains of soil stay put rather than blowing away in the wind like the fine gray dust that coats every surface of the Dead Zone. Taking another apple from the tree, she tucks it into her pocket to give to her dad later.

Turning to look at the black door, Echo longs to walk through it despite the temptations this strange new world has to offer. That door is like an oasis in a desert to her thirsty eyes.

It's her only option. She has to make sure that whatever happens next leads her there. What's the point in having food in your belly if your heart is empty?

A movement beside the door gets her attention and she sees Chase pressed up against the netting. He hasn't let her down, just like she knew he wouldn't. She pats her shirt pocket, her way of telling him that soon they'll be together. The rest of their life is about to begin. She's more certain than ever that the black door won't just lead her to the life she's chosen for herself, it's the only life she wants.

A bee flies past, and Echo instinctively ducks, even though being stung early in proceedings is exactly what she wants. The medics are standing by with their vials of adrenacure. If she's smart, she can get this whole thing over in minutes.

"Watch out!" cries Avid, snapping back into the tense ball of energy he'd been only moments before.

Echo's heart pumps so hard she can almost hear it over the hum of the bees. Harsha was right. It's definitely a hum. A relentless one that makes her want to cover her ears and crouch into a small ball like she used to as a girl to block out the whimpering sounds her mother made in the middle of the night.

The bee flies on and Echo follows it.

"Echo!" Avid shrieks. "Where are you going?"

"Leave her," says Jupiter, perhaps understanding better than anyone that sometimes it's important to walk your own path in life.

The bee weaves its way around the trees, Echo trailing behind as soft grass tickles her ankles, and her fingertips brush the surprisingly rough bark of the trunks. The unfamiliar sensations set her on edge, reminding her that while she may only be on the other side of a net, she's a million miles from home.

Trying not to lose sight of the bee, she debates how she can get it to sting her without alerting its hundreds of siblings and causing them to swarm. Usually, the people who walk out of the Betadome are the ones who are stung once, maybe twice. Too many stings, and no amount of adrenacure in the world is going to help.

Unless she's an Immune, of course. Then, she'll feel nothing more than a pinch.

No purple rash will spread across her body.

No swelling. No itching. No closing of her airway.

But there's no way that will happen. She's a Vulnerable, not an Immune. Her home is through the black door.

The bee takes a sharp turn and Echo quickens her pace, slamming directly into the firm chest of a tall guy with the greenest eyes she's ever seen.

"Sorry," he murmurs, even though she was the one to crash into him.

"You're one of them," she blurts out. She's never met anyone from the Green Zone before. Do they all have eyes the color of their name?

He goes to say something but turns his head and lets out a stifled sneeze.

"Sorry," he says again.

"You're very polite." She tilts her head, wondering if his eyes are simply reflecting the color of all the foliage that surrounds them. "Are you okay?"

"I'm fine," he says, pointing to the trees. "There must be some dust in the trees, that's all."

Echo knows that now isn't the time to find anything amusing but this is quite funny. The guy's a Green Born and the trees are making him sneeze.

She breaks into a smile and he returns it, although there's

puzzlement in his expression as if he's not quite sure what they're smiling at.

"River!" calls a girl with the same green eyes. Except instead of confusion, hers are filled with fear.

There's a bee crawling up her arm and another circling her head.

"Flora!" He rushes to her side, trying to swipe away the bees, only seeming to make them angrier.

Echo glances aside, knowing what's about to happen. This is just like her dream.

Looking back at Chase, she takes the pouch out of her pocket, letting him know she's not prepared to take any chances.

He has both hands pressed against the net and they lock eyes for short moments that feel impossibly long.

I'm sorry, he mouths.

She shakes her head, not understanding what he's talking about. He has nothing to be sorry for. He's here, standing by the black door like she'd asked him to. He kept his promise to her. Just like always.

Squatting down behind a tree so nobody can see, she unwraps the pouch and holds it in her shaking hands to study the contents.

Pollen. Her secret weapon. The key to her future. The precious substance that bees find impossible to resist.

Her brow furrows to see the contents are brown. For some reason, she'd expected it to be yellow. If she didn't know any better, she'd think this was nothing more than dirt.

She quickly rubs the pollen on her arms, coating them in her guarantee to get back to Chase.

Standing, she moves away from the tree and nods at him, only for him to mouth the words again.

I'm sorry.

She looks at her brown-stained arms and icy realization slides down her spine.

The pollen looks like dirt because it is dirt. He's sorry because instead of working with her to build a future together, he's stubbornly put her first.

"How could you?" she whispers, unable to tear her eyes from the guy who betrayed her. "How?"

A new determination roils in her gut. A determination to do whatever she has to do to leave through the black door, so that instead of kissing Chase, she can make him face up to what he's done. Why didn't he just refuse her request to get her some pollen? She thought he had more guts than that. Is it possible he doesn't love her in the way she loves him?

She turns away and marches back to the green-eyed candidates who are most certainly twins. The girl twin has two bees circling her now, the boy twin continuing to swipe at them. Echo's seen this happen from the other side of the net a hundred times. This scenario only ever has one possible outcome. But this boy is acting as if he can change something that's already set in stone.

"There's nothing you can do," she tells him. "It's her they want."

"Get back," he yells at Echo, waving his hands at her now instead. "You're making it worse. Get back!"

Echo remains with her feet planted, hoping to attract a stray bee in the frenzy. Hoping Chase sees her get bitten and realizes she's a Vulnerable. Hoping he regrets not trying to help her, as the result would have been the same whether she was coated in pollen or not.

A high-pitched scream has her spinning on her heel and she sees Avid running through the Betadome with his arms waving as a thick swarm follows him. He stumbles over a large tree root and falls to the ground. Rolling around, he crushes dozens of bees into the grass and Echo's stomach fills with dread.

There aren't many rules in the Betadome, but this will be frowned upon by the medics. These bees are the only thing keeping this planet alive. The Green Zone worships these tiny creatures. Echo already knows there's no way anyone will administer the adrenacure in time to save someone who purposefully killed so many of them.

She runs closer to Avid, her heart breaking all over again. He hadn't wanted to come in here and she'd practically forced him, thinking a bee sting would be a better way to go than starving to death. Or maybe death wouldn't come at all. But now she's not so sure. The way he's howling in pain seems far worse than any of the other options.

"It's okay," she tells him, scanning the Betadome for a medic. "I'll get you help."

The bees are covering him in a moving blanket of black and gold. Undoubtedly, it's already too late.

"Medic!" she shouts. "Over here! We need a medic!"

But either nobody hears her, or nobody wants to, as there's not a medic to be found.

Avid thrashes on the ground, his face swelling, his hands turning purple as the bees sting him again.

And again.

Over and over.

If she gets too close and the bees turn on her, there won't be anyone to help her either. Why hadn't she made sure she got stung earlier? If she hadn't been so caught up trying to find Chase in the crowd, this would all be over by now and she'd be on her way back home to her dad.

"I can't breathe," Avid gasps. "Please help me."

Echo is torn. To go closer to him is certain death. To turn her back is to go against who she is as a person. It would make her no better than the Vulnerables who refuse to care for those sick with the scurge. She'd rather die than be like that.

With four quick steps, she's by Avid's side. She crouches, wanting to take his hand, but it's covered with too many bees. They're crawling up his arms, his neck, his face. His eyes are squeezed closed, his breath coming in ragged gasps. Each time he parts his lips to draw in more air, bees crawl into his mouth.

"I'm here," she tells him. "I'm right here. I'm not going to leave you."

She brushes Avid's face, trying to clear the bees from his eyes, and one stings her on the thumb. She winces, accepting that soon she'll be lying right next to Avid on the ground.

"Medic," he says, the word barely audible.

Echo looks around. She sees a medic beside Jupiter giving them a shot. Another two are helping Green Zone candidates. The girl twin is still attracting the bees' attention but doesn't seem to have been stung just yet. Her brother continues to do his best to lure the bees away. And continues to fail just as miserably.

"The medics are coming," Echo says, hating that the last words Avid will hear are a lie. But the gift of hope seems like the only thing she can give him right now.

He doesn't respond.

The bees lift off Avid in one synchronized movement. No adrenacure can help him now.

He's gone.

She braces herself, searching for Chase's dark eyes in the crowd. As soon as this swarm catches the scent of her Vulnerable pheromones, they'll turn on her. She might be furious with Chase, but right now, in her last moments, he feels like he's all she's got. She loved him at first sight when she was a small girl, but it seems she can't turn her feelings off with the same sudden switch.

She pulls herself into a stand, wanting to run to Chase. To press her hands against the net and feel close to him one last time.

But she can't. He betrayed her and she's too hurt. Too stubborn. Too annoyingly proud.

He smiles at her, which only confuses her more because it's a smile she hasn't seen on his face before—equal parts happy and sad.

Then she sees what he must have noticed.

The bees that had lifted from Avid are flying back to their hive. And the sting on her thumb barely even hurts.

"Come back!" she calls to the traitorous insects, willing them to return. Except, they continue to treat her like she's invisible.

Like she's...an Immune.

"No!" she cries. This can't be. It's a mistake. It has to be!

She runs toward the green-eyed twins, determined to make this right.

The bees just need more time to sense her.

She's not giving up.

Not now.

Not ever.

The Dead Zone is her home.

CHAPTER
FOUR

RIVER

T he two bees buzzing around Flora's head quickly become three. Then four. River's conscious there are other people moving around the Betadome, including the girl with the surprisingly beautiful features who ran into him, but he ignores all of them.

All that matters is Flora.

"River," she whispers. "It's happening."

Like hell it is.

A fifth bee appears, landing on Flora's neck. She stiffens, her eyes bulging and her face going pale. Without thinking, River brushes it away. He's spent all his life learning about these amazing insects. How essential they are. How the people of the Green Zone honor and celebrate their very existence.

But right now, all he can think of is how dangerous they are. That by ensuring their survival, humans inadvertently made them deadly.

Their venom is highly toxic.

They can sting multiple times.

That some poor soul from the Dead Zone just died.

The bee buzzes away, only to curve around and return. It's then that River's panicked brain remembers what else has been drummed into him since childhood. The reason everyone in the Green Zone prizes calmness. Smooth, steady movements. Peace and quiet.

Superbees are highly aggressive.

It shoots toward Flora like a bullet, the buzzing around them seeming to amplify. Uncaring of the consequences, River jams his hand between the bee and Flora's soft skin. There's a prick on the back of his hand and his heart lurches.

"River!" Flora gasps. "You shouldn't have done that!"

He shakes his hand. "I'm as Immune as you are," he says determinedly.

The sting grows to a mild burn. The wheezing that he's been trying to hide since entering the Betadome increases.

But there's no instant rash. No explosive swelling. His airway remains open.

He grabs Flora's hand. "We need to move."

Obviously there's something about this location that's drawing bees to them.

She shakes her head as she lets him drag her along. "River, it's not—"

She gasps and he spins around, his pulse jackknifing through his veins as they both freeze. He hears the hum. Feels the very air vibrate.

But he still refuses to believe what he sees.

It's no longer four or five bees they have to face. Not even ten or twenty. A swarm is coming for them, like a black, ominous cloud.

Before River can move, a girl—the beautiful, dark-haired girl from before—leaps between them and the approaching menace. She waves her arms wildly. "I'm here, you little bastards. Take me!"

"What are you doing?" River gasps.

But the girl ignores him, arms waving as if she's calling the bees to her. River releases his sister's hand and strides over, trying to subdue her movements. "Stop! You'll only agitate them further."

Like any animal primed for aggression, bees are triggered by anything they perceive as a threat. Loud noises and sharp movements are a beacon to them. It triggers the kill or be killed programming now a part of their DNA. They're already on high alert after the sirens that had marked the start of the Confirmation.

But the girl is faster than he expected, easily slipping out of his repeated attempts to grasp her. And each time, she shouts louder. Jumps higher.

"Come and get me!"

"It's me you want!"

"I'm over here!"

The bees descend, the mass of menacing buzzing growing louder. Terror like he's never known before grips River. Bees are the foundation of life.

But they're also the harbingers of death.

And the girl beside him is doing everything she can to rain that annihilation down on her.

The swarm shoots straight for them. Too frozen with fear to move, all River can do is raise his arms to protect his face. The girl opens her arms up like she's basking in sunlight after a life in the dark.

The hum intensifies, the darkness multiplies.

And then divides around them as if they just cleaved the swarm in two.

The bees come together again behind River and the girl, never losing momentum. They have a target. And it's not them.

Flora stumbles a few steps back as the deadly mass closes

around her. She cries out once. Twice. Her arms flail at being caught in a web of death.

And then she drops, her only sound garbled, gasping breaths.

River rushes to her, uncaring of the bees still peppering her. He swats them away, all his learning of peace and calm gone in the face of his sister's desperate fight for life. Her face is already swelling, her skin starting to take on the color of a bruise.

"Medic!" he screams. "Medic!"

The white suited woman is there before he can draw in more air to shout again. She kneels beside Flora, jamming a fat, white tube into her leg. The jolt triggers the thick needle inside and Flora winces as it pierces her thigh.

Rapidly injecting adrenacure into her muscles.

She grips her leg at the pain, curling into herself as she lets out a sob. River sits back on his haunches, relieved. Crying means she can breathe. His sister won't be dying today.

"Get them away from me!" comes a screech.

River looks up to see another Vulnerable engulfed in bees. The savage insects are in a rage now. There are multiple threats within their haven. Their pheromones are everywhere.

And they intend on exterminating it.

The Vulnerable collapses, his entire body writhing as he tries to flick and twist and swat the bees away. "Medic," he croaks.

The medic that just attended to Flora rushes over, only to see Cascade now falling beneath a cloud of furious buzzing. Then Leif.

There's no way the medic will be able to get to them all in time. The bee's venom works too quickly.

She takes a sharp right and reaches Cascade, quickly injecting her with adrenacure. The Vulnerable is next, but as she reaches him, the hands that were scrabbling at her medical belt come up empty.

She's out of adrenacure.

Her shoulders sag as she watches the last twitching movements of the Vulnerable. River tears his gaze away from the grizzly scene, only to discover it's being replicated in every sector of the Betadome.

Vulnerables and Immunes are falling alike. Equal in this one moment in time as death circles, looking for another victim.

The medics are doing what they can. But they can only get to people so fast. And there's only so much adrenacure.

River turns back to his twin, struggling to breathe through his constricted chest. He was so sure today would be the beginning of the rest of their lives. A future that he's looked forward to with everything he has. But at least his sister is alive. That's a positive he can cling to.

Flora sits up, face still puffy, the red mark of a sting on her neck. She's one of the lucky ones. She survived.

The spark that flickered to life, the one that almost felt like hope, is quickly snuffed out.

Except she's not an Immune.

"Flora," he chokes.

She looks up at him, green eyes pools of apology. "I'm so sorry, River."

"It'll be fine," he says. "We'll figure something out."

She shakes her head, indicating for him to help her up. "There's nothing to figure out. You're going to have to accept—"

"No," he snaps as they both come to their feet. "This isn't how it was supposed to go."

Before Flora can answer, a voice rings through the Betadome, somehow soft and calm, yet still carrying the power of authority.

Their father's voice.

"The Confirmation is complete," he intones.

A siren sounds, a muted howl that's also crying through River's soul. Its piercing sound is unmistakable. As real as the moments unfolding before him.

He's an Immune. Flora's not.

They're about to be torn apart. Forever.

There are hushed cheers from the side of the Green Zone. Subdued shuffles from the Dead Zone. And a sluggish, listless thud in River's devastated chest.

His father glances at the medics. "Please escort the confirmed Vulnerables to the black door."

The medics do as they're told because they're no longer medics. They're now guards. No one's tried to defy the Green Zone leader's decree in many years by making a desperate dash for the green door, but they need to make sure.

The Green Zone must be protected at all costs. It's the last bastion of human survival.

The medic that had tended to Flora less than ten minutes ago appears by her side, indicating for Flora to move. Her features are barely visible within the mesh of her suit, leaving River to wonder how this Immune feels. She just saved Flora's life.

And is now signing her death sentence.

Flora turns to River and throws her arms around him. "It's okay," she whispers beside his ear. "This is the way it's supposed to be."

His heart and soul simultaneously scream one word.

No!

He holds his sister tightly. Tighter than he ever has. Tighter than every time she cried because of their father's emotionally distant ways. Tighter than the time she reacted to the medication given to her for a cut on her foot and ended up in the infirmary. Tighter than the day they found out their mother was dead.

River holds her as if he's never letting go.

The medic-guard clears her throat. "It's time to leave."

"Go away," growls River. "Get away from us."

Flora goes to pull back, but he bands his arms around her like steel. "River," she whispers, her voice breaking.

He's never questioned the rules of the Green Zone. He understands why they're so vital. Which means he needs to let her go.

But...he can't.

Then hands are pushing between them, trying to pry them apart. River doesn't move, doesn't loosen his hold. His entire body is frozen in shock and denial. Four words are on a loop in his head.

This can't be happening.

The hands start to tug with earnest, digging deeper in between them, pulling harder. Then Flora releases River and lets them do this.

Allows them to draw her away.

He scrabbles, trying to get a hold of her again, but she's too fast. She's spent her life evading his teasing and tickling. She knows the right angle to twist, how to duck his desperate clutches.

"No!" He means to shout the word. To scream out the anguish that's billowing in him like a black balloon. But it comes out as a tormented whisper. A useless denial against the forces of nature.

Flora is a Vulnerable.

The guard quickly herds her to join the others and they form a line, trudging toward the black door. River watches, a painful fracture rupturing through his heart. Flora's his twin. They've been inseparable since birth. He's watching his future being torn to shreds until there's nothing left.

The black door opens, and the teens walk through. All Vulnerables now. All destined to live a life with the slow death of the scurge or a swift death thanks to a rogue bee hanging over their heads.

And Flora's one of them.

She glances over her shoulder as she passes through, her dark hair and pixie face framed by the drab colors of the Dead Zone. He'll never hear her say 'viridescent' ever again. A tear glistens on her cheek. She raises a hand, pressing her fingers to her lips.

Then she's gone.

The hum of the bees fills River's ears, becoming white noise in his stunned mind. His whole body has gone numb.

His father moves to the center of the Betadome and lifts his arms. "Two Immunes are joining us this year."

The muted cheers barely puncture River's detached daze. The people of the Green Zone may be celebrating, but he wishes this day never happened.

Then his father's words register.

Two Immunes?

River blinks. He always imagined it would be two, maybe even more, like the Year of Plenty. He and Flora would raise their arms in victory. They'd be smiling so hard it hurt.

But Flora's prediction was right. Only two teens will be walking through the green door today. And it's not who he thought it would be.

Turning, he discovers someone coming to stand beside him. The girl.

She looks as shell-shocked as he feels.

But he doubts her world has been forever altered. That the

future she imagined for herself has been cruelly snatched away. Coming to the Green Zone would be a dream come true for someone like her, a Dead Born.

River straightens, wondering how he's going to get through what's coming next. Especially with her by his side.

The one who agitated the bees surrounding Flora.

The one who stole her place in the Green Zone.

CHAPTER
FIVE
ECHO

Leaving the Betadome is even more frightening than entering it. Back then, Echo had a plan. A path forward. A whole future mapped out. And now...

She has nothing.

She clutches at the locket her father gave her, willing her feet to move toward the green door when all she wants to do is run home.

Nobody's ever refused to accept their place in the Green Zone. Sure, there have been a few Dead Born Immunes who've hesitated, looking at the black door with expressions filled with guilt, but each and every one of them has turned their back on it.

"Come on," says the boy twin beside her. *River*, his sister had called him. "It's time to leave."

"Go ahead," she says. "I'm not coming."

He blinks at her with those incredibly green eyes. "What do you mean? This isn't a choice. You're an Immune."

She shakes her head. "I'm going home."

"The Green Zone is your home now." These words seem to

have a bad taste on his tongue. "I thought you'd be grateful. Everyone wants to be an Immune."

He breaks into a series of sneezes and Echo looks toward Chase, who's still standing with his hands pressed dangerously against the net, watching her with that same happy-sad smile. This whole thing is his fault. If he'd given her the pollen like she'd asked him to, she wouldn't be having this pointless conversation right now.

She tears her eyes away.

"I see." River nods in Chase's direction as he recovers from his sneezing fit. "You don't want to leave your brother."

She doesn't correct him about their relationship.

"Well, thanks to you, I have to leave my sister, so let's get moving." He takes her by the arm, urging her toward the door, but stopping short of forcing her. It reminds her of the way she'd led Avid into the Betadome. Which ultimately had led him to his death. It feels very much like that will be the same outcome here if she allows herself to go.

"I'm not coming." She plants her feet on the soft grass. "My father needs me. He's sick."

"Well, if you don't come, your rations will be cut," River tells her, seeming to lose his patience. "It'll be just like you refused to attend your Confirmation. Then your sick father will have to share his rations with you. Is that what you want?"

Her mouth gapes. She can't possibly let that happen. Her father needs every morsel of food he can get. And she'd rather eat dirt than take anything from Chase after what he did to her. It seems whatever path she walks from this point, she's doomed.

"We have to go," River says. "The Immunes are expected to leave together. Trust me, I'd rather it wasn't you coming with me, either."

If what River's told her is true, she really doesn't have any other choice. It's no wonder she's never seen an Immune walk out through the black door.

The green door swings open. This time, there's no smoke to walk through. The bees are welcome to come and go as they please between the Betadome and the Green Zone.

Just like Echo is now.

She looks down at the pin prick of a bee sting on her thumb, hardly daring to believe this is true.

River pulls gently on her arm. "Come on."

She shakes off his grip and takes two steps away, delaying the inevitable. "Just give me a minute."

River throws out his hands.

"I'm coming with you." She holds up a finger. "I just need one minute."

Running to Chase, she reaches the net and presses her palms against his, the thick wire separating them. But they're connected all the same. She needs an answer. She can't go through that green door until she understands why he betrayed her.

"I'm not really sorry," he says, his eyes shining so brightly his grief almost looks like excitement. "I'm glad you're an Immune."

Her hands withdraw like the net has been electrified. "You lied to me. You don't want a future with me."

"No, Echo!" He clutches at the net, the holes in it too small for him to get his fingertips through. "I do want that. But what future do we have here? Now you've got a chance. A real chance. This is a good thing."

She swallows, unsure how she feels about that. All those times he'd snuck through the net to steal food from the Green Zone, she'd thought he was a guy who knew how to take risks. She'd thought he had a plan to even the score between the factions.

"I can help you," she says, needing to find some good in this situation. "From the inside."

Chase nods as if welcoming her to an answer he'd worked out long ago. It seems he does have a plan. And perhaps her becoming an Immune had a whole lot more to do with it than she'd realized. Is that why he didn't help her?

"Look after my father," she says, stepping back from the net. "And Nola. And the others. *Please.* Can I trust you to do that?"

He narrows his eyes as his hands fall to his sides. "You don't trust me?"

"You lied to me, Chase." She steps back again, seeing River's sister stumbling through the crowd of Vulnerables.

"You can trust me," he says, putting a hand over his heart.

"And look after her." Echo points to Flora, feeling a kinship with the girl who woke up in one colony only to find herself having to lie down to sleep on the other side of the net tonight. "She's going to need a friend."

Chase turns to see who she's pointing at and Echo takes that moment to leave. So many more words need to be spoken, yet it feels like all of them have already been said.

She runs back to River, who's still waiting for her.

"That was more than a minute," he tells her.

"I asked him to look after your sister," she says.

River makes a strangled noise at the mention of his sister as he leads her to the green door.

The leader of the Green Zone is waiting for them at the door.

Oren.

Echo's heard of him before, of course. Everyone has. She's seen him at previous Confirmations. But this is her first time seeing him up close. The whites of his eyes and teeth are a brilliant white to match the color of his clothes. His complexion is clear, his hair shiny, and his fingernails strong and clean. No doubt, all this perfection is the result of good nutrition.

"Be in peace," he says as they walk past him.

Neither River nor Echo reply. Echo because she isn't sure if she's meant to. And River because he's very clearly seething. Or is he grieving? It's hard to tell.

"Be in peace," Oren says, a little louder.

"Are you kidding me?" River's voice is soft despite the anger simmering beneath his words. "Your daughter just got sent to the Dead Zone and you're wishing me peace?"

Echo draws in a sudden breath. River is Oren's son? And his own daughter hadn't made it through. Maybe River has a right to be mad. His father should be devastated.

"Be in peace," Oren repeats more firmly.

River scowls. "Be in peace."

Satisfied, Oren turns his gaze to Echo, sweeping his eyes up and down her with an inscrutable expression.

"Be in peace," Echo says, deciding if she's going to find a way back to the Dead Zone, she'd be wise not to make trouble.

Oren nods his approval. "I like a fast learner. Welcome home."

Echo blanches. This will never be her home.

River steps toward the crowd of Immunes who are all smiling, a sea of white in their tight-fitting trousers, and figure-hugging shirts. Echo shakes her head as she follows him, wondering if something happened to her hearing in the Beta-dome. She can see the crowd clapping, their hands springing together and apart in front of their chests, but they're not making a single sound.

"Why can't I hear anything?" she asks, catching up to River.

"There's nothing to hear." He looks at her, confused. "We like to be quiet in the Green Zone. It relaxes the bees. You'd be wise to learn how to keep your voice down. You probably don't realize but it's quite...high pitched."

Echo's eyes widen. This guy is even worse than Chase! First, he blames her for his sister being Vulnerable, and now he's accusing her of screaming when all she'd done was ask a perfectly reasonable question. Next, he'll probably tell her she needs to take a bath.

Oren holds up a hand and the already quiet crowd falls silent.

"We have two Immunes Confirmed this year," he says. "Thank you for making them welcome. First, we have my son, River, who you already know."

The crowd launches into their silent clapping, genuine smiles plastered on their perfect faces.

"And..." Oren leans toward River and drops his voice to a hush. "What's her name?"

River shrugs and Echo rolls her eyes. "My name's Echo."

"And Echo. Our first Dead Born Immune for over five years. Welcome to the Green Zone, Echo."

The crowd silently cheers for her and she stands there stunned as she looks beyond the people to take in her new surroundings.

The sky looks so clear without the barrier of a net shielding it that she has to hold up a hand to shade her eyes. Beneath the expanse of blue is nothing but green, stretching far out to the horizon. There are dark green trees, light green shrubs and a thousand shades between. She wonders if these people have words for all these kinds of greens? Back home—her real home —they only have one word for this rarely seen color. But here it's in abundance. She can see fields with rows of plants growing food just like Chase had described. Birds soar overhead and she watches as they head to the Sting and circle the giant spike-like structure before flying off again.

"Let us feast!" says Oren, his voice rolling like a gentle wave across his people.

He nods at a trim, middle-aged woman with a sharply cut blonde bob, who rushes forward holding a white suit in her arms.

"For you to wear to the feast," she says to Echo, flashing her perfectly white teeth as she smiles. Her voice sounds like it's dripping with the honey from the Betadome. "I'll take you to get changed."

"She might need a bath first," says River, looking at her dirt-stained arms.

"I knew you were going to say that," Echo snaps, marching away to follow the woman, deciding she'd be happy to go anywhere as long as it gets her away from River. Hopefully, once this feast is over she can have nothing more to do with him.

"My name's Daphne," the woman says, as a white egg-shaped object slides up beside them.

Echo jumps. "What the—"

"It's a pod," says Daphne. "It's how we move around. Don't you have these where you're from?"

Echo shakes her head, wondering how much the two colonies actually know about each other. She'd never heard of this strange mode of transport before.

A door on the pod rises up with a gentle hiss and Daphne motions for Echo to climb in.

"Is it safe?" she asks.

Daphne laughs. It sounds more like a fairy tinkling some bells than an actual sound a human might make.

Echo climbs into the pod, relieved when Daphne gets in beside her. Somehow, it feels less dangerous if she's prepared to get into this contraption herself.

"The Confirmation has now concluded," says Daphne.

Echo is about to say she'd already worked this out when Daphne's voice continues. Except her mouth isn't moving...

"What's going on?" Echo sits bolt upright and Daphne laughs again, pointing to a small screen in front of them.

There's an image of Daphne, smiling out from the screen as she explains the feast is about to begin.

"I make all the announcements for our colony," says the real Daphne. "I'm afraid you'll have to get used to hearing my voice around here."

"Oh." Echo nods, not having seen a television screen before but having heard of their existence. She hadn't realized how realistic the image would be. It's like having a teeny-tiny Daphne traveling in the pod with them.

"Be in peace," the smaller Daphne says before the screen goes blank.

"Be in peace," Echo mumbles back.

The door slides closed and the pod takes off, the movement pressing Echo against the back of her molded seat. She sits in stunned silence as the pod zooms them toward the Sting faster than Echo's ever moved before. The trees become a blur of green, and a sick feeling builds in her stomach. Surely, walking would be a far healthier way for these ridiculously healthy people to live?

In what seems like an impossibly short space of time, they arrive at the Sting and the pod's door slides open. Echo can't climb out fast enough, not sure she ever wants to get back in one of those things.

Daphne is beside her, almost like she'd floated out of the pod, urging her toward the entrance. When looking at the tower from the Dead Zone it looks like it's made out of one smooth silver surface. But this close up, she can see it's covered in millions of shiny, hexagonal-shaped panels of glass, soaring up toward the clouds.

Pausing at the doorway, Echo isn't sure she trusts a structure this tall to remain standing above her head. But then again, if it comes crashing down, at least this very white and green nightmare will be over.

She follows Daphne through a door that somehow knows to slide open the moment they draw near. They pass through an airlock, then walk into an open area and Echo looks up at a series of balconies on the six sides of the hexagon, stretching up as far as she can see. Aren't these people worried they might fall?

Daphne takes her arm and leads her past a trolley of glass water bottles and down a short passageway to a door.

"You'll find everything you need in the bathroom." She hands Echo the suit and puts a gentle hand on her back, pushing her forward. "Once you're ready, follow this passageway right to the end where you'll find a set of glass doors."

Echo nods, glad to be left alone. For a moment there, she'd thought Daphne was going to insist on helping her dress.

Pushing open the door, she wonders about the word *bathroom*. A whole room for a bath seems a ridiculously luxurious concept. Back home, they sponge themselves down with bowls of water using cloths that are almost as dirty before the wash as after. Absolutely nobody has a bath, purely because the idea of carrying that much water would require far more effort than it's worth. Who carries the water here? Is that why they're so keen to welcome her? Perhaps she's destined to become nothing more than a slave.

The room she finds herself in is even whiter than the suits of the Immunes. The glare of light bouncing off the hexagonal tiles and polished glass surfaces is blinding. There's not even a bath, which is strange. There is a strange chair-shaped thing, but it doesn't look very comfortable to sit on as there's a large hole in the seat.

Echo sets her clean suit down on a low bench next to a plush folded towel, wondering where the bowl of water might be. How on earth is she meant to get clean with nothing to dip her towel into? Daphne had said everything she'd need would be in here.

Going to the back wall and stepping behind a glass panel, she takes hold of a silver handle and pulls on it, thinking it might open a drawer. Maybe the washbowl is in there?

She startles as water pours from some holes in the ceiling like warm summer rain, completely drenching her. If it didn't feel so good, she'd jump right out, but it fills her with bliss and she tilts back her head to drink in the liquid. Brown whirlpools swirl at her feet as years of filth runs down the drain, and she concedes that perhaps River might have had a point.

Spotting a jar filled with a thick, pink gel on a shelf, she pours some into her hands and sniffs at it. It smells so good that her tongue darts out and she licks it, but it tastes even worse than her dad's cabbage broth.

Wanting to get as clean as she possibly can, she strips off her soaked clothes, and rubs the gel on her body, noticing how it cleans her skin, leaving it feeling soft and fresh. No wonder everyone here smells so good. This rain machine is incredible! How many buckets must it take to fill it up?

After a while, her fingertips start to pucker and she fiddles with the silver handle and the rain stops. Reaching for the towel, she pats herself dry then wraps it around her hair to soak up the drips. She slips into the clothes Daphne had left for her, marveling at how soft the fabric feels on her skin, then combs out her hair with a white brush that's been left on the counter.

There's a large mirror and she stands in front of it, barely recognizing herself. Nobody has mirrors in the Dead Zone, not wanting to see the evidence of the hard lives they live. But here, she can see why someone might want to admire themselves.

Because the girl standing before her is not the Echo she knows. This girl has a mane of dark silky hair, clean skin and clothes the color of freshly fallen snow. She looks just like the people who'd silently welcomed her to her new home. If it weren't for the locket, just visible from the neckline of her shirt, she'd wonder if this was a trick and she was looking at someone else.

How had Nola adjusted to life in the Dead Zone after being raised in a place that makes rain fall from the ceiling? And how is Flora possibly going to cope?

Deciding that she can't think about these things now, Echo kicks her old clothes into a corner of the rain machine. It feels disloyal to leave this part of her behind and the apple she'd picked for her father rolls out of her pocket and across the floor as if it agrees.

"I'm so sorry, Dad." She scoops up the apple and takes a bite. It's not as sweet as the one she'd eaten in the Betadome and she can't tell if that's because it isn't, or if it's because she wishes she wasn't the one eating it.

She slips on the set of soft-soled shoes Daphne had given her, finishes the apple, and leaves the bathroom, following the passageway until she finds the set of glass doors.

Taking a deep breath, and running her hand down her damp hair, she steps forward, not surprised this time when the doors sense her and slide obediently apart. She walks through another airlock and finds herself outdoors in a place so foreign she's not sure where to look first.

The doors have opened onto a large hexagonal-shaped atrium—a room that's both indoors as well as out. There are trees in large pots and garden beds bursting with fruits and flowers. Overhead, a grapevine twines its way through an arbor, the fruit hanging down in tempting bunches of purple and green. Tables have been set out in long lines and decorated with vases filled with more flowers and platters loaded with food of so many shapes and colors that she can't identify what most of it is. Some are so full that their contents are spilling out onto the white tablecloths. Trolleys with glass water bottles have been placed around the room. Clearly, these people like to keep well hydrated.

Bees buzz from the flowers to the food and the people gathered don't seem at all bothered by them. Echo reminds herself that she doesn't need to be, either. These tiny creatures are responsible for pollinating all the food she sees before her. And they're not in the slightest bit interested in her. She can't even see the mark on her thumb anymore.

"Echo," says Oren, appearing beside her. "We've been waiting for you."

She nods, wondering if she should have hurried.

He leads her toward a platform at the front of the atrium. As she passes the tables, people get to their feet and clap silently to welcome her. River is standing at a small table on the platform with an empty chair beside him. He's wearing a crown fashioned from vine leaves and seems to have stood under the rain himself, as he looks far neater than he had when she'd last seen him. His dark hair has been brushed back and his green eyes are even more piercing. If she didn't dislike him, she'd possibly describe him as handsome. As she climbs the steps of the platform and gets closer to him, she notices against her will that he smells as good as he looks. The gel he'd used in the rain machine seems to have been made from earthy wood scents rather than flowers and it's annoyingly masculine.

He indicates the empty chair and she stands behind it as Oren places a matching crown on her head. It doesn't sit comfortably and as her hand flutters to it, she realizes that's because it's hexagonal. Is everything in the Green Zone this shape? There are a whole other bunch of shapes they could try out, such as a circle for something that goes around your head. For people who seem so smart, they sure have a lot to learn.

"They're waiting for you to sit," says River, placing a hand on the back of her chair. "And don't worry. After today, nobody's going to pay you this much attention."

She sits on the soft white pillow on the chair, sinking into it. River takes his seat, then the rest of the room does the same.

A large screen at the front of the room lights up with Daphne's face. It seems she wasn't joking when she said Echo would need to get used to hearing her voice around here.

"The Confirmation feast will now begin," Daphne announces. "Be in peace."

Oren goes to the front of the stage and clears his throat. "Welcome, as we gather to celebrate our two new Immunes. The earth has continued to look after us and provide Immunity in abundance."

Echo frowns. Two immunes out of the number of teens who went into the Betadome doesn't exactly seem abundant to her.

"Please, let's take a moment," Oren continues. "To show our gratitude for the hardworking creatures who've made all of this possible."

Everyone in the room bows their heads at once and Echo finds herself doing the same. She knew the Green Zone thought highly of the bees, but this is a whole new level. They're worshiping them like some kind of higher species.

Seeming to decide that enough gratitude has been shown, Oren leaves the platform. The people begin to fill their plates, talking softly to each other as they patiently wait their turn. If this much food was put in a roomful of Vulnerables, there'd be a riot in a matter of seconds. This is possibly the most spectacular and depressing celebration she's ever seen.

River points to Echo's empty plate.

"After you," he says with a frown. "I'm not hungry."

Echo looks at the platters laid out in front of her. On this one table is more food than she's possibly seen in her life. There's no way that everyone here will be able to make even a dent in this extravagance. She has no idea where to start.

"What happens to the leftovers?" she asks, reaching for a strange purple fruit that's been cut in half with tiny seeds peppering its yellow insides.

River shrugs like it's of no importance. "Those who couldn't be here today will eat it. What's left after that will be put toward the Dead Zone rations. The scraps will be used as compost."

"But..." Echo can hardly believe what she's hearing. It's no wonder her colony is starving if they're surviving on leftovers, only one place in the pecking order up from compost.

"You have to eat something," River says, pouring water into both their glasses. "At least take something so it looks like you're eating."

"But..." Echo puts some food on her plate. "This is an outrage!"

"Shh." He glares at her, his green eyes flaring. "I told you to learn to keep your voice down."

"We're starving in the Dead Zone," she says, not bothering to lower her voice. "People are dying of the scurge because the little food we get isn't enough to keep us healthy. Surely, there's a fairer way to distribute all of this?"

"It's the way it's always been," he says.

"And it's the way it's going to be for your precious sister," she snaps. "Don't you care about that?"

River drops his fork and it clatters to his empty plate. Every head in the room turns to look at him.

"Sorry!" He smiles, trying to soothe them. "Just a little accident. Won't happen again."

"Right now, Flora is probably eating a tiny potato for dinner," says Echo. "If she's lucky."

"I know." River's voice fills with anguish. "You don't think it hurts me to know that? Why do you think I can't eat?"

Echo stabs a cube of bright pink fleshy fruit with large black pips and shoves it in her mouth, chewing loudly as she glares at River, doing her best not to feel sorry for him. As much as she's having a very bad day, it's clear that he is, too. Saying goodbye to his twin couldn't be easy.

"You should eat," she says with her mouth still full. "We eat to live, not to enjoy ourselves. You starving yourself is making a mockery of Flora's future."

She shoves another piece of fruit in her mouth, this time noticing the intense sweetness. Taking a spoon, she attacks the yellow flesh of the purple fruit she'd put on her plate earlier and scoops it out. Wincing at the tartness, she crunches down on the seeds, already feeling the nutrients being sucked up by her body to feed her depleted cells.

"Flora's future would have been just fine if you hadn't interfered," he mumbles into the slice of orange he's picked up.

Echo rolls her eyes as she reaches for a piece of bread coated in a sticky red substance. If he wants to blame her for his sister being a Vulnerable, then that's his problem. She had nothing to do with those bees making a claim on Flora. Thankfully, after this feast, River said nobody would pay her any attention. Which she's going to make certain includes him.

Oren returns to the platform and stands in front of their table. "Are you enjoying your meal?"

Echo nods as she chews on the bread, unable to believe anything in life could taste so good. She reaches for her glass and takes a sip of water to clear her mouth. It tastes strange with so many new flavors still dancing around on her taste buds.

"Excellent," says Oren. "I hope my son has been telling you all about what you can expect in your new life here?"

"Oh, he's been extremely helpful," she says, feeling this is in no way a lie. He's already taught her a lot about the Green Zone, whether he intended to or not.

"Excellent." Oren rubs his hands together. "He'll make a wonderful mentor."

"A what?" Echo's heart thuds. She's not familiar with that word, but if it means what she thinks it does, then that's never going to happen.

River goes to protest, but Oren holds up his hand. "Green Born Immunes always mentor the Dead Borns. My son has probably just forgotten as it's been so long since we had an Immune from your colony."

"Surely, we can find someone else," says River. "Someone better suited to the job."

"You're suited just fine," says Oren. "You'll do a great job."

"I don't need a mentor." Echo doesn't like this idea any more than River clearly does. "Like you said earlier, I'm a fast learner."

Oren waves his hands as if to wipe away her words. "It will be my son's pleasure to help you orientate. Won't it, River?"

River crosses his arms and nods.

"Be in peace," says Oren, smiling.

"Be in peace," River reluctantly replies.

Echo pokes another piece of bread into her mouth and licks the stickiness from her lips. Be in peace, her ass!

Chase may have lied to her, but he was right about everything else he ever told her. It's not right for such a divide to exist between colonies.

She's been sent here for a reason. And now she knows what it is.

She's going to orientate, just like Oren suggested.

Then she's going to blow this colony sky high.

CHAPTER
SIX
RIVER

River's hands are hot fists beneath the table as his father turns to the people of the Green Zone and slowly raises his arms.

Silence ripples through them as they instantly subdue. Oren has something to say.

River focuses on his breathing as his throat constricts even further, not sure he's ready for what's coming next. The pain of today has stolen so much from him. Annihilated so many things he took for granted. The free flow of air in and out of his lungs.

Having Flora by his side.

Happiness in his future.

The girl—Echo—shifts beside him. "What now?" she mutters under her breath.

Daphne's voice floats across the room like a gentle breeze as her face flickers back onto the large screen at the front of the atrium. "It's now time for the Choosing. Our new Immunes will learn the important role they will play in our colony. Be in peace."

"I already know what my role is," Echo says even more quietly, as the screen goes blank.

River doesn't know what that means, but he's too focused on adjusting to his new world. A world without air or Flora or a tomorrow to look forward to.

His father takes a step forward. "Humankind has already stood on the brink of extinction," he begins. Somehow, his father's always had the ability to keep his voice low and controlled, and yet convey great conviction. It has the people here sitting a little straighter, several of them nodding. "We progressively killed a single species, despite the dire warnings. Ecosystems collapsed. Then economies. Wars came next as countries fought for diminishing resources."

Although he's heard these words many times before, River bows his head. This is the legacy they now all live with.

His father gazes out toward the horizon. "The world inevitably became a Dead Zone." He glances back at his people. All sitting within an oasis surrounded by a sea of death. "Until we discovered a few could survive the superbees." He scans the people of the colony, his eyes stopping on Echo. "Immunity is a privilege. And with privilege comes responsibility."

People nod more vigorously, a few even having to curb themselves before they foolishly move too fast.

"We are the future of humanity."

The weight of responsibility settles on River's shoulders and he finds himself shifting in his chair. The Immunes are the chosen few. The only ones who can keep humankind alive. It was his father's same calm conviction that had him believing he was one of them. Looking forward to carrying that mantle.

But he was so sure Flora was, too.

And somehow, this Echo girl is instead.

His world was built on shifting grains of sand, every one of them consisting of nothing but assumptions and blind hope.

How does he carry such responsibility on a foundation like that?

"And to ensure the survival of our people for all the tomorrows to come, we must work," continues his father. "Give. Sacrifice."

"Did he just say sacrifice?" gasps Echo.

River's spine stiffens. He's lost his twin. While she's gained everything.

His father turns as someone enters the atrium, carrying a platter, its contents covered in a white cloth. "We all have a role to play."

River stands, indicating for Echo to do the same. Grudgingly, suspicion stamped on her face, she joins him. He recognizes the person carrying the platter and his stomach clenches.

Clover smiles at him despite her red-rimmed eyes. Cascade, her younger sister, was in the Betadome.

She walked through the black door with Flora. Now a Vulnerable.

Essentially dead to them.

Clover stops beside his father, lifting the platter. He removes the white cloth with a smooth, almost silent motion, revealing what's beneath. River senses Echo still, although he doubts she's really unwound during the entirety of the feast. It's clear she doesn't trust the people who have shared so generously with her.

Focusing on the carved piece of wood on the platter, River pushes away the thought he's expected to mentor such a prickly, ungrateful girl. Not when he has no intention of doing it.

"Your future awaits," his father says, almost a note of warmth in his voice.

River glances at him, stilling when he sees his father's

looking at Echo. His brow is smooth, his mouth almost soft. As if he likes her...

A hot, burning sensation pools in River's gut, corroding his stomach from the inside out. He accepted long ago his father would never look at him like that. But Flora never stopped hoping. Trying to please him.

And now Oren's gifting that to a Dead Born.

Clover steps toward River, the platter trembling a little. A strand of her shoulder-length blonde hair has stuck to her cheek. Probably because she's been crying. Clover's always felt things intensely. But her lips tip up in a tremulous smile. She glances down at what she's proffered him.

His future.

The carved timber sitting on the platter is shaped like a large piece of honeycomb, twelve hexagonal cells in three rows. Within each is a rolled piece of paper, looking like twelve cream pupae. Each one waiting to emerge. To be unfurled, revealing the holder's role in the Green Zone.

Each role within each cell is one currently needed by the colony. Allocated to the Immune by the forces of fate.

River always thought he was ready for this.

Now, he's not so sure.

The platter rises an inch and Clover's thumb subtly, almost imperceptibly, brushes the cell in the bottom right corner. His breath stills.

He and Clover grew up together. A year older and Immune, she's the one who told him what the world beyond the Sting looks like. Lush. Beautiful. Abundant. She knows how much he wants to be out there, working the gardens. Helping the Green Zone flourish.

Is she giving him a hint where that role is?

Could something finally go right today?

He reaches in, pinching the edge of the paper and pulling it out. Quickly unrolling it, he scans the words that will be printed there.

But there's only one.

Eden.

His gaze shoots to Clover. "Eden?" he breathes.

Yes, it's a garden. The garden of tomorrow, in fact. But it's within the Sting, located several floors up. It houses the plants that man's wars and destruction almost wiped from existence. Endangered species, some thought to have been extinct until a fragile seedling or surprising shrub was found, all given a second chance.

After thousands, probably millions, of species were lost, it's important, valuable work, but it's not the sun-drenched, air alive with humming, green-scented garden he's always dreamed of being a part of.

Clover smiles, a flicker of something warm shifting in her honey-colored eyes. "Congratulations, River."

Did she know? Has she chosen for him to work with her?

Numbly, he passes the note to his father, who reads his fate aloud. "River has been chosen for Eden."

There's a round of silent applause and River steps back, a hollow smile on his face.

Expectant faces return as everyone in the atrium focuses on Echo. She raises her chin and steps toward the platter. Barely glancing at the man-made honeycomb, she pulls out a small scroll of her own and frowns down at it. She passes it to Oren without speaking.

"Learning and Bounty," he reads aloud, and Echo's frown deepens, clearly confused.

River sucks in a sharp breath. *No.* Echo's in the LaB. Where Flora once was.

His father does something River's seen very few times in his life. Especially since his mother died. He smiles.

"Echo has been chosen for the LaB."

There's more silent applause, although a few people glance at each other, no doubt wondering what a Dead Born, with no knowledge of their world, can contribute to the LaB.

"A bountiful Confirmation and now a fortuitous Choosing," his father announces. "Be in peace."

"Be in peace," the room murmurs back.

Daphne's face flickers back onto the screen. "The Choosing is now complete. Please continue to enjoy the fruits of our land as we return to our feast."

The people of the Green Zone talk among themselves, throwing surreptitious glances toward the raised platform as River and Echo take their seats again. Each look seems to compound the weight in his chest.

He pushes to his feet. He needs to get out of here.

His father is just stepping off the platform when he turns to see River now standing. "You're going to give Echo a tour of her new role and room? Excellent idea."

The unmistakable smile on his father's face is a punch to River's gut. He almost tells his father to do it himself if he's so happy to have the girl here. "I'm...ah...tired."

"It won't take long. I'm sure she's exhausted, too. It's been a big day for you both."

A pivotal day. A monumental one. One that leaves River sick with grief.

He nods numbly. "Of course."

He'll show Echo the LaB, find out where her room is, then disappear into his own. He wants today over with.

"Wonderful," his father says warmly. River doesn't think he's ever heard him say that word, let alone use that tone.

As his father walks away, River turns to Echo. "Have you had enough?"

She glances at the plates of food around her, jams another

piece of bread in her mouth and stands. "I have. I'm not used to eating so much all at once. Unlike you."

River spins on his heel and steps off the platform, heading to the door that will take them to the back exit. His resolve to not respond to that statement snaps the moment they exit the atrium.

He spins around and scowls at her. "You could be a bit more grateful."

She narrows her dark eyes at him. "Were you grateful you were chosen for Eden?" she retorts. "Are you grateful that I'm here? Another Immune for your precious colony?"

He jerks back, shocked at her anger just as much as her words. "I'm...dealing with some stuff." She was there. She saw that he lost Flora.

She crosses her arms. "Of course, a Green Born would only see their pain and no one else's."

River pushes his face forward so they're only inches apart. "We do what needs to be done."

"By turning your back on others' suffering?" Echo shoots back.

Yes. They have to.

Just like adrenacure, there's only so much food and water to go around. And if the Immunes were to share everything they have, they risk their own survival.

If that happens, humanity ends.

Plus, they give the Dead Zone food rations. They're not totally heartless. They don't leave them with nothing.

Anger, fueled by everything that's happened today, flushes through River's veins. He shoves his face forward until they're almost nose to nose. "You don't see it, do you?"

Echo's own eyes flare with dark fire. "I've seen what I need to see."

Suddenly, he realizes how close they are. And for some

reason, all River can think of is how Echo looked when she first entered the atrium. Her hair seemed longer somehow, even darker, now that it's clean. Like a curtain of silk, it cascaded over her shoulders and framed her sun-kissed skin and dark eyes. Her body had been encased in the white suits he's been surrounded by all his life, but it hadn't looked like anything he'd seen before. He'd seen the curves the suit hugged. The lean lines.

And then she'd lifted her chin. Met the gazes of the crowd surrounding her, and entered the atrium like she owned it, that same dark fire smoldering in her eyes that he's seeing now.

Echo is strong. A survivor. And a beautiful one.

It's a compelling mix he wishes he hadn't noticed as she blinks back at him.

"River?" comes a tremulous voice.

He spins around to find Clover standing a few feet away. She glances at Echo then back at him. "I can't believe they're gone." Her face crumples and she buries it in her hands, her shoulders shaking.

He strides over, engulfing her in his arms. "I know," he says. "I know."

The pain of today shreds him all over again as Clover collapses against his chest. "I thought Cascade would be here along with Flora. That we'd all be celebrating together," she weeps.

River's eyes close as his own tears sting. Clover understands how he feels. What he's lost. "Me, too."

She pulls back, looking up at him. "At least we'll be together, working in Eden."

The moment during the Choosing when she drew his attention to the corner cell flashes through his mind. "Why did you do that? You know I wanted to work in the gardens."

She stiffens. "They didn't need helpers in the gardens." Her eyes well with tears. "I thought you'd be happy with your allocation."

Her words strangely mirror what Echo just said to him. But for some reason, they don't trigger the same defensiveness. But then again, she's not...unsettling like Echo is.

"Sorry, it's a lot to take in, that's all." He softens his face. "I look forward to helping the colony in any way I can."

A smile melts over Clover's face. "Me, too."

The not-so-subtle clearing of a throat has them turning to Echo. She raises a dark brow. "The LaB?"

"You're giving her a tour?" Clover asks, looking alarmed. "Oh, that's right, you're her mentor."

River clenches his jaw. "Yes." Although once he's shown Echo the LaB, he needs to talk to his father. He can't be expected to spend time with this girl. Not after what it cost him for her to be here. "Although, I'm going to talk to Oren."

He hasn't called him Father or Dad since he was a child.

For some reason, Clover looks relieved. She steps away. "Be in peace," she says, although it seems more of a question than a statement.

River nods. He wonders when he'll feel anything resembling peace again. "Be in peace."

Clover beams at him even though he gave her nothing more than the standard response. "I'm going to help at the feast."

She spins around, her blonde hair flying out, and walks away. A quick glance over her shoulder, and she disappears through the door.

"Come on," says River, heading to the elevator on their left. "The LaB is a few floors up."

"You're going to try and get out of being my mentor, aren't you?"

"Yes," he says, not meaning it to sound so curt. "I don't think I'm the best person for that role," he adds more gently.

"Because you irrationally blame me for your sister being a Vulnerable? Or because your girlfriend won't like it?"

River glares at her, choosing to ignore the first statement. "She's not my girlfriend. Clover and I grew up together. She's more like a sister to me."

Echo follows him as he steps into the elevator. "I'm not sure she got that memo."

Deciding not to respond again, River presses the hexagonal button for the twentieth floor. The elevator silently glides upward as he steps away, trying to create as much space between them as possible.

Echo clutches her stomach with one hand as she presses her other to the white wall. "How do you people get used to moving so fast?"

River glances around, having never considered her question. "It's how we get around."

They come to a stop and she stumbles out the moment the doors open. "Well, a whole lot of stuff you think is normal, really isn't."

Once again not responding as his jaw tightens, River follows her out. The sooner their time together is over, the better.

He stops beside Echo, who's now frozen to the spot, gazing around with wide eyes.

"This is the place of Learning and Bounty," says River, also scanning the space they're now in, trying to see it through Echo's eyes.

The LaB is large, taking up the entire floor of the Sting, although part of it is off limits to those without the proper authority. Brightly lit, almost every surface is platinum white, multiple computer screens blinking with the information that

Flora loved so much. Six glass hexagonal columns are spaced around, reaching from the floor to the ceiling. Most contain plants of various shapes and sizes. Two contain bees. He always thought it looked sterile and cold, but Echo probably hasn't seen technology like this. In fact, the whole of the Green Zone must be quite alien to her.

"We produce adrenacure here," he explains. "And study the superbees."

No one knows why a select handful of the population are Immune. The fate of humanity depends on finding that out.

Before she can answer, a head pops out from behind one of the vegetation filled biomes. "River!" Reed calls out. Red-haired and freckle faced, he pushes up his glasses as he hurries toward them. "I heard the news. Is there anything I can do to help?"

River's gut clenches. Reed is practically a permanent fixture in the LaB. He worked alongside Flora when she was up here. He knows how close she and River are. And yet, there's nothing he can do. No one can.

Flora's never coming back.

River's gaze slides away. "I'll be fine," he lies. He clears his throat. "Echo has been chosen for the LaB."

Reed's face lights up. "Great!" He pushes his glasses up again. "Did you want a tour? This place is amazing."

"Ah, sure," says Echo.

"We'll start with the *tremuloides* species. They're quite fascinating."

Waving an arm like Echo's a princess entering her domain, he leads her to the glass biome he was studying a moment ago.

River watches them move away, frowning. He's always liked Reed's permanently enthusiastic personality, but for some reason, he doesn't like the warm welcome he's extending Echo. Doesn't he realize who she is? And what if that friendliness is more than just polite interest... He would've had to notice how beautiful Echo is.

River's about to follow them when he hears the soft rustle of material behind him. He turns to find his father stepping out of his office, which is situated behind an opaque glass wall in the LaB. He grabs River's arm and pulls him back in with him.

The moment the door's shut, River steps away, more uncomfortable with proximity to his father than Echo. "How did you beat us up here?"

His father waves his hand as if the question isn't important. "I need to talk to you. In private."

River glances around the office they're now in, the opaque glass walls definitely affording them privacy. His father has never been...secretive. He's always led the Green Zone with integrity, honesty and strength. "About what?"

"About Echo. And your mentoring of her."

River stiffens. He's never defied his father. Never.

But this is the one thing he can't do.

He's hurting too bad, and Echo is too closely tied to that pain.

"Oren—" he starts.

"Hear me out, River. This is important." His father glances around as if to make sure they're alone. "I need someone I can trust."

Those words have River's attention. His father trusts him?

"As you know, Echo is a Dead Born. She's not familiar with our ways."

"No, she's not."

"We need to make sure she understands why we do things the way we do."

River frowns, conscious there are layers to his father's words. He's right. Echo's seen the blessings of the Green Zone, but not the responsibility that comes with them.

"We can't afford any trouble," his father continues, his gaze intense. "We need to make sure she's...assimilating."

Echo, the girl who can't stomach their world, needs to accept she's one of them now. River frowns. "And if she doesn't?"

His father raises his chin, his face hardening. "Immune or not, the colony always comes first."

With a hard glare so River understands what that means, he turns him around and pushes him back out of the office. "Don't let me down, son."

River finds himself back out in the main area of the LaB, blinking like he just exited from a cave.

His father just called him son.

And gave him a task.

One that gives him a surefire way to get rid of Echo for good.

CHAPTER
SEVEN
ECHO

E cho wakes and for one blissful moment she thinks she's back home on her mat. Then the sterile smell hits her, wafting up her nostrils like an antiseptic cloud.

She looks around her new room. Which is also Flora's old room. Just another reason for River to resent her. Part of her wonders if Oren assigned it to her for that very reason. He seems to be making sure Echo and River are in each other's orbit. He either wants them to be best friends or worst enemies. River's made it clear which one of those options he prefers.

There aren't many clues to Flora's personality in this room. Nor in any of the other rooms Echo had snuck a peek in as she'd walked past. Back home, people fill their homes with objects that have no purpose other than to make their owner smile when they look at them. The house Echo shared with her father has a row of primitive figurines sitting on a shelf that she'd carved out of rocks as a young girl. Beside them is a flower she made out of a piece of yellow plastic by shredding it into petal-shaped sections and attaching it to a stick.

There's nothing like that here. It's just white walls. White furniture. A white closet filled with fresh white suits all in Echo's size. And the most comfortable bed on this entire planet. No lumps. No dips. No pointy bits to dig into her back. She even has a pillow.

Pulling the sheets up to her chin, she revels in their crispness. Maybe she won't get out of this bed. Not ever. She'll lie in here and refuse to move, just like Nola in her chair.

She sighs. What she'd give to talk to Nola right now. To find out how she coped with being ejected from one life and sent to live another. Although, maybe she'd be the worst person to ask for advice. Because Nola hadn't coped well at all. And if Echo stays in this ridiculously comfortable bed, she'll fare no better. If she's going to make a difference in this world and find a way to bring down the Green Zone, then it starts with getting up.

In a minute or two...

Soft music pipes into her room. It has a peaceful rhythm, its purpose no doubt to gently rouse the precious Green Borns from their sleep. The sound of water trickling through pipes starts up as her new neighbors obediently start their day without having to collect a single drop of this precious liquid themselves.

"Good morning, Green Zone," Daphne's voice drifts across the music. "We hope you slept well. It's time to wake up and contribute to your colony. Be in peace."

Deciding she'd better get on with it, Echo swings her legs out of bed, feeling unsteady for a moment when her feet don't immediately hit the floor. She goes to the small room the Green Borns call a bathroom and uses the chair with the hole in it, having finally figured out its purpose late last night when she couldn't find a bedpan.

She needs to play nice today, having realized that's going to be the best way to extract as much information as she can about this place. River might hate her, but his father seems to like her, and he's the one with the power around here. Keeping him on her side is important. That Clover chick, who's clearly in love with River, is going to be a waste of time, but Reed is worth investing in. He seems to know his way around the LaB like he was born there.

Splashing water on her face, Echo drinks some in and sloshes it around in her mouth. Just like at the feast, it has a strange taste to it, although that could either be the pipes, or more likely the fact she's never tasted clean water before. Just another thing to get used to.

She notices a stain on her shirt from the feast, so changes into a fresh one, dropping the old one through a chute at the bottom of the cupboard. Thankfully, washing dirty clothes hadn't been her allocated task at the Choosing. It's almost too good to be true that she'd somehow gotten lucky enough to have been placed in the epicenter of this colony. The LaB is bursting with secrets—she could practically feel them oozing out of the walls when Reed had shown her around.

All she needs is the patience to do this right and she might just be able to improve the lives of everyone in her entire colony. It's not right that she was the only Dead Born to go to bed last night with a full stomach.

Leaving her room, she waits outside River's door as she'd been asked. She knocks and when there's no answer, she presses her ear to the smooth panel. Silence bounces back. Maybe he left without her? He made it pretty clear when he'd been asked to mentor her that he'd rather do anything else.

She counts to sixty. One minute. That seems fair. And when his door still fails to open, she walks off down the hallway. She spent her life waiting for Chase. There's no way she's going to waste more time on a guy who doesn't want anything to do with her.

Feeling like she's skating across the shiny floor tiles, she heads to the walkway along the balcony in the center of the Sting. She pauses to look over the railing, holding onto her stomach to see how far down the ground is. Why does everything inside this giant structure need to be so high or fast or hexagonal? It's like the people think they're the very insects they worship so much.

She steps away from the railing and takes the elevator to the LaB, wincing as it lurches into motion and avoiding looking out the glass panels. Watching the world rush past so fast makes her stomach flip.

She exits the elevator and approaches the double doors to the LaB. They open like a set of arms ready to embrace her. Reed is waiting for her, his orange hair reflecting the harsh lighting and glowing almost as much as his smile.

"Hello." He pushes his glasses up higher on his nose. "Where's your mentor?"

Echo shrugs. "He's either hiding from me in his room, or he left without me."

The smile falls from Reed's face. "Oren won't be impressed. The colony appoints the Dead Born Immunes a mentor for a reason."

"Maybe he just slept in," she says, wondering why she feels the need to defend a guy who's made it clear he wants nothing to do with her. "To be honest, I really didn't wait very long for him."

"Not you, too." Reed shakes his head and chuckles. "Why do all the girls love him so much?"

"They do?" Echo is a little surprised. It was clear that Clover has feelings for River, but other girls, too? Maybe they like tall, green-eyed and jaded in this colony.

Reed leans forward. "What's his secret? It's the way he looks after everyone, isn't it? Girls are a sucker for those kind-hearted types of guys."

"I'm sorry?" Echo straightens her back, genuinely confused. "Are we still talking about River? Because—"

"There you are!" River bursts into the LaB, panting heavily. His hair is ruffled and he has dark circles underneath his eyes. "Why didn't you wait for me?"

Echo cocks a brow at Reed, words not needed to get her point across. Kind-hearted, her ass!

"What's going on?" Oren appears in that way of his, as if he materialized out of thin air. "Did River not escort you here as I asked him to?"

River's face turns a deep shade of pink and Reed takes a few steps back, not wanting to be involved. This guy is smart, even if he seems to have the wrong idea about what kind of person he thinks River is.

Echo considers covering for River and telling Oren they came here together, but before she gets the chance, River steps forward.

"We had a m-misunderstanding," River stammers.

"Is this true?" Oren asks her.

"Yes." Echo crosses her arms, then uncrosses them, not wanting to appear defensive. "I did wait for him, but not for long enough. I thought he wasn't in his room, so I left or I'd have been late. I'm very keen to get started and learn how I can contribute to my new colony."

Something lights in Oren's eyes and she knows she chose the right words. He shifts his gaze to River accusingly.

"I had trouble waking up again." River's shoulders slump. "I was only a couple of minutes late coming out of my room and she'd already gone."

"Like River said, it was just a misunderstanding." Echo is

unable to help feeling sorry for the guy. "It won't happen again."

Oren nods, his disappointment seeming to be directed at his son. He turns to Echo. "Please come directly to me if you have any other difficulties settling in."

"That's very kind of you," she says. "And I'm sorry again for the misunderstanding. River's been very helpful."

"I'm pleased to hear that." Oren shoots River a doubtful look and walks away, disappearing behind an opaque glass wall.

"Why did you do that?" River snaps.

"Do what?" She tilts her head. "Be nice, you mean? Does it surprise you that a Dead Born can be nice?"

He lets out a sigh and she resists the urge to smooth down his tousled hair. He's annoyingly cute first thing in the morning, even if it looks like he didn't actually sleep.

"I mean, why did you lie to Oren?" he clarifies. "I haven't been helpful to you at all."

"Oh." She shrugs. "I could have waited a bit longer for you, I suppose."

"You're acting differently to yesterday." River studies her with a frown. "What are you up to?"

Her eyes flare and she works to compose herself. It seems Reed isn't the only clever one around here.

"It's amazing what a good sleep does for you." She stretches her arms over her head, trying to change the conversation. "Flora's bed was like sleeping on a cloud."

He winces at the sound of his twin's name, successfully distracted from his suspicions about Echo's motives.

"Where do you think she slept last night?" he asks quietly. His pain is clear and she pushes down more guilt that she'd brought up his sister.

"Did you lie awake all night thinking about her?" she asks,

wondering if there's a grain of truth in what Reed had said about River. Maybe he is kind—just not to Echo so far.

He shakes his head. "The opposite, actually. I slept deeply. Does that make me a bad brother?"

"No." She touches him on the arm, understanding him more in this moment than she had all day yesterday. "Sometimes our brains need a rest from thinking about all the bad things."

His green eyes flood with concern. "Will your brother take care of her, like you asked him to?"

She's confused for a moment, then remembers River had assumed Chase was her brother. She still doesn't want to correct him because that will require her to figure out exactly what Chase is to her. Ex-friend? Ex-neighbor? Ex-boyfriend? Ex-confidant? Ex-the-guy-who-meant-everything-to-her-and-she-still-can't-believe-he-betrayed-her-like-that?

She lets her hand fall back to her side. "Chase will look out for her. I don't know for sure where she would have slept, though. It usually takes the Green Born Vulnerables a while to find a place to claim as their own."

"Claim?" He pounces on this word like she'd fired a bullet. "You mean you don't allocate them a place to live? What kind of a colony are you?"

She crosses her arms, taking a step back. "The kind of colony that doesn't have available homes just sitting there ready to allocate. But we're not savages if that's what's worrying you. Flora might be hungry and her back may be aching from sleeping on the ground, but she'll be alive."

He blinks rapidly like he can wipe away his concern for his sister. "I need to get to Eden. And Reed's waiting for you. We have work to do for our colony."

"Thanks, mentor." She gives him a smile, genuinely wanting to take away some of his pain. He might have grown up in a life of luxury, but it seems his heart can break just like anyone else's. Maybe there's hope to form some kind of friendship with this guy, after all. At the very least, perhaps they can form a truce.

River doesn't return her smile. He walks away with his shoulders hunched like he's carrying the weight of his sister on them.

Pushing down the complicated emotions River stirs up inside her, Echo joins Reed, who's busy at a long counter, lining up syringes on a mat.

"Hey." Reed looks up. "We've got a lot to do, so I hope you have more energy than your mentor seems to have today."

"What are we doing?" She gives him an efficient nod, not wanting to think about River anymore.

"Time to replenish our adrenacure shots." Reed continues laying out syringes. "We totally wiped out our supply yesterday. Happens every year."

"Maybe you should have replenished them *before* the Confirmation," she suggests, thinking of the horrible way Avid had died. "Then we'd have had enough."

"We can only make a limited supply. And they have a shelf-life of a month." He places the last syringe down in a line of what must be at least a hundred. "Unfortunately, we're short on donors right now."

"I don't understand." She runs a hand through her dark hair. "What's a donor? And what do they donate?"

"Their adrenaline." He nods toward a large red door with the word *RESTRICTED* emblazoned across it. "It's a delicate process to extract."

"How's it done?" she asks, itching to get behind that door.

"That's not something you want to find out." He laughs in such a way it sets every nerve of hers on edge.

"And what if I do?" she asks.

"Echo, no. Don't go there." His face becomes serious and he lowers his voice. "You're extremely lucky to be an Immune. And you've landed one of the best jobs in the colony. You could have spent your life washing dishes or unblocking toilets. Don't mess it up by asking too many questions. It's not good for the colony."

"Okay." Echo holds up her hands, despite having just decided she's going to find out how the adrenaline is extracted as a matter of urgent priority.

The doors to the Restricted Area swing open and a man with a trolley walks out. Echo peers into the open space behind him but sees only darkness.

The man wordlessly wheels his trolley to Reed. He looks even more exhausted than River. There are lines around his bloodshot eyes and a puffiness to his skin. His hair is gray and thinning on top. He looks nothing like any of the other Green Borns.

"Hello, I'm Echo," she says, deciding this is someone she needs to meet. "I'm new here."

The man looks at her and the wrinkled lines on his face grow deeper.

"It's okay." Reed steps in front of Echo. "We'll take it from here."

A large grunt erupts from the man and he walks quickly back to the Restricted Area.

"Who was that?" Echo asks, stepping out from behind Reed trying to get another glimpse of what's behind the door as he passes through.

"That's Tuff." Reed moves a box of vials from the trolley to the counter, not seeming to want to give her any more details.

"But who is he?" Echo helps him unpack the trolley.

"He works in the Restricted Area." Reed pushes the empty trolley out of their way. "And if you keep asking questions, then you'll end up looking exactly like him. So, as I said earlier, I advise you to back off."

Echo holds up her palms. "Consider my back to be off."

Reed sets about showing Echo how to sterilize the equipment they're using and fill the syringes with the correct amount of liquid from the mysterious vials Tuff had brought out. It's tedious work and Reed insists on watching her every move.

"I've got it," she tells him, not enjoying his close proximity.

"We always do this as a pair." He moves back marginally. "It could be lethal to get the dose wrong, or if an air bubble gets in. It's protocol."

Echo nods, biting her tongue from telling him it's also lethal when the adrenacure is given to someone from another colony when you need it yourself.

"Tuff's an unusual name," she says instead, unable to get the strange man out of her mind. "It's not like everyone else's names around here."

Reed shoots her a warning look. "Nor is Echo."

She fills the next syringe, letting in a huge air bubble as what he just said sinks in. "You mean he's a Dead Born?"

"I never said that." He takes the syringe from her and works out the air bubble.

"How do I meet him?" she presses. What better ally to have in this colony than someone who understands exactly how she's grown up. Sure, Tuff might look a little scary, but he's a Dead Born. Which means she already trusts him more than anyone else around here. If she can befriend him, maybe he's her key to the Restricted Area.

Reed hands her the syringe and sighs. "You know why River doesn't like you, don't you?"

"He blames me for Flora being a Vulnerable," she says. "Which is ridiculous."

"It's not that." Reed watches closely as she continues on with her work. "Well, not just that."

"Then what is it?" She pauses to jam a gloved hand on her hip.

"Flora asked too many questions as well," he warns. "You're exactly like her."

"Not exactly," says Echo. "She's a Vulnerable. I'm an Immune. Which means I'm one of you and you should trust me. So, how do I get to talk to Tuff?"

"You don't." Reed's voice is firm. "Leave it, Echo. I told you, it's not good for the colony to ask so many questions."

Echo nods.

"Besides, there's no point going down that path," Reed adds. "Tuff hasn't said a single word since his Confirmation. He's a mute."

Echo's heart sinks, but then she steadies herself. There are plenty of ways to talk without actually saying anything. She'll get him to answer her questions, even if he doesn't use words. Once he learns what they have in common, surely he'll trust her?

She fills the next syringe perfectly and Reed nods his approval as she moves onto another, then the next.

"You're a fast learner," he says, checking her work.

"That's what Oren told me." She looks toward the opaque glass wall he'd disappeared behind earlier.

"It's important work we do here," Reed says enthusiastically. "The survival of every last human life left on this planet depends on it."

"Do you think some lives are worth more than others?" she asks as she fills the next syringe that will no doubt be used to save a Green Born.

"Not at all." Reed shakes his head.

Anger bubbles in Echo's gut at the easy way he can dismiss this. "Yet in the Dead Z—"

"You don't understand." Reed sets down the vial he's holding and looks her directly in the eye. "The colonies have been set up this way to ensure everyone's survival. Without the work we do in here and the crops we grow out there, nobody would still be alive. The bees would have wiped all of us out by now. Is that what you want?"

She shakes her head. "I just want—"

"Equality." He cuts her off again. "I know what you want. But it's not realistic. The only reason the Vulnerables are still alive is because of the Immunes. So, instead of bemoaning all the things the Dead Zone doesn't have, why don't you stop for a moment and think about all the things it *does* have? A net for protection. Rations to feed the people. A chance each year to live a better life—just like you are now. Without us, instead of being Dead Borns, they'd just be...Dead."

Echo breaks eye contact, unsure about how any of that makes her feel. What he's saying is true. The Vulnerables would never survive without the Immunes. But it still doesn't make any of this right.

There has to be a better way. One where neither colony gets destroyed in the process.

She just needs to work out what that is.

CHAPTER
EIGHT
RIVER

River steps through the doors of Eden and draws in the familiar scents of cultured green. It looks like it did yesterday, and the day before that, and the day before that. He should feel comforted. It should help him find some sort of equilibrium.

But he struggles to find any feelings of peace or warmth.

Maybe it's because he slept so deeply his head still feels wooly and his limbs heavy. His mouth is as desiccated as the Dead Zone, so he grabs one of the glass bottles of water beside the door and takes a long drink. The bottles are stationed everywhere throughout the Green Zone. As you enter a room. As you exit the Sting. In small, shaded stands along the paths that wind through the verdant gardens.

Water is as abundant as food in the Green Zone. It's important to look after the Immunes.

For the first time in his seventeen years, River finds himself wondering what the world of the Dead Zone looks like. How is Flora? Does she at least have easy access to water? Echo's words of needing to claim somewhere to live punch through him, no less painful than the first time he heard them. She'd be thirsty. Hungry. Lost. And conscious it's inevitable she'll develop the scurge.

And yet he slept the sleep of the dead last night. What sort of brother is he?

Echo said he needed a break from all the bad things, and for a brief flash, he wonders at the empathy he saw lurking in the depths of her gaze. What bad things has she had to disappear into sleep to forget? Frowning, he pushes the thought away. He can't afford to think like that. Not for a Dead Born who rejects everything his colony stands for.

A Dead Born he's been tasked with watching.

Not feeling much better even though the gritty taste has been washed from his mouth, River enters Eden more fully. Taking up most of the floor of the Sting, the first half is encased in a dome of hexagonal panes of glass, allowing sunlight to stream through onto the garden beds.

He walks slowly down the ordered paths that intersect dozens of garden beds. The closest ones are raised beds with hundreds of seedlings, ordered and carefully propagated. Further on are floor level garden beds with plants of every height, all looking lush and healthy. He has to remind himself each and every species is here because it's fighting to survive.

Several feet further and he reaches the glass doors where the dome ends. Stepping through, River finds himself amongst a forest of more mature vegetation open to the elements. Here, the plants adjust to the world they'll be introduced to, the final stage before they're incorporated into the growing expanse that is the Green Zone.

River walks on, leaves brushing his face and green filling his lungs. He reaches the railing at the end and grips it. The Green Zone is fifteen floors below, but it's not what grabs his attention. Eden faces away from the Dead Zone, so all that stretches out is the expanse of desert that largely comprises the continent they live on. Land scarred by the almost-extinction of a key species, then war, then starvation. And ultimately death, not just of humans, but of millions of other species.

Immunes aren't just fighting to save themselves. They're fighting to save what's left of this ravaged and ruined world.

His hands tighten around the railing, a soft breeze brushing his face. Would a Dead Born ever understand what they're up against? What must be done to salvage what little there is left?

His heart constricts painfully. That sacrifices must be made.

River wonders how the railing doesn't snap under his grip. If Echo doesn't realize what they're fighting for, then she'll be Forgotten. Exiled to the Dead Zone and never spoken of again, just like the few Green Borns who fail to abide by their laws. He frowns. Unless that's what she wants...

"I thought I heard someone enter." Clover appears behind him, a smile lighting up her face. "Be in peace, River," she says warmly as she comes to stand beside him.

"Be in peace," he says automatically. He took feeling at peace for granted along with everything else he had in his life.

She moves closer, her smile dipping as she glances up at his hair. "Didn't sleep so well, huh?"

He reaches up, finding it a ruffled mess. All because Echo didn't bother waiting for him and he panicked, rushing off to find her. His father's given him a task, and he won't let him down. "Yeah," River mutters. "Something like that."

Clover steps closer, her fingers combing the wild locks down. "I like it," she says huskily. "It's kind of cute."

River blinks. Cute? Echo certainly didn't think it was cute. He turns to look back over the barren vista, not entirely comfortable with Clover touching him like that. "So, what are our tasks for the day?"

"We're focusing on the *Rauvolfia* seedlings. The latest batch is moving out here."

He nods, liking the idea of keeping busy. And serpentwood is an important ingredient in adrenacure. Their stocks will be low after the Confirmation.

If Flora hadn't had a dose, she'd be dead.

"Let's get started then," says River, turning and taking a step to make his way back into the dome.

But Clover doesn't move. She hunches her shoulders, her head dropping down. "I'll be there in a minute," she says. "You go."

"Is everything okay?" he asks, returning to stand beside her.

She looks up at him with tear filled eyes. "I miss Cascade," she whispers.

River smiles, trying to lighten the mood. Dwelling on this isn't good for anyone. "You're forgetting how much you two fought."

Sometimes the screaming matches could be heard across entire floors.

"We might not be as close as you and Flora, but she's still my sister," says Clover, frowning a little.

Abashed, his smile falls. "Of course. You love her."

Her forehead smooths out as she nods. "I worry for her, you know?"

His own grief once more clenching at his insides, River swallows. "Echo said they'll be okay."

"The Dead Born?" Clover asks archly. "Of course, she'd say that. She'll tell you whatever you want to hear."

He blinks. Was that what the touch on the arm was about? Was the empathy and compassion all an act? And yet,

Echo's been nothing but honest with him. Prickly, but honest.

He doesn't get a chance to follow the confusing train of thought because Clover throws herself into his chest, sobbing. He wraps his arms around her instinctively, holding her as her shoulders shake.

"Flora and Cascade are Vulnerables," he says through his tight throat. "There's nothing we can do."

Clover looks up, face pale and cheeks wet. "At least we have each other."

"And an entire colony," he reminds her. "And our important work to focus on."

Clover's faint frown is back. "Yes, that, too."

River steps back, smiling once more. "Let's get propagating, shall we?"

She clamps her hand over her mouth as she giggles. "River," she admonishes.

He flushes as he realizes what she just insinuated. He rubs the back of his head. "I meant the serpentwood."

Clover giggles again. "Sure you did." She spins toward the door, giving him a coy glance over her shoulder before making her way back to the dome.

River follows, unsure whether the undercurrents he's sensing are just his imagination. Surely Clover is just messing with him. She's like a sister, and they've both lost a sibling to the Confirmation. Wrong person. Wrong timing.

He rubs his hand down his face. He obviously slept poorly as well as deeply. His mind is a muddle this morning.

Inside the dome, Clover is beside a large plot full of cardboard tube stock containing serpentwood saplings about knee height. "We're transplanting, then moving."

"Sure thing."

River's worked in Eden many times before. In fact, he spent

as much time here as Flora did in the LaB. He enjoyed the work, although that was when he believed he was preparing himself for his role in the gardens. Eden's just not where he imagined himself...

Then again, he didn't imagine himself quite so alone, either.

He's just bent over to pick up a sapling when the doors to Eden slide open. River instantly straightens, wondering if his father has come to visit. Probably to chastise him again for failing his first morning of his task. He needs to monitor if Echo is assimilating. If she's following the rules.

And even on day one she didn't bother waiting for him, ignoring one of the first things asked of her.

But it's not Oren who strides through the doors. Instead, a familiar Green Born stumbles in, sways, and quickly rights himself.

"Urgh, it's Vernon," mutters Clover as she rolls her eyes.

"Ah, Eden," Vernon calls, throwing his arms out wide, one hand clutching a half-full glass bottle. "The garden of tomorrow."

River approaches him, shaking his head. "Vernon, isn't it a bit early—"

"To play Sting roulette?" demands Vernon in a too-loud voice. "It's never too early for that, dear boy."

Clover rushes forward. "Vernon, we're trying to work here. Please, you need to leave."

Vernon arches a bushy brow at her, combing his fingers through his unkempt beard. "So you can save us all, my sweet Clover?"

"I'm not your anything," she snaps, making River's eyebrows shoot up.

He knows Vernon is only tolerated in the colony. But Clover's being...rude.

River steps around her just as Vernon lurches. Clover retreats as the man begins to fall, but River quickly catches him. He slips beneath Vernon's arm, hoisting him back up. "Easy there, Vern."

He squints at River through bloodshot eyes. "You're very much like your mother."

River smiles. Most people can't get past the stained white suit and eye-stinging fumes to learn Vernon has a good heart. With somber eyes, he salutes River with his glass bottle and downs a large gulp. Although the contents are clear, they aren't water. It's perpetually half-full of the rice wine Vernon discovered he could brew.

But even through his permanently drunken haze, Vern recognized that River and Flora were still hurting long after they lost their mother. Oren acted like she was Forgotten, not dead, never mentioning her name. But Vernon would randomly pop into whatever floor they were on and tell them stories, reminding them of her bright mind and beautiful heart.

He made sure she was remembered.

"How about we take a walk in the gardens and clear your head?" offers River.

"No, thank you," says Vernon, leaning more and more against River. "My mind is perfectly clear."

"Of course, it is," River says good naturedly. "But I could use a breath of fresh air."

"They're preparing for the next Harvest Day," he says in a conspiratorial whisper. "They'll tell you that you're getting in the way."

River nods, realizing others probably tried to shoo Vernon away like Clover just did. "Maybe a rest in your room?"

"My room is a wonderful idea," announces Vernon. "Although I'm not tired, I do need more kasi." He waves his bottle around, showing the drink he named is almost gone, even though it's still early.

River glances at Clover. "I'll be back."

She frowns. "It shouldn't take too long."

He turns away before his own frown blossoms. He's hoping the people of Dead Zone show Flora and Cascade respect and consideration, even though they clearly don't fit in. He can't expect that if he's not willing to extend the same to Vern.

River half-walks, half-carries Vernon back to the elevator. Inside, he's just pressed the button for the residential floor when Vernon jostles into him. River catches him with a grunt, but still staggers under his weight. There's a brief moment where they stumble around the elevator before River can right them again.

"Sorry," rumbles Vernon, not sounding particularly apologetic.

"It's fine. The floor is deceptively flat just there."

Vern throws his head back and laughs as he slaps River on the back. "Just like your mother!"

He's right. River's mom had a dry sense of humor. His childhood had been full of laughter.

The elevator silently speeds up, and Vernon does what he always does when he's in one.

"Glassworks," Vernon announces cheerfully as they pass the sixteenth floor.

Where the glass bottles are made, along with all their crockery and LaB supplies.

They zip past the seventeenth floor. "Woodworkers."

For furniture and building supplies.

"Metal workers."

Vast piles of metal are dotted around Sting, remnants of a society of excess consumption and careless abandon when they no longer wanted it. The Sting was built in its entirety out of the smelted and melted materials in those piles. River doubts humanity will ever need to mine for metal again.

"Ooh, the LaB," Vernon announces with childish glee, and River quickly realizes why.

The elevator has stopped, and the doors are opening.

River glares at him, as he realizes they were traveling up the Sting and not down. He'd been so busy trying to keep Vern upright, he hadn't noticed. "This isn't the floor for your room."

"I'm playing Sting roulette," Vern states indignantly. "I didn't know where we'd end up."

It's the game Vernon plays where he enters the elevator, presses random buttons simultaneously, and sees which floor he ends up on. He must've done it when he jostled River when they first entered.

Before River can stop him, Vernon disengages himself and stumbles into the LaB. "The place of Learning and Bounty," he half-shouts with a flourish. "What a wonder of human creation!"

Reed rushes forward, waving his hands. "Vernon, you know you're not supposed to be in here!" Echo appears beside him, curious surprise on her face.

"I'm not supposed to be anywhere," he snaps back. "But I don't let that stop me."

He stumbles sideways, almost crashing into the cart of water bottles to his left, but River quickly slips under his arm and catches him.

Vernon looks down, grinning. "It almost happened again."

Reed's hands are on his hips. "Smashing all those bottles wasn't funny. Not only did we have to clean it up, but what if we were thirsty?"

"There's plenty of kasi to go around." Vernon waves his bottle, although it's empty now.

River picks up one of the bottles of water he's now beside. "Why don't you have some water, instead?"

Vernon knocks it away. "What are you trying to do, poison me? That stuff tastes foul."

"If kasi tastes anything like it smells, then you don't seem to mind drinking bird pee."

Vernon roars with laughter, but it's the giggle that weaves through the raucous sound that has River glancing up. He finds Echo's eyes are filled with mirth as she regards them.

Vernon quiets. "Now, who's this?"

She steps forward. "Hi, I'm Echo. The latest addition to this weird ass world."

Vernon bursts into laughter again. He turns to River. "I like her," he says in a mock whisper.

River has no idea what to say to that, but before he can answer, Vernon's legs give out, yanking them both down. To River's surprise, they don't crash to the floor.

Because Echo is now under Vern's other arm.

"Get him out of here," says Reed through gritted teeth.

Vernon leans down closer to Echo. "So much for *be in peace*, huh?"

She giggles again before looking to River. "Where are we taking him?"

River's lips twitch. "I was trying to get him to his room."

"To get more kasi."

"To sleep off the kasi," corrects River.

"But I'm not tired," slurs Vernon.

With a quick glance at each other, River and Echo maneuver Vernon back to the elevator. Inside, River makes sure he can't reach the buttons, but Vern doesn't try. Seems he's had enough of playing Sting roulette.

Silence and the heavy smell of kasi fill the elevator. Vern clears his throat. "My name's Vernon, by the way."

"Lovely to meet you, Vernon," says Echo warmly.

Vernon sags and River tries to take more of his weight. The guy will crush Echo if he keeps this up.

He doesn't seem to notice because he peers more closely at her. "You're like River, aren't you? A good one."

"I don't know about that..."

"You're in the elevator with me, aren't you?"

Echo glances at River, then quickly looks away. He focuses on the buttons as they light up one by one. He's not sure why, but things just became awkward.

Maybe it's because he didn't expect Echo to be in the elevator with him. Even Flora sometimes didn't have the patience for Vernon.

The doors open and River directs them to Vernon's room. Inside, they place him on the bed. River waits for an objection, but Vernon lies down and settles his head on the pillow. River pulls the blanket up like he has countless times before and tucks it around his shoulders.

Vernon snuggles down with almost childlike contentment. "River always looks after me," he mumbles. "Just like his mom did."

A second later, his soft snores fill the room. Leaving River with Echo, not really sure how they ended up here.

He clears his throat. "Thanks, ah, for helping."

Echo glances away, shrugging. "He looks a bit like my dad." She looks back, smiling. "If he was sober."

River finds himself smiling, too. "I don't think I've ever seen Vernon sober."

They simultaneously blink, then look away. This moment is just getting weirder and weirder.

He clears his throat again. "Well, we'd better get back to our roles."

Echo to the LaB, River to Eden. She nods, chewing her lip as she leads the way back to the elevator.

Once they're in, she reaches for the buttons before he gets a chance. "Actually, I have a better idea."

River's about to object, especially when he sees that she presses the button for the ground floor. Echo obviously isn't planning on going back to where she's supposed to be.

And he's her mentor.

Tasked with ensuring she plays by the rules. Rules she clearly has no interest in trying to keep.

NINE

ECHO

The horrified look on River's face is priceless.

Echo suppresses a smile as the elevator stops with a gentle thud at the ground floor. "You're not used to breaking rules, are you?"

"I...well...I..." His hand hovers near the elevator buttons. "Flora was the rule breaker out of the two of us."

"Flora's no longer here." She wonders how far she can push him. "Which means you need to loosen up a little."

"I need to get back to Eden," he says.

"Why?" She tilts her head. "So that Clover can continue to fawn over you."

"She didn't..." He turns a shade of pink. "She doesn't..."

"Oh, believe me, she does." Echo steps out of the elevator and beckons him to follow.

He takes a tentative step toward the open doors and she grabs hold of his arm and pulls him forward before they slide closed again.

"See." She smiles. "Breaking rules isn't so hard. You might

even find you enjoy it once you manage to pull that green rod out of your—"

"Echo," he warns.

Right. That's how far she can push him.

"Sorry," she mumbles. "It's just that ever since we got here, I've been dying to take a look at the gardens. I think as my mentor it's your duty to show me around. You know, in case I get lost."

"You can't get lost if you don't go out there," he huffs as they walk across the foyer toward the airlock at the entrance.

She nods, conceding he has a point. It's just that the Sting has been making her claustrophobic. She's practically spent her entire life outdoors, running through the dusty streets of the Dead Zone. Being locked up in a giant, sterile tower is starting to make her feel ill.

And besides, River really needs to loosen up. He's clearly suffering a great trauma, losing his sister like that, and she's not sure burying himself in work is going to help. This will be a good chance to figure out if there's any possible way the two of them can get along. Something that might benefit them both.

They step out into the fresh air and Echo raises her face to the sky, still marveling at how white the clouds look when not obstructed by a net.

"Where are we going?" River asks.

"Take me to your favorite place," she says. "Show me all the places you used to play in as a child."

He looks at her strangely, but his attention is stolen by a pod that rushes up to them.

Its doors whoosh open and Echo climbs in, relieved when River gets in beside her. Part of her thought he was going to run back inside the first moment he got the chance. Daphne is on the screen again, smiling as she announces that Harvest Day will be starting soon and all Immunes will need to either attend or present themselves at the Processing Center in the basement.

"Sounds like fun," says Echo, as Daphne's speech finishes and the pod waits for their instructions. "But where are we going now? Which one of your old hangouts are you taking me to first?"

He lets out a sigh, seeming to decide to tell her something. "The day of our Confirmation was the first time Flora and I had left the Sting. I don't have any hangouts."

"But...why?" Her face folds into a frown and she tries to smooth out her features to hide her shock.

"We didn't know if we were Immune." He seems to suppress an eye roll. "It wasn't safe."

"Oh." She blinks, the frown still stuck to her face. "But don't you have those white suit things with hoods to cover you up? The ones you were wearing before you went into the Betadome."

"They're only for Confirmation." He shifts uncomfortably. "They do a pretty good job of keeping out the bees, but they're not guaranteed. It's safer to stay inside the Sting."

"Wow, talk about being risk averse." She thinks of Nola and her paranoia about not letting any bees inside her home, and suddenly her strange behavior makes a little more sense. She'd always thought of the Green Borns as being free, but it seems they're even more repressed in some ways than her own colony.

River shrugs. "Some risks aren't worth taking. I only know the places I've stared at from the windows of the Sting."

"Then take me to your favorite one," she says. "The one you've stared at the most. Surely, you're curious to see it up close?"

He pulls his attention back to her as he considers what she's suggesting. "Okay then, we'll go to the cornfield."

River types something into a keypad and the pod takes off. This time, Echo is ready for the sudden movement and her stomach only complains a little bit.

"Interesting choice," she tells him.

He frowns. "What do you mean?"

"You chose one of the few places that doesn't depend on bees for pollination." She raises a brow.

"What do you know about growing corn?" he asks.

Now it's her turn to roll her eyes. "Just because I don't eat much of it, doesn't mean I don't know about it. We grow some corn, although our soil's not great so it doesn't really thrive."

He almost smiles at this. "Fair enough."

"So, why?" she presses.

He looks out the window. "I like the way the leaves all move together in the breeze. I've always wondered what it would be like to walk amongst the stalks. It looks...fun."

"You haven't had a lot of fun in your life, have you?" She hopes she hasn't pushed him too far again. It's just that in all the times she imagined what life might have been like growing up in the Green Zone, never once did she imagine they were stuck inside a building looking out at the world, instead of climbing trees and throwing apples at each other as they laughed until their full bellies ached.

"Depends on your perspective," River says. "I'm pretty sure my childhood was more fun than yours."

"I think we need to call a truce." Echo sticks out her hand. "How about I stop making assumptions about your life, and you stop making them about mine?"

He looks at her hand as if shaking it is something that requires serious consideration, but to her relief he takes it. His skin is soft and warm. Different to Chase's. And she finds she's the one to pull back first, confused about how it makes her feel.

The pod comes to a halt and she lurches forward in her

seat, then looks out at the vast cornfield that stretches before them. The land is blanketed in lush green, broken up by dark lines where there's space to walk between the neatly planted rows of corn. She can see why this place might appeal to River. There's a calming symmetry with its mathematical layout. And not a hint of a hexagon anywhere in sight.

River clambers out the pod and extends his hand to help her.

She pretends she doesn't notice, not wanting the feeling of his skin against hers again quite so soon.

He wipes his palm on his white trousers, and sniffs. For a moment she thinks she's offended him, until she notices he's having difficulty breathing.

"You okay?" she asks.

"Just adjusting to the outside air." He sneezes twice in quick succession. "It's fine."

She walks slowly toward the field to give him space, almost feeling sorry for the guy. He's spent his entire life inside a building, only to discover when he finally leaves it that he's allergic to the outdoors. And to make it worse, he doesn't want to admit it.

Seeming to have recovered, he catches up to her and falls into step.

A gentle breeze caresses the field and the long stalks whisper to Echo as she walks into one of the corn rows. The cool shade envelops her and she shivers, unsure if it's the temperature or the sheer magic of this place. There's enough corn growing here to feed everyone in her colony twice over. Surely, there has to be a way to smuggle some of it back home? Not leftovers from a feast, or meager boxes of rations, but fresh corn, straight from the field, ready to be cooked and eaten or ground into flour to make bread.

"What are you thinking?" River asks and she realizes her hands are clenched tightly into fists.

"That I can see why you like this place," she answers, trying to stick as closely as she can to the truth. "Is it like how you imagined from the window?"

"It's even better," he says. "I just wish Flora could see it. She'd love it here."

A loud squawk catches Echo's attention and her head snaps up in the same way as all Dead Borns when there's the chance of filling your belly with meat.

"What is it?" River seems confused.

The bird cries out again and she puts up her hand to silence River, then runs in the direction of the noise. If she's quick, she can get to it first.

She stumbles, but quickly regains her balance and picks up her pace, determined to prove she doesn't need Chase when it comes to hunting prey. She can do this.

Listening intently as she tries to keep her footsteps light, she hears the bird again and makes a swift turn to the left, seeing an injured raven lying in the middle of the path. She grinds to a halt and crouches beside it.

The jet black bird is trying to flap its wings but there's a string caught around one of them, meaning it can't get enough momentum to lift itself from the ground.

She swoops on it, picking it up by its body, feeling its tiny heart racing against her palm. It's a drum beat of victory and she holds the squawking creature in the air as River comes running to her.

"I got it!" she cries, beaming with pride. "And it's huge! Enough to feed both of us."

"What are you doing?" He looks stricken as he reaches for the bird and she moves it away. "Put it down!"

"Are you crazy?" She turns her body to protect her bounty.

When she snaps its neck, she wants it to be a clean break. "I said I'd share. You don't have to confiscate it."

"Confiscate?" He runs his hand through his crop of dark hair. "I don't want to confiscate it."

She tucks the frightened creature to her chest, wishing River would leave her alone so she could put it out of its misery quickly.

"Then what do you want to do with it?" she asks.

"Rescue it," he says. "We don't need to eat animals here. We have plenty." He sweeps out his arms, indicating the thousands of heads of corn that surround them.

"But..." She keeps her grip on the bird, not prepared to let go. "But it's just an animal."

He nods, putting his hands gently on the raven. "And it doesn't need to die for us."

Her eyes widen. "I thought it was only bees you worship here."

"We don't worship bees." He grips the bird and she reluctantly lets him take it into his hands. "We respect them, just like we respect every other animal. The world needs all kinds of creatures to thrive. That's why we work so hard to protect them."

He turns the bird over and untangles the string binding its wing. The animal holds still, almost as if it knows he's helping it. Is this what Reed meant about River having a kind heart? First the drunk guy, now the bird. And she can't deny he's been awfully worried about Flora.

River stands up the bird on his hand and holds it high above his head. It shakes itself out, then takes off into the sky. Echo watches it with moisture seeping into her mouth, mourning the meal she could have had.

"I can't believe you let it go," she says, as the bird becomes a mere speck against the clouds.

"And I can't believe you didn't want to," he replies.

"That's because you've never been hungry." Her shoulders slump. "You've never had to take a creature's life to save your own."

He studies her for a moment, his eyes filling with concern. "Is it really that bad where you come from?"

"It is." She nods slowly, seeing an opportunity to bring him to her side. "Will you help me change it? We have to do something. Think of Flora."

He looks stricken. "There's nothing I can do."

"You're the leader's son! Surely, you can do something?"

He lets out a long breath. "Flora's the leader's daughter and look how far that got her."

Echo suppresses a sigh. Instead of this outing drawing them closer and helping them find common ground, they seem to be discovering just how different they really are. Talking is getting them nowhere. She thinks back to how she used to make friends as a girl. Back in the days when she didn't have to worry about colonies and cures and changing the world. Life may have been difficult in the Dead Zone but in many ways it was also far simpler, with happiness more easily won.

"I'm going to teach you a game," she says, knowing this next move is a risk.

"We don't play games in the Green Zone." River crosses his arms. "Our work here is serious. The future of the entire planet depends on us."

She shakes her head. "Nope. I'm not buying that."

"It's true," he insists. "Without all the systems we've put in place to—"

"I don't mean that." She waves a hand at him. "Reed already gave me that lecture. I get it. We couldn't live without all the important stuff you do. I mean, I'm not buying that you don't have time for games. Everybody needs to have a little fun sometimes."

"Echo—"

She slaps her palm against his upper arm. "You're it!"

"I'm what?" He furrows his brow as he rubs his arm.

"It!" she cries. "You're it. And you'll stay *it* until you tag me back."

She takes off deeper into the cornfield with no idea if he'll follow.

When she hears his footsteps pounding the ground behind her, she lets out possibly her first genuine smile since she'd stepped into the Betadome.

Darting between some stalks, she reverses her direction and increases her pace. In the short time she's been in the Green Zone, she's already learned more than she thought possible. Not everything is black and white—or black and green in this case. Perhaps both colonies can learn from each other to create a better world for *everyone*.

Including River.

It's time to show him the meaning of the word fun.

CHAPTER
TEN
RIVER

River stops after only a few feet, hands on his hips, unsure why he's already a little short of breath. What is he doing? He's not going to chase Echo. This is not what Green Borns do. Fast movements like that are dangerous. It's like she's trying to draw bees to her.

He frowns. Like she did at the Confirmation.

For the first time since then, River wonders why Echo would do that. Did she have a death wish? He frowns even deeper. Echo's a fighter, she doesn't strike him as someone who wants to die.

But that means she didn't want to be Immune.

"Come on, River." Her voice filters through the cornstalks on his right. "Right now, a Dead Born is outwitting a Green Born."

He angles his head, guessing she's only a few yards away. The game wasn't a front for her to run away. She's actually trying to have...fun.

Well, if she's attempting to introduce him to how they do

things in the Dead Zone, then he's going to show her how it's done in the Green Zone.

Taking several steps backward, he finds a particularly bushy cornstalk and slips behind it, arranging a few other strips of leaves to shield himself.

And waits.

Just as he suspected, it doesn't take long. This rapid change of events suggests that Echo is impulsive. Probably not big on patience. While River's grown up having to be patient, sheltered within the Sting, waiting to start his life.

"Are you really okay with me winning?" Her voice sounds closer. "Because I won't let you forget it."

He grins before he realizes he's doing it. Echo would do exactly that.

But he doesn't move. Her taunting won't draw him out.

Seconds pass, River conscious of how loud his breathing is no matter how much he tries to quiet it. It's like there's something caught in his throat, making it rasp.

"River?"

The teasing lilt is fading, replaced by a hint of suspicion. Once again, Echo's a few feet closer.

A grassy leaf tickles River's nose and he has to clap his hand over his mouth to stop a sneeze.

His eyes water as the need increases and he rubs furiously at his nose. Not now!

Echo appears, pushing cornstalks out of her way with sharp shoves, a frown on her face. "Of course he didn't play," she mutters to herself. "He wouldn't know how to."

She trudges straight past him, her bottom lip protruding in a pout that draws his eyes. Why does this girl have to be so beautiful?

"He's probably taken the pod back," she continues, practically growling the words. "And now I'm going to have to learn to use that just like the rain machine and the chair with the hole."

River blinks. His world is far more alien to her than he realized if she didn't know how to use the shower or the bathroom. The Dead Zone is more primitive than he was made to believe.

She stomps on, her shoes leaving deep impressions in the soft soil. Stomping is also something people of the Green Zone don't do.

The need to sneeze hasn't gone away, so the moment she's gone past his hiding spot, River leaps out. He touches her elbow, then jumps back. "You're it!"

The words are quickly followed by a sneeze. Then another. And another.

Through watery eyes he sees the surprise fade from Echo's face, replaced by a blossoming smile. With lightning-fast movements, she taps his arm, spins around and runs. "Back at you. You're it!"

"What?" he calls after her. "It doesn't work like that!"

Laughter rises through the leafy green foliage. "It most certainly does."

Knowing the same strategy won't work twice, River breaks into a run. He'll show her that Green Borns might be serious and focused, but that doesn't mean they'll let a challenge go uncontested.

He sees a flash of Echo's ebony hair as she darts between some cornstalks and he injects more speed. This time, he'll tag her and get the hell out of there. Maybe even call game over.

Before he can stop himself, River sneezes again. Except as he tries to draw air back in, it gets caught in his throat. As if it's too narrow. He doubles over, coughing, his hands braced on his knees.

"Echo," he calls out weakly. His lungs feel like they're shrinking.

"I'm not falling for that!" she calls out. "Oldest trick in the book! After the hide and wait strategy, that is."

River no longer has enough breath to tell her he's not faking. In fact, there no longer seems to be enough air, period.

He tightens his grip on his knees, trying to focus on drawing in the precious gas. But it's like his throat is little more than a constricted straw and his lungs have a steel band around them.

Panic claws at him, increasing his breathing as he desperately seeks oxygen. Without air, he'll die.

A pain pierces his chest. The cornstalks and leaves blur as his head spins. He stumbles, his pulse a roar in his ears. His legs weaken and he knows he's about to fall.

"River!" He looks up, finding Echo in front of him. She grips his shoulders, leaning in so their gazes are level. "What's happening?"

He shakes his head, pointing to his throat. He has no idea what's going on. Only that he's suffocating.

Within a few minutes, he'll be dead.

"Look at me, River," Echo says sharply.

He tries. He really does. But the world is swimming. Fading. Going black around the edges.

Her warm hands grip his face, drawing it closer to hers. "Look at me. Focus on my breathing."

On her breathing? When he can't do it himself?

He tries to shake his head as his mouth works, but her grip won't let him move. Her dark gaze becomes all he can see. His new center of gravity.

"Breathe in," she says, pulling in an exaggerated breath. "Just like me."

River grasps the anchor she's thrown him, trying to imitate

her actions as if he's forgotten how to do something as basic as breathing. But all he can draw in is a trickle of air. And his lungs have shrunk so much they ache.

"That's it," Echo says encouragingly. "In, out."

Her warm hands cup his face as she rhythmically draws air in and out, matching her breathing to his choppy gasps.

But her eyes remain calm. In fact, there's so much calm pouring from her, it seems to neutralize the panic rolling off him in waves. Although his lungs still refuse to work, his pulse slows.

"That's it. In," she says warmly. "Out."

The world stops spinning. Then the pain in his chest eases. A little more oxygen reaches his starving cells.

Echo smiles. "You've got this, River. Small, slow breaths." She slows her own breathing a little. "Just like me."

The sound of his own wheezing reaches River's ears past the thundering of his heart. Then the rustling of the cornstalks. And eventually, Echo's own measured breaths counting out his own.

Her hands slip away from his cheeks as she takes a step back, her smile growing. "Wow, you really go to some extreme lengths to get out of playing a game of tag."

He straightens, surprised, then reaches out and taps her shoulder. "You're it," he says, his voice breathier than he'd like.

What just happened?

Echo's eyes twinkle despite the concern in their depths. "Fine then, you win this round." She arches an eyebrow. "Although it's the best of three."

River shakes his head, marveling at this young woman who just saved him, and is now allowing him to salvage his pride. Except he's in no state to try and figure that out right now. He feels like he just lapped the acres of cornfields. Puffed and exhausted.

Echo angles her head. "I think we should get back to the pod."

He nods, relieved when he takes a few steps and his legs hold up. They make their way back through the cornstalks silently and River can feel Echo's gaze on him. He focuses on keeping his shallow breathing even and steady. He never wants to experience that again.

The moment they're out of the cornfield, River straightens a little more. The sight that he used to study from the window in his room is nothing like he imagined. The beauty is there in its symmetry and creamy crowns of tassels and the rolling waves of green. But he never considered it hid dangers as well. That the cool shadows could be deadly.

They reach the pod and River climbs in, welcoming the soothing, familiar white. Echo sits beside him, hands clasped and silent, although still sneaking glances from the corner of her eye. It's possibly the longest period he's been with her when she wasn't talking.

Daphne repeats her Harvest Day announcement from earlier, the doors close and the pod whisks them away. River leans back in his molded seat, the band around his chest loosening a little more. Breathing has never felt so good.

"You've got your color back," Echo observes, breaking the silence.

"Yeah. Feeling better."

She angles her body so she can face him. "You want to tell me what happened back there?"

He looks away. "I have no idea. It's never happened before." He turns back to her. "Nothing to be worried about, though."

Her black brows jolt up her forehead. "I don't think—"

"I doubt it'll happen again. I just got out of breath and freaked out."

"That's not what I saw. You were—"

River shakes his head. He doesn't want to talk about this. "Why did you try to attract the bees during the Confirmation?"

Echo startles at the change in topic, even drawing back a little in her seat. Then it's her turn to look away. "I didn't want to be Immune."

Relieved she's not being stubborn about his little breathing fit, he leans forward a little. "So you could be with your brother?" River can understand that. He'd give anything to be with Flora again.

"Ah, Chase isn't my brother."

Something in Echo's tone has River shifting back again. Another assumption he's made. Of course someone as beautiful and strong as Echo has someone waiting for her back at her colony. She's probably played tag with him hundreds of times.

"And you loved him so much that you wanted to stay," he says thoughtfully.

She frowns. "Something like that."

It seems River wasn't the only one looking forward to a life that was never meant to be. And he's learned that even a life in the Green Zone would be a poor second choice compared to being with those you care about.

And he's supposed to make that transition a little easier.

"The pods work by touch," he says, remembering what she said in the cornfield about having to learn everything herself. "There's a console on your right, just like I have one on my left. You enter the grid location you want to go to using letters and numbers."

She glances down, eyes narrowing as she sees the white buttons barely legible beneath opaque glass. "Right. My dad taught me my letters, so I should be able to get the hang of it."

"I'll get you a map of the Green Zone so you can memorize the grid references."

She looks, a smile blazing across her face. "Thanks. That would be great."

His lungs feeling a little tight again, River nods. "And thanks for...ah...helping me back there."

A twinkle creeps into her dark eyes. "For the one-off breathing glitch?" The warm feeling fades as he narrows his eyes, but Echo raises her hands. "Don't mention it."

Settling back into his seat, River lets the sights of the Green Zone fly past him. Echo mentioned everything moves too fast here, and yet, he's the one reeling. Things are changing too fast for him to keep up. Who is this girl? And what will she mean for his colony? Echo didn't want to be here, and yet she's trying to assimilate. At the same time, she hasn't forgotten the Dead Zone. In fact, she seems to champion it.

And that's a threat to their way of life. To each and every life they're passing by.

He glances at her out of the corner of his eye, finding her pensively staring out her window. The only way he can really find out the answers to those questions is to spend time with Echo. Mentor her. Play these games she thinks up.

Without assumptions. Without the defenses. So she comes to trust him.

That's probably what his father wanted him to do all along.

The pod slows to a smooth stop and River realizes they're back at the Sting. He climbs out, finding he can breathe almost normally again. The moment in the cornfield was obviously some sort of panic attack. A culmination of everything that's happened.

Feeling a little better, he climbs out, extending his hand so Echo can do the same. She hesitates for a second then takes it, her palm bringing back memories of her hands on his face. So warm and soothing. Her touch and her gaze are what grounded him.

She steps out, her gaze fluttering up to his. Can she sense that something's shifted?

River quickly yanks his hand back. There's no way of knowing if Echo is friend or foe. Here to assimilate or to destroy.

"Echo, I've been looking for you."

River stiffens as he hears his father's voice. Oren has rarely sought out himself or Flora. He turns to find him exiting the Sting, an unrecognizable expression on his face.

Oren's soft smile is the epitome of warm and welcoming.

Echo smiles back. "We were just taking a tour of the Green Zone. The cornfields are beautiful."

Every muscle locks even more. Please don't let Echo tell his father about what happened there. He's only just trusted River with a task. And River may have found a way to have Oren turn one of those smiles on him.

"I see," he says, glancing at River. "You're taking your mentorship role seriously."

River nods, feeling a little like he's standing to attention. "Of course. I welcome the chance to serve my colony."

"Good," says Oren. He turns back to Echo. "Harvest Day will be commencing soon. Reed's wanting to show you something in the LaB beforehand."

"Of course," she replies.

Oren turns and walks back into the Sting, having expected that answer.

Echo takes two steps forward then hesitates. "Are you okay?"

River nods. "I feel fine," he says, ignoring the weakness in his limbs. He's just tired despite the deep, dreamless sleep of last night. "And, ah, thanks again."

She didn't tell his father what happened in the cornfields.

She shrugs, moving toward the doors once more. "Don't

mention it," she says. She's just reached the large glass doors when she stops and turns, her smile once again gracing her beautiful features. "That's what friends are for."

She steps through, following his father, leaving River rooted to the spot.

He'd just decided friends are what they need to be.

That it's the best way to fulfill his father's wishes. To protect his colony.

Then why did his heart just stop, stutter, and kick off again at a gallop?

CHAPTER

ELEVEN

ECHO

Echo picks up a glass bottle at the entrance to the LaB and guzzles the water. She's thirsty after her outing with River. An outing that hadn't exactly gone to plan but wasn't a complete disaster either. Sure, River had almost died, but...he hadn't.

"What are you so happy about?" Reed asks, looking up from his bench.

"Nothing." She wipes the grin from her face, not sure if it was the memory of helping River that was making her smile or simply River himself. He's not such a bad guy when he lets his guard down. They'd actually been having fun before his lungs had forgotten how to breathe.

"That took a while," says Reed. "Was Vernon difficult?"

"No, he was fine," she says quickly, not wanting to get the old guy into trouble. It seems he's already worn out his welcome. "River and I took a break outside. He's helping me get my bearings."

"Glad he has time to take a break." Reed looks back down at his work.

"It was my idea." Echo sighs. Is she going to spend the rest of her life in the Green Zone making excuses for people? Life hadn't felt like that in the Dead Zone. They were freer somehow.

"I wanted to show you something," says Reed.

"So I heard." She sets down the empty water bottle on the trolley and approaches Reed. "We ran into Oren. He mentioned something about Harvest Day. What even is that?"

"We all have to contribute to the colony by helping out with the crops," he explains. "At regular intervals, depending on the season, a Harvest Day is declared. I would have thought your mentor would've explained this?"

"He was busy explaining other things," she says. "He showed me the cornfield, and how the pods work."

Reed raises an unimpressed eyebrow. "Echo, I need you to commit to the LaB. It's your chosen task. No more unauthorized excursions, okay?"

She's about to point out she didn't exactly *choose* this task but decides to hold her tongue. Like Reed pointed out earlier, there are far worse places to work.

"I'm committed," she says, avoiding explicitly agreeing to what he just asked. "What are we working on next? How do we get the adrenacure syringes into those tube things the medics use to administer them?"

Reed tilts his head toward the bench behind him and she sees he's already done it.

"Oh." She grimaces. "Sorry about that. What's next then? What did you want to show me?"

"Come over here." He pats the chair beside him. "This is going to blow your mind."

Liking the sound of that, she scoots over and sits down so she can see his computer screen.

"I've been analyzing blood samples." He points at some

complicated graphs on his screen and she wishes her reading skills were a little more refined. "Some from Immunes and some from Vulnerables."

"Where do you get the Vulnerable samples?" she asks, not having heard of anyone in her colony providing their blood.

"We take them from our Green Borns before their Confirmation," he says. "They're all on file here. If they don't pass, we categorize them as Vulnerable. We're working on figuring out what's different between the two groups."

Reed has Echo's full interest now. "And if you figure out the difference, do you think you can make the Vulnerables into Immunes?"

"It's possible." He smiles. "Although, we've been working tirelessly on this for decades with no luck. Some think it's impossible, but I refuse to accept that. We're just missing something. All we need to do is work out what it is."

Echo's eyes widen. This could be exactly the answer they're looking for. What better way to unite the colonies than for *everyone* to be an Immune? They could remove the net, let the bees come in to pollinate the Dead Zone's crops and regenerate the dusty soil. Maybe they could do it all in time to save her father. It's ambitious, but just like Reed said, it's possible.

"This could change everything," she says in a revered hush, feeling a little ashamed for skipping out of the Sting earlier when such important work was at stake. "How can I help?"

Reed removes a syringe from his drawer and sets it down on a cloth. "Getting a sample of your blood would help. We don't have too many Dead Born Immunes to sample."

She nods, willing to do whatever it takes. "You have Tuff, though?"

Reed nods. "The more samples we have, the better."

Echo rolls up her sleeve while Reed prepares the syringe.

"How quickly do you think we could roll this out?" she

asks. "How soon could we administer something like this to the Dead Zone?"

"Whoa." Reed laughs. "Don't get ahead of yourself. Didn't you hear what I said? We've been working on this for decades without success. And even if we have a breakthrough, I'm not sure it would be in the best interests of the colony to give something like that to the Dead Borns."

Echo's eyes narrow. "What do you mean? Wouldn't that be the entire aim? You said you could make Vulnerables into Immunes."

"I said, we might be able to. I also said that many think it's impossible." Reed waves the syringe in the air. "But if we succeed, we'd need to consider the needs of our colony first."

Echo's mouth flaps open. This is like the Betadome all over again, with Flora getting a shot of adrenacure while Avid was left to die. It seems the Green Zone don't really care about the Dead Zone at all.

"What possible benefit would it have not to help the Dead Zone?" She pulls back her arm as the syringe gets closer.

Reed shrugs. "I didn't say we wouldn't help them. Just that we'd have to consider the needs of our own colony first. Can you imagine the anarchy if we simply removed the net and everyone could march on into the Green Zone? We have rules. Systems. An established way of life. That could all be under threat."

"And your systems mean more than my colony's lives?" Echo glares at Reed.

He looks a bit unsure of himself. "No...I just mean that...it doesn't matter. Besides, this is your colony now."

Echo stands and pulls down her sleeve. "You know, I think I might give the blood sample a miss for now."

Reed pales as he glances at the opaque glass wall. "But... why? You can't do that!"

"I'm just considering my own needs before the rest of the colony." She gives him a tight-lipped smile. "I have an established way my body likes to run, and losing blood might place that under threat."

"But you must!" Reed grips her by the wrist.

She yanks away. "Get your hands off me."

"But, Echo!" His voice is filled with desperation now and it's scaring her.

Daphne's soft tones filter through the speakers in the LaB. *"Good afternoon, everyone. Harvest Day is now commencing. Please make your way out to the fields. And remember, if you're unable to help for any reason, you must go to the Processing Center immediately. Thank you for your important contribution to our colony. Be in peace."*

Echo seizes this as her chance and marches away from Reed, not wanting to share any air with someone filled with so much prejudice. People are people. The side of the net they were born on doesn't change that.

She gets to the elevator and presses the hexagonal button.

"Echo!" Reed calls from the door of the LaB. "Come back. Let's talk about this."

"I'm contributing to our colony." She smiles sweetly at him. "It's very important."

"Echo," Reed pleads.

The elevator doors slide open and she sees it's completely full of people.

"Sorry," she murmurs to the people as she pushes her way in, knowing there's no way Reed is going to be able to squash himself in there, too.

The doors close and the elevator begins a slow descent, stopping at each floor to greet more disappointed faces of people trying to get inside.

"Hello, Echo," says a honey-coated voice that's quickly become very familiar.

"Is that you, Daphne?" Echo tries to see past the tall man pressed up against her but it's no use.

"It is." Daphne laughs. "It's time to connect with the Earth and do our bit for the colony. I'm glad you're joining us."

Echo's relieved Daphne can't see her grimace. Helping the Green Zone is the last thing she wants to do right now. But being outside in the gardens might be nice. At least it gets her away from Reed.

The elevator eventually reaches the ground floor and they spill out into the foyer to join the sea of people drifting toward the airlock to get outside. A few remain in the elevator, continuing on to the basement to help in the Processing Center.

Despite the number of people, everyone is calm, a stark contrast to the rage that's boiling inside Echo. Just when she was starting to see that maybe the Green Zone had layers that weren't all bad, Reed has to come along and say something like that. Can't he see that the colonies can learn from each other? The Dead Zone has plenty they can teach this bunch of stuck-up, rule-following, bee-loving hypocrites.

Echo darts behind a well-rounded woman so Daphne doesn't find her. She needs to be alone right now. Well, as alone as she can be given she's completely surrounded by people.

She makes her way outside and is corralled into a pod with three other Green Borns and taken to a field she hasn't been to before. It's filled with crops all in neat rows, just like the corn-field, with a huge variety of produce. She can see peppers, broccoli, tomatoes, berries and a hundred other things she doesn't know the names of. People are already hard at work, carrying baskets and filling them with food. A few of them have stains down the front of their shirts and around their lips from sampling some of what they've collected.

At that moment, Echo can't help but hate every single one of these people.

She draws in a deep breath as she exits the pod and reminds herself to be better than that. Hate is a strong word. These people have no idea of how tough life is inside the net. If they knew, surely they wouldn't be so accepting of it. They can't possibly all be like Reed.

A man passes Echo an empty basket and she walks down one of the rows until she reaches the very end where nobody else is working. There's a group of trees that stretch out beyond the field, all brimming with unripened fruit. This place is like paradise. It's so hard to take it all in.

Someone stands from behind a tomato bush and Echo steps back, her eyes widening when she sees who it is.

She ambles closer.

"Hello," she says, trying her best to sound friendly. "Tuff, isn't it? Reed told me your name. I met you in the LaB when we were making adrenacure."

She knows she's rambling to make up for his lack of words. But this could be her one chance to talk to this guy. It's almost like fate has thrown them together.

Tuff roughly tears a few tomatoes from the bush, ignoring her, just like he had in the LaB. He looks a little younger out here in the sunshine. Perhaps it's the effect of being outside. Or maybe it's simply because he's out of the dark shadows of the Restricted Area and whatever work he has to do in there that seems to have turned every strand of his hair gray.

"I heard a rumor about you," she says, keeping her tone light. "Reed told me you're a Dead Born. Like me. I'm a Dead Born."

She waits for this information to sink in, but he doesn't react.

"Don't you want to know about your family?" she asks. "Maybe I know them."

Tuff continues with his work as if she hadn't spoken at all. Except for one thing.

His hands are shaking.

"There's a lot I could tell you," Echo continues. "And maybe a few things you could tell me. If you wanted to, of course."

She flinches, hoping she hasn't been too heavy-handed. She wants to make friends with him, not strike up some kind of deal.

"Are you happy here?" she asks. "You don't look happy, if you don't mind me saying so. I'm not especially happy either. I miss my dad. And my friends."

She doesn't say Chase's name, although that's who she means, even though he's the last person on this planet she wants to miss.

"I know it was only yesterday that I saw them, but it feels so..." She lets her voice trail away as Tuff turns his back on her and walks purposefully away, his contribution to Harvest Day over.

"It feels so lonely here," she finishes, the irony not escaping her that she said the final part of this sentence to herself.

Deciding she has no choice but to let Tuff go for the moment, Echo wanders further down the vegetable patch, picking a few ripe tomatoes that he missed. Unable to resist, she bites into one and closes her eyes as sweetness floods her mouth. It's incredible what this colony has been able to achieve. As she finishes the last bite, the taste of guilt overpowers the sweetness. How can she eat this when her father has so little that his body is beginning to shut down in protest?

It's quiet out here, with only the soft hum of voices floating to her on the breeze. There's a calmness in this colony. Perhaps that's what Reed is so worried about? Because while saving the Dead Zone is something that must happen if they get the chance, he's right in thinking it will completely disrupt the Immunes' way of life. The Vulnerables aren't used to following rules or thinking about the good of the colony before their own personal welfare. Which would no doubt mean an end to the peaceful existence outside the net. The LaB might not be able to make so many amazing discoveries, the Earth may not be preserved in the careful way it's being cared for now, species of plants and animals may become extinct. But that has to be worth it to save the Dead Borns, doesn't it? Or are potential future lives worth more than those who live and breathe today?

A bee buzzes past, pausing as if considering Echo for a moment, then flies on. With her heart beating double time, she resists the urge to swat at it, knowing it won't hurt her, and thinking about what a strange feeling that is. All her life, she's been taught to be afraid of these small creatures and now she doesn't have to give them a second thought. They're her friends, responsible for pollinating all the food that surrounds her. Without them, everything would be...dead.

She leans forward to pluck a few bright red strawberries and her locket falls out of her shirt and dangles down in front of her.

She's been waiting for the right moment to open it since her father gave it to her. Is that now? What could possibly be inside that she needed to wait until she was in the Green Zone to open?

Curiosity builds inside her like a storm and she snaps open the clasp, gasping to see what's inside.

Seeds.

She tips them into her hand and studies them with no idea

what they could possibly be. Too small for pumpkin? Not big enough for strawberries? And now she knows why her father wanted her to open the locket here. The soil back home wouldn't be fertile enough for these poor seeds to sprout. But more plants are the last possible thing anybody in the Green Zone could possibly need! She looks around her at the prolific crops and tucks the seeds back into the locket and re-fastens the clasp.

"Sorry, Dad," she says. "I'm bringing these home to plant."

When the vaccine has been found and offered to everyone, not just those who were lucky enough to be born in this privileged colony.

When the net has been torn open to let the bees in.

When the soil in the Dead Zone has regenerated and is ready to support new life.

That's where she'll plant these seeds.

At home. Her *real* home.

She picks up her basket, ready to fill it with whatever she can find. She just wants to return to her room and collapse on the cloud she's allowed to call her bed. But as she steps forward, a rock lands at her feet.

She glances up, wondering if a bird could have possibly dropped it. But then she notices a note tied around it, so she picks it up.

"Who threw this?" she calls out, wondering if River had taken her suggestion of playing games a little too far. That rock almost hit her on the head! Some thanks for saving his life earlier.

A blurry movement in the orchard catches her attention and she squints into the shadows, knowing it's already too late to follow whoever it might have been.

Untying the note, she smooths it out on her knee, hoping

the letters her father taught her are enough to make sense of the scribbly lines on this paper.

"M...me...mee...t. Meet." She sighs, certain she has the first word correct. "M...me."

She lifts her gaze back to the trees, wondering if it could possibly have been Chase that she'd seen.

"Meet me," she says, studying the note again. "He...her... No! Here. Meet me here."

Her breath comes in gasps and she hopes she's not about to have some kind of episode like River in the cornfield. Determination lighting inside her, she pushes on to figure out the rest of the note.

"Meet me here at..." She squints like that's going to make the next word clearer. Because it's a long one. "Mi...mid...nit... midnit." What on earth is midnit?

Then it hits her what the note says. Midnight! *Meet me here at midnight.*

But meet who here at midnight?

And what could they possibly want?

CHAPTER
TWELVE
RIVER

River's watched countless Harvest Days. He and Flora used to press their palms to the glass wall in the elevator as they'd headed down to the Processing Center, their breath fogging up the glass.

"What do you think it smells like?" Flora would ask, her eyes wide.

"Sweet," said River. "Lush." He'd grin at her and they'd say the next word simultaneously.

"Viridescent."

And now that he's standing here, in the midst of a field of pumpkins, it's everything they thought it would be. The acres of large, lobed leaves shading sprawling stems are most definitely viridescent. Beneath the smells of rich earth and moist vegetation is the scent of pollen and nectar, carrying the barest hint of the honey they'll become.

Around him, the people of his colony move smoothly and quietly, picking pumpkins the colors of a brilliant sunset. They smile at each other, at the harvest they've been blessed with, and at the buzzing insects winding their way through it all.

And yet it's nothing like he imagined.

He never pictured he'd be so...alone.

A pang of grief has River's chest constricting. What's Flora doing now? How hungry is she? Has she made friends, someone who can help her learn the ways of the Dead Zone?

Does she resent him for being on this side of the Betadome?

The pain clogs his throat, feeling jagged and hard. How does he move forward, carrying this loss and pain and guilt?

River stills when a bee passes close to his ear. His pulse accelerates. He knows technically it's not a threat, but he can't stop the alarm that shivers down his spine. These tiny animals are deadly to most of the human population.

Including his twin sister.

To his surprise the bee lands on his sleeve, lacy, translucent wings twitching. With wide eyes, River watches as the bee crawls toward his wrist. Her black and gold striped abdomen pumps as her legs move in wave-like synchronicity, large balls of pollen tucked on the rear ones.

She circles his arm as she continues, and River twists it as he watches her reach his exposed skin. The faintest of tickling registers as she crawls up to his palm.

There, in the center of his hand, the bee stops, her abdomen still working as she pumps air through her body. Blinking, River realizes he's holding the most dangerous creature on this planet.

Humanity's greatest threat.

And yet, their only salvation.

There's no life without bees.

The tiny insect's wings flutter and she lifts into the air, her legs dangling as she turns in the direction of the Betadome. River watches, silent and still, as she flies away. She has her own colony to care for. She's more than willing to do what it takes to ensure its survival.

Which is exactly what River should be doing, rather than focusing on what he's lost.

It's his first Harvest Day. The day the bounty of their colony is celebrated. This food feeds them and the surplus goes to the Dead Zone. He jolts as he realizes this could be something he could do to help his sister. If there are a glut of pumpkins, surely a larger proportion will be sent there.

River's about to get picking when a white-clad body appears beside him.

"They're beautiful, inspiring creatures, aren't they?"

River turns sharply, surprised that it's his father. He glances in the direction the bee flew away. "Yes, they are."

Oren clasps his hands, drawing in a deep breath. "I do love Harvest Day. It always reminds me why everything we do is so important."

River simply nods. He's not used to having conversations with his father.

A man walks past carrying two pumpkins, and he nods deferentially to Oren. "Be in peace," he murmurs.

"Be in peace," Oren responds just as calmly.

River expects him to walk away after that. His visits on Harvest Day are generally a token appearance before rushing back to the Sting. He's no doubt moving through each of the fields, showing his face as he revels in the amazing beauty of the Green Zone.

Acting as if he never had a daughter.

The bitter thought takes River by surprise. His father has always been emotionless and aloof. He shouldn't expect any different.

Except Oren has welcomed Echo with smiles and warmth.

His father remains standing beside him. As if this is normal. Uncomfortable, River's about to walk away when Oren speaks in a low voice.

"How is our new member...assimilating?" he asks.

River stiffens as he realizes why Oren is actually here, talking to him.

He wants to know how his favorite colony member is going. Flashes of Echo's laughing face among the cornstalks rise in River's mind. It's like she'd been playing among them all her life. And then Echo helping him when he had the weird breathing issue.

But then so does her question when they were talking about the Dead Zone.

Will you help me change it?

What would his father say if he heard Echo say that? But for some reason, River doesn't mention it. There's too much conflicting information whirling in his head. Right alongside the conflicting emotions...

"Slowly," he says. "She finds our way of life foreign."

"Of course she would. The Dead Zone is a completely different colony to the Green Zone. A period of adjustment to all these blessings is to be expected."

River suppresses a frown. Flora would be experiencing the same adjustment, but to the emptiness of the Dead Zone, and yet their father isn't concerned about her welfare. "Echo's not acting like she feels lucky to be here."

Oren shifts as he clasps his hands behind his back. "Then how does she feel?"

"I don't know," says River through gritted teeth, conscious that's not the answer his father would be looking for.

"Then find out," Oren says in a low voice, his jaw just as tight. "If she's not willing to become one of us, then she can't stay."

"How am I supposed to tell? She's smart. She could fake it."

"We need a sample of her blood. That will be the first sign she's one of us." His gaze snaps to River, hard and intense. "And there isn't much time."

Before River can ask why a sample of Echo's blood is so important, or why it's so urgent, his father spins on his heel and stalks away.

Daphne passes him, carrying bottles of water. She smiles. "Be in peace, Oren."

"Be in peace," his father responds, his voice as cool and calm as always. Like the tension that River sensed a moment ago never existed.

River turns and walks down one of the rows in the field, frowning. There are layers to his father. He's been so welcoming with Echo. Gracing her with smiles River didn't know existed. And yet he was just talking of her being Forgotten if she doesn't fit in. Have those smiles been nothing but a ploy?

Tucking his head down, River keeps walking, lost in thought. Strangely enough, lying isn't something he ever associated with his father, which now seems rather naïve. It's just that he always believed Oren's aloofness had to do with the strain of leading the colony with truth and integrity. It's how River justified it. Made peace with it.

Except right now, he feels anything but peace.

For the millionth time, River wishes Flora were here. She'd be someone he could talk to. Someone to help him untangle the mess that everything is becoming.

There's a tap on his shoulder and he spins around, half expecting his father to be there and already bracing himself. But it's Clover, beaming up at him. "You walked straight past me," she giggles.

"Oh, sorry. I wasn't, ah, paying attention."

She moves a little closer. "You certainly were a moment ago."

River's brow crinkles. "Huh?"

Clover's smile grows even wider. "When you were standing with your father. I saw you watching me."

River blinks, aware that a flush is creeping up his cheeks. He didn't even know Clover was here, let alone was he watching her. But how does he tell her that without hurting her feelings? "Oh, I, was, ah—"

"It's okay," she assures, blue eyes twinkling as they flicker to his pink cheeks. "I was watching you, too."

He blinks again, not really sure how this conversation took this turn. "Look, Clover—"

"You seemed to be having an intense conversation."

Glad for the change of topic, River nods. "All conversations with my father are intense."

Another step, and Clover's right in front of him. He's about to take a step backward when she presses a hand to his chest. "I know things are a bit complicated between you two. That's why I want you to know you don't need to do this alone, River."

"Ah, thanks."

He needs to back away. Get her hand off him. Something that will tell her this is far from comfortable for him. But without hurting her. Clover's lost her sister, like he has. She'd be just as fragile emotionally.

She smiles, her face now soft as her eyelashes flutter. "We get each other. I think that's why I've always been drawn to you..."

There's no mistaking the inviting warmth pooling in Clover's blue gaze, and yet, it leaves River cold. It never occurred to him that they could be a match. Not once.

But Clover believes he was watching her. That they have a connection. How could he have been so blind?

And what the hell is he supposed to do now?

River clears his throat, but before he can speak, there's a grunt behind him. A second later, someone slams into his back. He's knocked forward, quickly grabbing Clover so he doesn't bowl her over.

"Oh," she says in surprise, only to grip him back. "So strong," she breathes, her hands tightening around his biceps.

Great. Just what he needs.

Clover glances over his shoulder to see who just rammed into him and frowns. "Oh," she repeats, almost distastefully.

"Shorry," comes a slurred voice.

River releases Clover and turns around, glad to create some space between them. Vernon grins at him as he tries to steady himself. "Hello," he says cheerily.

Reaching out to steady him, River smiles. "Hey, Vern. I didn't know you were helping in the pumpkin patch."

Vernon sways closer to River. "I was trying to spike the water bottles," he says in a hushed voice, glancing down at the two bottles tucked underneath his arm. "Let everyone else get a taste of the good stuff."

"I doubt Daphne would let you anywhere near them."

Vern frowns grouchily. "She wouldn't even take a sip so I could show her." But his expression quickly clears as his eyes twinkle. "Then I saw you needed a bit of a hand."

River's lips twitch as he realizes Vern could see his discomfort. "I was fine," he whispers back, conscious that Clover is a few feet away.

Vern snorts. "Yeah, you had it all under control." He steps around River, holding up a half-empty bottle to Clover. "Thirsty, darlin'?"

Clover smiles tightly. "No, I'm fine."

"You sure? There's plenty to go around."

This time, Clover recoils as if Vernon just lurched toward her. "I said I'm fine."

Vernon elbows River. "Seems I can't tell when someone isn't wanting to take me up on my offer."

Hiding his double take at Vernon's words, River slips his arm through his. "Come on, let's get you back to the Sting."

"But Harvest Day isn't over!" he says in mock horror.

Even though Vern's right—everyone is expected to be in the fields for Harvest Day—River sets forward. "We'll find you something to eat in the tents then."

Vern grumbles but allows himself to be led. He grins at Clover as they walk past. "Happy Harvest Day."

River throws her an apologetic smile as they pass, having to work on keeping it in place when he sees the disgust on Clover's face as she regards Vernon. It's quickly replaced by her own smile as she looks at River. "I'll see you in Eden."

Nodding even though he's not looking forward to it, River hurries past, still supporting Vernon. He slows once they're a short distance away. "Thanks Vern, I didn't see that coming."

"That's because you have a good heart, boy. And you do what everyone else around here does—you trust everything is what it seems."

River frowns. "Why wouldn't I?"

Vernon chuckles, although the sound is almost bitter. "Exactly. Why wouldn't you?" He shakes his head. "Anyway, I suspect that girl's going to be persistent." He winks at River. "She's trying to get in before the rest."

Conscious Vernon just changed the subject, River stops, uneasy. He's already got the sense his father's behavior isn't everything it seems. "Why wouldn't I?" he asks again.

"Ignore the ravings of a drunk man." Vernon waves his half-empty bottle under River's nose. "Let's have a drink."

River's eyes narrow. "You use that to keep people away, don't you?"

Vernon's face slackens before he quickly schools his features again. "Darned clever boy," he mutters.

River's about to insist that his question is answered when a bee zips between them and straight into Vernon's bottle. The amplified buzzing sound is cut short as it lands in the liquid.

Vernon curses. Squatting down, he tips the contents onto the soil. The bee lands on the dirt, glistening with moisture. Pushing to his feet, Vernon shakes his head. "I'm more than happy to share, little one. But no swimming in the kasi, okay?"

A faint humming rises, suggesting the bee's already drying off. River shakes his head. "At least someone wants some of that stuff."

Vernon chuckles and they watch as the bee slowly lifts into the air, heading straight back to the bottle in Vern's hand. "Oh no you don't, little one," he says, moving the bottle away. "Go get yourself some pumpkin flowers."

The bee lands on his wrist, and a second later Vernon winces and hisses. He glances down in surprise and the bee flies away, leaving behind a small, raised lump.

"It stung you," River says, his eyebrows hiked.

"Obviously wasn't happy I cut its swim short," grunts Vernon, flicking away the remnants of the sting.

River nods, knowing it's not a big deal. Although they do everything they can to be peaceful and calm, people are occasionally stung in the Green Zone. The bee's aggressive tendencies can be easily triggered.

But everyone is an Immune. Just like River in the Betadome, the sting will be little more than a burning feeling that quickly passes.

Except Vernon's eyes widen as his hand flies to his throat. He sucks in a raspy breath, only for it to be cut short.

"Vern?" River asks, concerned.

The bottle drops to the ground with a hollow thud as Vernon staggers backward. "River," he whispers, eyes impossibly wider.

River catches him as his knees give out, and he quickly slips under his shoulder. "Looks like you're going back to the Sting after all."

Even though it should be impossible, Vernon's reacting to being stung.

They've taken two steps when Vernon collapses, landing on a sprawling pumpkin plant with a grunt. Alarmed, River kneels beside him. He gasps when he sees the purple tinge climbing up his friend's throat. Vernon grabs River's suit, his face pale and panicked. His mouth works, but no words come out.

River looks around frantically. "Medic," he shouts. "Medic!"

Vernon's hand slips away as if his strength is waning fast, his breath now coming in shallow gasps as he lays among the foliage. River leans closer, heart tripping out a panicked beat. "It's okay. Help is coming."

Vernon's eyes flicker as he struggles to breathe. "Riv..."

"Sh, don't talk." He needs to save his breath. "Everything's going to be fine."

But Vernon shakes his head, a frantic gleam appearing in his eyes. "Question... everything..." he gasps through lips that are rapidly turning blue.

"Step away," says a voice behind him.

River looks up to find two medics holding a stretcher. He scrambles backward, giving them room to lift Vernon. He watches with disbelieving eyes as they rush away, transferring him to the nearest pod.

As the pod silently slips along its track, River reassures his thundering heart that Vernon will be fine.

He's Immune.

Or is that the first thing River needs to question?

CHAPTER
THIRTEEN

ECHO

The elevator begins its descent and Echo sighs in relief. She'd half expected it wouldn't run at this late hour. Just another way to keep the Immunes imprisoned in this glittering tower they call home.

But the elevator is working. As is her heart—at triple speed. If she can get out of the Sting and over to the orchard without anyone seeing her, she'll find out who threw the rock with the note attached.

She has a few suspects.

It could be Tuff. Perhaps he hadn't wanted to be seen talking to her out in the open, but under the cover of darkness he can tell her everything she wants to know.

It could be Clover, warning her to stay away from River.

It could be River himself, testing to see if she'll break more rules.

It could even be Oren. Although, she doubts he'd need to send secret notes to talk to her in private.

The elevator comes to a halt at the ground floor and she drags her mind away from one more rock-wielding suspect.

Chase.

Too late. The thought sweeps through her mind before she can stop it. The guy who she wants to both kiss and kill is a dangerous option, mainly because she has no idea what she wants to say to him. He betrayed her. If he'd given her the pollen like she'd asked him to, she'd be back home right now. Maybe even tucked into the crook of Chase's arm while they slept.

But he'd taken her future—*their* future—into his own hands. And now she's not really sure how she feels about him. Her heart had been so full of Chase before her Confirmation, and his betrayal has left her with an empty space. A space that if she's not careful, a certain green-eyed mentor might just edge himself into. Because as much as she'd gotten off on the wrong foot with River when they first met, she saw a completely different side to him today. A fun side. A loyal side. A side that showed her his heart is in the right place, even if sometimes his words are not. She doubts he'd give Flora a package of dirt if she asked for pollen.

With a bitter taste settling in the back of her throat, she passes through the airlock and steps out into the night, wondering if Oren has cameras at the entrance. That seems very much like something he'd do.

She covers her face with her hand and decides to head to the orchard on foot. The risk of being traced or followed in a pod seems too high. This is clearly a secret rendezvous, and she'd like to keep it that way. She hasn't been getting too many answers out in the open. This is her best chance yet to find out what the Immunes are really up to on this side of the net.

It's quite a distance, but she's used to walking. It's not like she had any other option growing up. She quickens her pace, enjoying the cool air in her lungs. It's different out here at night. The gentle hum of people talking and pods moving is replaced by the sound of crickets chirping and the occasional owl hooting. Darkness shields the view of the crops, leaving only strange shadows that crisscross each other as starlight twinkles through the leaves of the tall trees that line the road.

She breaks into a jog, unsure exactly how much time has passed since she slipped out of her room and tiptoed past River's door. Hopefully whoever wants to talk to her will wait a few minutes if she's late.

Taking the path that leads to the vegetable gardens, she's glad she mapped all this out in her mind as she'd left Harvest Day to return to the Sting. She'd never have been able to find her way back otherwise. Especially in the dark. It would have been easier if it were a full moon, but she's grateful for the stars to light her way.

Stumbling on a stick on the path, she makes her way down the first row of vegetables, heading toward the dark line of trees she can see at the very end.

It's only just before she reaches the orchard that fear floods through her. What if whoever wants to meet her, plans to hurt her? What if it's Reed with a syringe wanting to take her blood by force? What if Tuff wants to be the only Dead Born who works in the LaB? What if Clover wants to do more than just warn her?

Shaking these thoughts away, Echo slows her pace, straightens her spine and marches forward. She faced a cage full of killer bees and survived. She can do this.

She steps from the dabbled light into the darkness and blinks.

"I'm here," she says, cautiously. "Show yourself."

Her heart is pounding now and she draws in a breath as she waits.

There's the rustle of leaves and a set of hands covers her

eyes as someone pulls her to their chest, in just the way Chase had the morning of her Confirmation.

She turns and his hands fall from her eyes as familiar arms wrap themselves around her. She doesn't need moonlight or sunlight or the brightest bulb in the Sting to show her who this is.

Her heart takes on a new beat as she draws in the feeling of being close to Chase once more. Except, it's different to how she used to feel. She still loves him, of course. That's not a feeling anyone can turn off like a switch, but everything feels tainted now.

"Echo," Chase says, tipping up her chin as his lips brush across hers.

Surprising even herself that she doesn't want the kiss she'd dreamed of since she was a girl, she turns her face away, pressing her cheek against his chest instead.

Not seeming to notice, he lets his hands slide down her arms until he's holding her hands.

"I'm so happy to see you," he says.

She lets go of him, trying and failing to conjure the same level of warmth. "You tricked me."

"And I said I was sorry."

"And you also said you weren't really sorry." She searches for his gaze in the darkness, even though she knows she'll never find it.

"I didn't want to lie to you," he says. "I wanted to tell you the truth."

"So, why didn't you?" She crosses her arms, giving him no chance of reaching for her hands again. "Did you think I couldn't handle the truth? Because let me tell you, finding out you lied to me has been a whole lot more difficult to process."

"You're being stubborn," he says. "Like you always are. I

knew if I refused to get you the pollen, you'd get some yourself. I had to stop you. I had to let you take the chance."

"Why?" she asks again, surprised at how angry she feels. "Because you know what's right for me? Or did this have more to do with what's right for you?"

"I...but...Echo..." He lets out a sigh. "I *am* sorry for what I did. But I'm also not sorry. Was what I did really that bad?"

He puts a hand on her upper arms and she shakes him away. She's not so much angry at what he did. She's angry that he ruined what they had. That it didn't seem as important to him as it was her.

"Why are you here, Chase?" she asks. "If you were so keen to get rid of me, why can't you just let me go? Are you that desperate to have someone on the inside?"

"I have to tell you something." His voice is solemn, even though he shouldn't have anything to be unhappy about given everything played out exactly as he wanted it to.

"Will it be the truth this time?" she snaps. "Or is this another one of your games?"

"Your father is dead." His words slam into her chest and he reaches for her again.

Collapsing into him as her legs threaten to give way, she drags in a deep breath and steadies herself.

"You're lying." She tries to pull away, realizing she can no longer trust a word this guy says.

But Chase holds her so tightly she can feel the beating of his heart through his worn shirt. "He died this morning. I knew you'd want to know."

"But I just saw him yesterday!" Her head spins as she fights against both the physical contact and Chase's words. *This cannot be true.*

"He was sicker than anyone realized," says Chase. "It seems

he was staying strong for you. When I went to check in on him this morning, like you asked me to, he'd...gone."

"No." She speaks firmly, as if denying what he's telling her can make it a lie. "No."

"He was so proud of you." Chase continues to hold her and she stops fighting him for a moment as she tries to understand. "He was so happy to hear you were Immune. Once he knew you'd gone to the Green Zone, he must have let go."

"I don't believe you." She wrenches herself free and drags some cool air into her lungs. "You lied about the pollen, and you're lying about this."

"Why would I lie about this?" he asks. "For what possible reason?"

She shakes her head even though he can't see her as she tries to answer his question.

To get her to come home? No, he already proved she's exactly where he wants her to be.

To upset her? Maybe. But surely, he knows he's already upset her enough.

Because he's a pathological liar? Right now, this seems the most likely option.

"Echo, it's true," Chase says in such a way that she has to believe him.

Her legs buckle and she drops to the ground as silent tears choke her.

Chase is beside her in a moment with a hand rubbing her back, saying soothing words she can no longer hear.

Her father is dead. She's never going to see him again. Ever. And she wasn't there to hold his hand as he let go.

She clutches her locket as she rocks back and forth, her most precious possession now even more precious. It's the last thing her father gave her. And over the years he gave her so much.

"I need to see him," she says.

Chase's hand pauses on her back. "It's too late, Echo. He's gone. There's nothing you can do for him now."

"Take me home with you," she begs. "Please, Chase. I don't belong here. I should never have left."

Maybe her father would still be alive if she'd refused to step foot in the Betadome.

"You can't." Chase sounds panicked. "You have to stay here."

"Why, Chase? I don't care if they cut off my rations." She uncurls herself and sits up straight.

"Because we need you here," he says firmly. "You said you'd help."

"Who's *we*?" Her voice is little more than a whisper as she wonders who exactly she's agreed to help.

"It's better if you don't know," he says. "And we don't have time now for me to explain."

She falls silent, disappointed at being treated like a pawn in Chase's game, but too exhausted to fight him. It's hard enough trying to process that her father is really gone.

"Can you leave food?" he asks. "Right here behind this tree. As much as you can wherever you can. I'll distribute it."

"Is that all?" she asks, disappointed at how menial the task seems. If she's going to help him, she'd like to do more than just feed him.

"For now. When I have further instructions for you, I'll put them in this hollow." He pats a small divot in the tree trunk. "It's just not safe for you to go back home just now."

"It's never been safe." She gets to her feet, needing to end this conversation and return to her soft cloud of a bed so she can let her tears for her father fall.

"But especially now." Chase stands, seeming to know

better than to try to touch her again. "You remember that Green Born you asked me to look out for? The girl?"

"Flora." Echo really doesn't care about River's twin right now. Not when her father is dead. But she finds herself listening intently anyway because she knows someone who does care about her.

"That's the one," says Chase. "Flora. She's gone. Nobody knows where she is. She completely vanished."

There's a gasp and the sound of the crunching of dried leaves behind Echo. She spins around to see a shadow behind her, instinctively holding up her hands to shield herself from attack.

"Who's there?" she asks, her heart pounding once more.

"It's me," says River, taking a few steps forward. "And what do you mean, *she's vanished?* Where's my sister?"

Echo turns back to Chase, only to find darkness. It's as if he was never there.

She stands with River, breathing heavily in the darkness, each mourning their losses and nursing their fears. For two people who were supposed to have achieved the ultimate dream of being Confirmed as Immune, right now the future doesn't feel so bright.

CHAPTER
FOURTEEN
RIVER

"What did he mean, Flora's disappeared?" River repeats through a tight, dry throat.

"I..." Echo's little more than an outline in the dark night as she shuffles one way then the other as if the answer is hiding among the trunks of the fruit trees. "I don't know."

River's about to demand some answers—who she met, why, and what any of this means for his sister—when he registers the hitch in Echo's voice. It's faint, almost lost in the hesitation of her words, but he recognizes it. The deep, slicing pain of loss.

Because he's felt it himself.

"Your father," he says quietly. It took time to sneak up on Echo and her friend, so River didn't hear everything. But he heard enough.

A sob punctures the air, quickly cut off as Echo clamps a hand over her mouth. It muffles her words as much as the tears. "He can't be..."

"I'm so sorry, Echo."

He sees the movement because he's expecting it. Echo's

146

shadowy form dips as her legs give out. River leaps forward and catches her before she crumples to the orchard floor. He scoops her up, holding her against his chest.

She curls into a ball in his arms, not so much to seek comfort, but as if she's fighting to hold herself together. Another sob erupts, jagged and harsh. And then another. And another. His own heart aching, River turns and carries her out of the orchard.

When Flora was Confirmed a Vulnerable, it had felt like his foundations had been ripped away. It was knowing his father was watching that had kept him upright.

But Echo's foundation *was* her father. And she's alone in the Green Zone, a world away from everything she knows. She has nothing to brace her. Nothing to stop her from falling apart.

Echo continues to cry as he heads to the nearest pod. He held Flora after they lost their mother, alongside his own grief. He just hopes doing the same for Echo will offer her some comfort.

The white pod glows gently in the dark, acting like a muted beacon. River climbs inside, ending up with Echo on his lap. For long seconds, he's not sure what to do. The gentle light within shows the devastation on her face. Liquid eyes. Stained cheeks. Trembling lips.

Echo was obviously close with her father. She's taking this hard.

And River's nothing to her. Another Green Born.

Does he continue to hold her, or should he shift her to the seat beside him? For a fleeting moment, he thinks of the boy she met. Chase. The one who's not her brother. Shouldn't he be the one comforting her, instead of running away at the first disturbance?

"My father... He's dead," Echo whispers, as if she's testing the words. Maybe sampling what that new reality feels and looks like. Her dark gaze rises to his. "I...I just can't..."

"I know," he whispers. "It feels like you'll never be able to go on."

Echo will, though. She'll keep moving forward, her strength and courage carrying her through. The same strength and courage her father instilled in her. But she doesn't want to hear that now. The pain is too encompassing. It's swallowing her whole.

Echo's back bows under the weight of her grief and she buries her face in his chest, gripping his shirt with white-knuckled intensity. Quickly typing in the coordinates for the Sting, River wraps his arms around her once more, holding her just as tightly.

He leans back as the pod silently slips through the night. "Tell me about him," he says gently. "Tell me about your father."

Since Flora's been gone, he's discovered exactly how harsh a punishment being Forgotten is. Losing someone is hard enough. Acting as if they never existed means the wound can never heal.

His chest tightens. And now Flora's disappeared.

Echo draws in a shuddering breath and for long moments, says nothing. River wonders if he should've stayed quiet.

"He was convinced I was an Immune," she whispers. "He didn't come to the Confirmation because he believed I'd be leaving. I was sure we'd have more time."

The tears start afresh, but River doesn't stop. "What else?" he coaxes.

"He...he liked to carve. Out of stone." Echo hiccups. "We needed to save wood for fires in case the bees got through the net."

The smoke is the only second line of defense they'd have.

"What else?"

The sobs subside as Echo thinks. "He was the most generous person I know. I was twelve before I learned that I was eating far more than my allocated rations. Dad had been giving me half of his, pretending that's how much I was entitled to." A shudder has her hunching in tighter. "It's probably why he died young, even by our standards."

The sobs return, ripping through Echo's body, making her seem fragile and vulnerable. They're two words River hasn't associated with her. Not until now.

The pod comes to a standstill and River realizes they've arrived at the Sting. The doors open and he climbs out, Echo still in his arms.

"He loved you," he says softly as he walks toward the airlock. "He did everything he could to ensure you survived, and that's a beautiful thing."

Echo nods, the tears glistening beneath the lights of the building. She tucks her head into his shoulder, either not wanting him to see them or finding the foyer too bright.

River carries her to the elevator, noticing for the first time how little opportunity there is for shadows to exist within the Sting. The soft, angled lighting and white walls make it feel like there's light everywhere.

Leaving nowhere to hide.

The elevator silently carries them up and he wonders where that thought came from. No one needs to hide in the Green Zone. There are no secrets and there's nothing to fear. It must be the protectiveness he's feeling toward Echo. She'd be feeling so exposed right now.

They come to a stop and the doors slide open. Walking quickly down the hexagonal corridor, River carries Echo to her room. He doesn't bother turning the lights on, wanting to give her the privacy of darkness.

Inside, he stops by the bed. "Echo—"

He stills as he looks down. She's fallen asleep, her head on his shoulder, damp tendrils of hair stuck to her cheeks.

Carefully, he lowers her onto the bed. She curls up and presses her face into the pillow the moment he releases her. River pulls the blanket up and tucks it around her shoulders. Echo barely stirs.

Glad she's deeply asleep, he tiptoes back out of the room. Tomorrow the pain will hit her all over again. The more rest she gets the better.

His room is next door and he doesn't bother turning the lights on in there, either. It seems he could use the protective cloak of darkness, too. Suddenly exhausted himself, he strips off his white suit and slips into loose shorts, the movements quick and automatic. It frees up his mind to go over what he learned tonight after he followed Echo.

Echo met with someone from the Dead Zone.

Her father is dead.

And Flora is missing.

River sits on the bed, his body feeling far heavier than it should. The future he dreamed about was a fairytale. He was so naive...

"River?"

He leaps to his feet as his heart vaults into his throat. "Who's there?"

The room is bathed in light, revealing Clover sitting on his bed. She smiles apologetically. "I came to talk to you tonight. When I found you were gone, I decided to wait."

While he was off following Echo after he heard her slip past, curious what she was up to. He never thought she was going to the orchard.

To meet a Dead Born.

River presses his fingertips to his temples. And now

Clover's in his room. How did things get so complicated, so fast?

Clover shuffles to the end of the bed. Her white nightgown hikes up past her knees, but she doesn't pull it down. "Where were you?"

"In the orchard. I thought I'd forgotten something there after Harvest Day," he lies, conscious he's covering for Echo. He just can't bring himself to land her in hot water right now. Not straight after learning about her father's death.

That will be a task for tomorrow.

Clover frowns. "Is everything okay?"

River shakes his head. "Nothing's okay."

"I'm here if you need a friend," she says softly. "I know how hard it's been to lose your sister."

The truth of Clover's words has his shoulders sinking. The thought of Flora, out in the Dead Zone, alone and scared has his heart twisting in his chest.

Clover tucks her knees up to her chin, hugging them. "I lost Cascade, too."

River sits down beside her, glad there's someone who understands what he's going through. He asks the question that's been burning through every cell since he heard the news about Flora. "If you knew that...Cascade was missing in the Dead Zone. That no one knew where she was. What would you do?"

Clover stiffens. "You think Flora's missing?"

"I overheard a conversation," he hedges. "She's disappeared. No one knows where she is."

"Oh, River. I'm so sorry." She unfolds herself and moves a little closer.

"What would you do, Clover? If it were your sister?" Someone she's loved all her life.

She frowns. "There's nothing I could do," she says, as if it's obvious. Her hand wraps around his. "Cascade's gone."

Practically Forgotten.

River knows that's the right answer. The answer that should be sitting right alongside the burning question, soothing it until it's little more than a hard piece of coal he has to swallow.

But the smoldering doesn't go away. It keeps scorching him from the inside out.

Clover presses a hand to his upper arm and River realizes for the first time he's shirtless. "You're not thinking of going to look for her, are you?"

"Of course not," he says quickly. "I was just...wondering."

"It hurts to lose them. I know it does. But you have to let her go, River."

He nods, staring at his hands, discovering they're clenched into tight fists. "You're right. I just have to hope everything will be fine."

His response seems to relax her. "I'm sure it will be. Flora's one of the smartest people I know." She leans in a little closer. "Except for you."

River shifts, recreating the distance between them. He can't deal with this right now. "I'm really tired, Clover, and you should get some rest. We both have to be in Eden tomorrow."

She hesitates, but then stands. "Sure. It's late." Padding in her bare feet, she pauses at the door. "If you need a friend, I'm here."

He nods, then realizing she may not be able to see, he clears his throat. "Thanks, Clover."

She leaves and he lets out a long breath. Clover may have some idea of what he's feeling, but she wants far more than friendship. It's something he's going to have to deal with.

Tomorrow.

He falls back onto the bed and stares at the ceiling he can't see. Tonight, his mind is going to be stuck in a loop. A merry-go-round of anguish. He's going to have to figure out how to let his twin go. Just like Clover has with Cascade.

Just like their father has with his only daughter.

River can't go after Flora. Green Borns don't go to the Dead Zone. Ever.

And yet, how can he sit here and do nothing? He spears his fingers into his hair, pushing his palms into his eyes so hard it hurts.

How can he act like she's already dead?

Or worse. Forgotten.

FIFTEEN

ECHO

Echo sits behind the large computer screen in the LaB and immediately rubs her temples.

"You can do this," she mutters to herself, talking not just about the impossible task Reed has set her, but generally breathing in and out when she knows her father is not.

She'd slept deeply for a few hours after her vague memories of River carrying her to her room. Her brain had been so overloaded it'd given her no choice but to shut down. Then she'd woken in the darkness, hugged her pillow and cried until the soft sounds of music had piped into her room to let her know it was time to face the day.

Her first instinct had been to pull the covers over her head, but then she'd given herself a stern talking to. She *cannot* let her father's death be in vain. The best way she can make things right and honor all the things he did for her is to do exactly what Chase has asked of her. She's in a unique position in the Green Zone. She has an important job to do. She can help make sure that nobody else has to lose their father in the same way she lost hers.

"Press the button on the top right to turn it on," says Reed from his desk, looking at her in confusion. "Please, tell me you've at least seen a computer before?"

"I'm a fast learner, remember." Pressing the button, she watches as the screen lights up and is filled with an image of a green field. It looks almost as beautiful as it does in real life and she's captivated once more that one color could have so many different shades.

"What do you call all these green colors?" She points at her screen, which Reed can just see if he leans back. "Do you have different names for all of them?"

He seems to find her question amusing. "There's emerald and jade and juniper and olive. Then we have lime green and sea green and avocado and sage. It's endless, really. Flora used to call them viridescent."

"I'm not even going to ask how to spell that." Echo smiles wearily.

She studies the photo, wondering which label applies to which color.

Reed turns back to his own screen. "Do you have different names for shades of gray where you're from?"

She can't tell if he's mocking her or if it's a serious question. "It's just gray." She studies the text box that's popped up in the center of the screen, sounding out the words in her head.

"What's a password mean?" she asks. "And why's Flora's name in this box?"

"Maybe this wasn't such a good idea." Reed sighs. "I didn't realize you had literally zero experience with computers."

"Then teach me." Echo gives him an encouraging smile, certain this computer must contain hundreds of secrets about the Green Zone.

"Echo." Reed leans back in his chair. "I can teach you a lot of things. But first I have to trust you. Which means you need to trust me."

She sighs, knowing exactly what he's talking about. "I'll give you my blood sample. You can take it as soon as we finish this. I promise."

She'd already decided not to be stubborn. She wants Reed to unlock the secret to their Immunity as much as he does. Even if his plans on how to use the information differ to hers.

"Today, Echo," he says. "We need it today."

"I already said you can take it today." She rolls her eyes then looks back at her screen. "So, why's Flora's name in this box?"

"That used to be her computer." Reed retrieves a syringe from his drawer, just a little too enthusiastically for Echo's liking. "And the password is what you type in to gain access to the files."

"What do I type?" Echo's fingers hover over the letters, hoping whatever the word is that it's shorter than that other one he'd used before for all the green colors. Viridognant? Or Vinosentant? Or whatever it was. But that's not important right now.

"The password is *River*." Reed rolls his eyes as he looks for something else in his drawer. "Not exactly original but at least it's easy to remember."

"Very cute." Echo presses the R key, then hesitates.

"R.I.V.E.R," spells Reed. "Just in case you write it differently where you're from."

It's obvious Reed is being kind to her, which reminds her of someone else who'd looked out for her feelings last night. The guy attached to the very name she's trying to type. River had been so understanding of the grief that had ripped her heart in two, despite the deep concern he must have been feeling for

Flora. She's not sure how she would have made her way back to the Sting without him.

The longer she's spending in this colony, the more kindness she's seeing amongst the multitude of misunderstandings these people seem to have about her own colony. If only she could talk to her dad about it. It's making her question literally everything she's ever known.

"What do I do now?" she asks, when the computer seems happy with the order of the letters she'd typed in.

Reed sets down the syringe and gets up from his chair to show her how to use the small white device beside the computer to move a little arrow on the screen.

"We're extracting DNA this week from some rare plant genuses and recording our findings here." He points to the screen. "Click on this file with the picture of the flower beside it."

She does as she's told and a box pops up with long lines of tiny text.

"Please tell me I don't have to read all this." Her brows raise as she looks at the jumble of words on the screen.

"No." He points to a blank line. "We'll just need to type our findings in here. I really only wanted you to learn the basics today. You'll get the hang of it, little by little."

She nods, not entirely sure that's true. This is like trying to learn a new language.

Reed passes her a piece of paper. "These are the plants we'll be extracting DNA from. Type a name into the blank box here. Just copy the letters you see, then click on a new line for the next name. Got it?"

Echo swallows as she looks at the length of the list. Or, rather, the length of the names of the plants on it. At least she only has to type them out and not try to pronounce any of them. "I've got it."

"Great." Reed sits back at his desk and looks in another drawer, setting a vial down on a clean cloth. "You get started on the list while I make sure everything here is sterile. I'd really like to get that blood sample out of the way so I don't forget."

"About that," she says, highly doubting he would forget something that seems to be so important to him. "I'm sorry I ran out on you yesterday when you tried to take the sample. I want to help. I *really* do. It's just that..."

Reed pushes his glasses up on his nose as he waits for her to continue.

She hesitates, wishing she had a clearer head for this conversation. "I'd like you to keep an open mind about how to use the Immunity if you happen to find it."

"This again." Reed is clearly unimpressed. "I already explained to you the consequences it could have for both colonies if we mess with the system we have in place. It's vital that—"

Echo holds up her hand to silence him, well aware she wasn't going to change such a firmly held view in one day. "I only asked that you keep an open mind. In the short time I've been here, I've already seen that things aren't as I assumed. All I'm asking is that you do the same. The Dead Borns are worth saving, too. That's all."

Reed nods slowly. "Okay. An open mind. I can give you that. But there are two things you need to accept in return. One—my mind being open doesn't mean I'll change it. And two—we've been searching for Immunity for decades and never been able to find it, so I'm really not sure this is an argument we're going to need to resolve in our lifetime."

"Deal." Echo knows this is as far as she is going to be able to push him for now. She picks up the list of plant genuses and searches the keyboard for the letter S. "Why aren't any of these letters in the right order?" she asks on a sigh." I thought A came first, not Q."

"Makes it easier to type," Reed says, sitting back at his desk. "You'll get the hang of it. You're a fast learner, remember?"

"Makes it easier, my ass," she mutters as she finds the E and starts looking for the R. Eventually she manages to finish the word and puts her hand on the white thing to move the arrow down. But, instead, the arrow shoots over to the right of the screen and she presses down as she tries to drag it over to the correct place.

A yellow triangle appears with a symbol inside it—a thick line and dot at the bottom of it, like an upside-down letter *i*. She squints at the text underneath.

This file is protected. Enter password.

She draws in a silent breath as she steadies her hands. This could be important. This has to be important!

Glancing at Reed to make sure he hasn't noticed, she quickly types in River's name, pleased she managed to do it a lot faster this time.

The computer beeps loudly and the triangle symbol bounces on the screen.

Reed jumps up and is back beside her in a second. "What are you doing? I told you not to click on anything else!"

"It was an accident!" She throws up her palms as her heart beats wildly.

He closes the triangle and returns the screen to the much less interesting list of plants.

"What was that?" she asks, trying to steady her breath.

"I don't actually know." He rakes his hands through his red hair. "It's Flora's. I haven't been able to open it either. But don't touch it again, okay? Snooping around won't get you anywhere. You're part of this colony now, remember?"

"I wasn't snooping." She crosses her arms, not making any promises. The first opportunity she gets, she's going to have another try at opening that file. But if the password isn't *River* what could it be? *Oren?* That seems a little unlikely. Besides, surely Reed would have tried that already.

"This was a terrible idea." Reed reaches across Echo and presses a button so the screen goes blank. "We'll just write our findings down and I can type them up later."

"I can do it," she protests. "Please, Reed. It was an honest mistake. I'm a bit distracted today, that's all. I'm missing my family. But I was just starting to get the hang of this computer. Apart from that last bit..."

Reed returns to the equipment on his desk. "You need to forget about your family. Your life's here now."

Echo glares at him. "I can't just forget."

"You can," Reed insists. "Plenty of people here have had to forget about people they love. It's the way it is. It's the way it has to be. Your duty is to your colony now."

Echo wills Daphne to announce something that would give her a reason to leave the room again. Although, that solved nothing last time. She can't keep running out on her problems. They only seem to find a way to follow her again.

Before she can decide what to say or what to do, the door to the Restricted Area opens and Tuff comes striding out. The unmistakable sound of painful groaning reverberates in the dark space behind him.

"What's going on?" Reed leaps in front of Echo like that has any chance of blocking out the awful noise.

A strangled sound escapes Tuff as if he wants to say something but his throat isn't willing to cooperate.

Echo leans out to see the door closing and the LaB falls silent aside from the clomping of Tuff's feet as he stomps out the main exit. Reed races after him, panic etched into the deep lines that have appeared on his forehead.

"Don't touch anything!" he calls to Echo. "I mean it! Touch nothing! I'll be back."

Echo sits frozen as she figures out what exactly she's going to touch first. Surely, Reed didn't expect her to comply with that?

She gets up and scurries over to the door to the Restricted Area and tries the handle, not surprised to find it locked. There's a keypad beside the door, a little like the one in the pods, and she types in a few combinations before giving up.

"Hello?" she calls, pressing her face against the cool metal of the door. "Who's in there? Hello! Do you need help?"

Realizing her efforts are no use, she dashes back to the computer, turns it on and clicks on the secret file, intentionally this time. Maybe the code to the door is in the file? If only she could get it open. Someone could be dying in there!

Her hands shake as her fingers hover over the keyboard. She hasn't got long. There's no way Reed will leave her for more than a few minutes. And if he catches her trying to access that file again, his open mind is going to slam firmly shut. She needs him on her side.

R.I.V.E.R. she types again, just in case she made a mistake like last time. The computer beeps and she jumps in her chair even though she was expecting it this time.

She tries O.R.E.N.

Beep!

O.R.A.N.—just in case she had her letters confused.

Beep!

F.L.O.R.A.

Beep!

R.E.E.D.

Beep!

T.U.F.F.

Beep!

There's a gasp at the door. "What is going on in here?"

Echo winces as she looks up, expecting Reed to be marching toward her with a face as red as his hair.

But it's River.

"Oh, thank goodness it's only you," she says.

"What are you doing?" he asks again, taking a few steps closer.

"Nothing," she says, closing the file and folding her hands in her lap so he can't see how they're shaking. "Just learning how to use a computer."

River looks around the LaB, not seeming to believe her. "Where's Reed?"

Echo gets up and rushes to River, lowering her voice when she reaches him. "Tuff came out of the Restricted Area and there was some groaning. Like a painful moaning noise. Tuff left all upset and Reed went after him. There's something awful going on in there, I just know it. You have to help me find out what it is."

River eyes her cautiously. "And what does that have to do with Flora's computer?"

"She has a secret file," says Echo. "One that even Reed can't open. I was trying to crack the pass—"

"Show me." River almost trips in his haste to get to Flora's computer. He sits down in front of it and Echo shows him where to find the file.

"Her password to her computer was your name, so I thought the file might be the same but it's not," she explains.

River starts typing, trying all the same names she'd previously tried and several more. "It has to be something else," he says. "Maybe a combination of letters and numbers."

Echo remembers what River had told her about the Green

Zone being laid out on a grid. "Did she have a favorite place? Maybe her password is the grid reference."

River's eyes widen. "That's genius." He starts to type something then seems to change his mind. "Except she didn't have a favorite place. Apart from the Sting."

"Then try that!" Echo is trembling now, no longer with nerves but pure excitement.

"Not you, too!" cries Reed from the doorway. "I told her not to touch anything."

Echo's head snaps up.

"Technically, she's not," says River. "I am."

Echo grins, liking this side of him.

Reed lets out a frustrated sigh. "Step away, River. It's not your place to be looking at that computer. It's property of the LaB."

"It was Flora's," says River. "There might be important information on there. A message for me, or something."

"Please don't make me tell your father about this," says Reed firmly. "This is LaB property and I've asked you to step away."

River pushes back the chair and holds up his hands. "Okay, okay. I'm stepping away."

"What happened with Tuff?" Echo asks, trying to deflect the conversation away from River.

"Nothing," says Reed, scratching at his chin, a clear tell that this is a lie.

"It didn't sound like nothing," she pushes.

"We need to close the LaB for the day." Reed tilts his head toward the door. "You both have to leave."

"But I work here," Echo protests.

Reed shuffles his feet. "Not today, you don't."

"But I thought you wanted my blood," she says, wanting to

see how important to him it is that they leave. "I'm ready for you to take my sample."

A pained expression crosses Reed's face.

"He wants your blood?" River asks. "Why?"

"Long story," says Echo, trying to give him a warning look to keep out of it.

Reed walks toward them and puts a hand on each of their backs. "I said the LaB's closed. Go and run around the cornfields or something."

"How did you know about that?" Echo plants her feet on the floor.

Reed's nostrils flare but he recovers quickly. "River told me. Didn't you, River?"

River locks eyes with Reed. "No, actually. I didn't."

Horror slides over Reed's face at River's show of disloyalty, and for one moment Echo thinks Reed might throw a punch.

"We're going." Echo tugs on River's arm. "Come on. Let's get out of here."

Whatever happened with Tuff, it's something serious. And there's no way Reed's going to tell them about it now. The best thing they can do is to clear their heads by getting out of this LaB and try to sneak back in later.

"What's LaB stand for again?" Echo asks as they step out into the entryway.

"Learning and Bounty," River replies.

She huffs. "Lies and Bullshit more like it."

"Echo!" River looks horrified, but the twinkle in his eye gives away his amusement.

"It's true." She marches toward the elevator. "There's something terrible going on here. And I'm determined to find out exactly what."

SIXTEEN

RIVER

Hours later, River finds himself standing outside the doors to the LaB, the silence of the night a little suffocating, swallowing past the lump in his throat. Echo's words that something terrible is happening in here have been on a loop since they left.

He defended the Green Zone at the time, just like he should, pointing out she's determined to find something wrong with her new home. That she's decided the Green Zone is evil because of the sacrifices that must be made.

She refuses to see the peace they've built. The beauty. And the future they're working so hard to forge.

Echo had gone quiet just like he expected her to. He'd stood in the elevator and watched her stalk away, spine stiff and head high. The moment the doors closed he'd sagged against the cool, white wall. He'd needed some time alone.

Especially considering he's made the decision to find Flora in the Dead Zone.

Now, he's standing outside the LaB once more, long after

everyone has gone to bed. His heart clamors against his ribs as his mind tries to process he's really doing this.

He's going to enter when he's not supposed to.

And he's going to find out what's on Flora's computer.

Vernon's words before he'd been taken away hiss through his mind. *Question everything.* Tomorrow, River intends on visiting him in the infirmary. Right now, he's going to honor that request.

"Isn't this against the rules?"

River gasps and spins around, that pounding heart now high in his throat. Echo is standing a few feet away, arms crossed and eyebrows raised.

"I mean, we were told to stay away," she says pointedly. "And I suspect that especially means at night, when no one else is here."

"Go back to your room," hisses River. "This has nothing to do with you."

Echo covers the short distance between them. "You're only here because I told you about Flora's computer. That has everything to do with me."

River curses under his breath. Why does she have to be so...tenacious?

"Go back to your room, Echo," he repeats through gritted teeth.

"No."

The refusal is short, simple. And determined.

It means River either has to get her to leave or abort his plans. He glances at the door. That computer is his last link to Flora. He needs to know what's on it.

He turns back to Echo, wishing it hadn't come to this. "If you don't leave now, I'll tell my father what you've been saying about this place. That you believe we should change."

"You do need to change," she says through narrowed eyes.

"He'll be very interested to hear that seeing as he wants to know if you're assimilating."

She draws back. "Your job is to spy on me?"

Guilt flushes River's cheeks, and he's glad it's shadowy in the softly lit corridor. "Everyone in the Green Zone knows how important it is to protect what we have." He crosses his arms. "My father needs to know whether you're willing to become one of us."

"And if I'm not?"

"You'll be returned to the Dead Zone and it will be like you were never here," he says, ignoring the pang in his chest. "You'll be Forgotten."

Echo's lips part as she draws in a sharp breath and the twinge is back, but this time tugging a whole lot harder. River clenches his jaw and tightens his arms. This is bigger than just him and Echo.

To his surprise, she takes a step forward, her eyes flashing with certainty. "You wouldn't do it."

"What?"

"You couldn't be responsible for inflicting Flora's fate on me or anyone else."

River's eyes widen in shock, only to quickly narrow once more. "You don't hold that high an opinion of me, remember? I'm Green Born."

"I can admit when I'm wrong," she says quietly, her dark eyes firmly holding his.

River's breath disintegrates as his arms unwind. In the silence and low light, a warm cocoon seems to enclose around them. He's highly conscious they're alone in ways they haven't been. That there are no prying eyes. His gaze drops to her lips.

They both step back simultaneously, fracturing the moment. "The point is," Echo says firmly, "that you're going in there to check out Flora's computer and I'm coming with you."

He huffs in exasperation. That was the third option he wasn't really willing to entertain, but it looks like he doesn't have much choice. "Just keep quiet," he mutters as he steps toward the doors.

"I followed you the whole way here and you didn't hear me," she points out, falling into step behind him.

River's back to gritting his teeth. He can't exactly say anything about that when he followed her to the orchard.

Inside, the LaB is dark and empty, which is exactly what he was hoping for. With eyes squinting to make out the shadows of benches and shelves, he slowly makes his way to Flora's computer.

"What exactly are you looking for?" Echo asks in a whisper.

He reaches it and carefully pulls over two stools. "I don't know," he says evasively. "I just want to see what she has on here."

Echo's silent as he starts up the computer, but she suddenly lets out a small gasp. "You've decided to go after her, haven't you?"

River doesn't answer. That's exactly what he's planning on doing. He just needs to see whether there's anything of interest on Flora's computer. Why she hid it under a secret password. He swallows. Whether she was keeping anything from him.

He focuses on the screen as it comes alive, bathing both their faces in pale light. At least he knows Echo won't follow him there.

She shuffles a little closer. "That's a really bad idea, River. As in a really, *really* bad idea."

"I wasn't asking you for your assessment of the situation."

"The Dead Zone is dangerous. Especially for a Green Born who decides to just turn up. You'll stick out like a flower in a desert."

"She's my twin, Echo. And she's missing. What sort of brother am I if I don't go looking for her?"

"A smart one. And one who wouldn't openly defy his father like that."

River looks away. That's exactly what she's been asking him to do all along.

She places a hand on his arm. "And one who knows his sister wouldn't want him dead."

That has his gaze snapping back. Her warm hand presses with urgency on his arm. Echo stares at him like this matters.

"Why are you so interested?" He moves his arm so he can wave his hand at the computer screen. He can feel that things are shifting between them. And it's a complication he could do without.

Echo chews her lip. "I think Flora has the code for the Restricted Area on there. That's why she has a special password."

"The Restricted Area is restricted for a reason."

"And have you ever wondered why that is?"

"Because it's not safe."

"After hearing the sounds coming out of there today, I totally agree."

River's lips press into a thin line. "Flora never mentioned the Restricted Area. I doubt it's on there."

"You're not just a little bit curious what goes on in there?"

"Not enough to break one of the golden rules of the Green Zone," he retorts.

"If Flora has the password to the Restricted Area, then we check it out," she says, her dark eyes full of challenge.

He huffs again. "Well, if we get infected with some extinct disease or stung by something even more dangerous than bees, then it's on you."

Echo inclines her head. "But if we find something that

breaks this place wide open, then you have to drink a whole bottle of kasi."

River suppresses a smile. This girl is always keeping him on his toes. "Deal."

He turns back to the computer and navigates to the file Echo showed him earlier. The screen fills with the box asking for the password.

"We were about to try the coordinates for the Sting," says Echo.

He nods, fingers hovering over the keyboard. Surely there's nothing in here but LaB data that Flora was being extra cautious with. She wouldn't have access to the Restricted Area. She wouldn't have kept secrets from him.

With quick strokes, he taps in the coordinates and presses Enter.

Beep.

The rejection sounds loud in the silent LaB and they both flinch and glance furtively around. It means it takes a few seconds for River to realize it wasn't the right password.

"What else could it be?" Echo whispers.

Typing quickly, River tries whatever he can think of. Greenzone. Sting. Even their mother's name—Magnolia.

Beep.

Beep.

Beep.

"This could take days," he says, frustrated.

"Considering you're not going to the Dead Zone, then you have plenty of time."

"There's a chance I won't know it," he points out. "She could've used something completely obscure that I'll never be able to guess."

Echo frowns. "But we have to get in there. She wouldn't have hidden something if it wasn't important."

River tries again. Immune. Greenborn. Betadome.

Beep.

Beep.

Beep.

With a frown, he types in any word that comes to mind, whether it makes sense or not. The air quickly fills with *beep* after *beep* after *beep*, each one feeling louder and more insistent than the last.

Echo's back curves on a sigh. "We can't give up. No matter how long it takes."

Except, with each objection from the computer, they risk someone hearing them and getting caught. River leans back, looking at her. "Or I could go to the Dead Zone, find my sister and ask."

Her eyes widen, the glow from the screen making them look large in her pale face. When she doesn't say anything, he knows he's struck a chord.

She can see it's a good idea.

Her brow scrunches down. "Then I'm coming with you."

"I don't think—"

"It wasn't an offer. It was an FYI."

River clamps his mouth shut. Dammit, that's also a good idea. With Echo, he'll be able to navigate the Dead Zone far quicker. He'll be able to find Flora sooner.

Plus, it'll distract Echo from this vendetta she has against the Green Zone. Maybe a reminder of where she came from will be just the thing she needs.

"Fine," he concedes, shutting down the computer. "You can come."

She nods curtly, her lashes flickering as if she just shuttered her gaze. It means he has no idea what her motivation is for going with him. "Why are you—"

Footsteps beyond the door of the LaB have them both

freezing. Simultaneously, they shoot to their feet, looking around frantically. River can't afford to get caught. Not now that he's decided he's going to the Dead Zone to look for Flora.

Not when he has no idea what the consequences are for such a blatant disregard of the rules.

The doors slide open. "Who's there?"

Oren's voice sends ice rippling down River's spine. Of all people to catch them, it had to be his father? He'll be furious.

And deeply disappointed.

"Kiss me," whispers Echo.

"What?"

Before the shock of what she's said has worn off, River does exactly that. He's not sure whether it's because it's a great decoy, or because he can't say no...

He wraps his arms around Echo and hauls her against him, bringing his lips down to hers only to find her already pushing up. Their lips crash and they both gasp. The heat is instantaneous. There's a moment of surprise, of hesitation, before they come together again. Their mouths connect. Passion combusts. Lips move with fervor as the need to consume ignites.

Echo's fingers spear into River's hair, gripping like she's holding onto dear life in the same way he is. His arms tighten, pressing all of her against all of him, making the fire burn even hotter. He never expected this.

And right now, there's nothing he wants more.

"What is the meaning of this?" his father almost roars.

They leap apart and River discovers light has filled the LaB. He blinks, finding his father standing in the doorway, thunder storming across his features. "What are you doing?" he growls at his son.

River straightens, realizing he has no idea. That kiss wasn't supposed to be like that. "We, ah..."

"I thought this would be the best place for privacy," says Echo, ducking her head. "Seems I was wrong."

Oren's gaze slowly shifts to her, nothing else moving as if he's frozen with fury. "You are—"

She presses her hands to her flushed cheeks. "So freaking embarrassed!" She glances at River but doesn't quite meet his gaze. "I'm so sorry. I shouldn't have...we shouldn't have..."

Without finishing the sentence, she scurries to the door, scooting around Oren. "We won't do it again, I promise," she squeaks.

She exits, shooting River a quick look once she's past Oren. One that's part embarrassment, part cheeky triumph.

River turns to his father as the doors close on Echo, crossing his arms as his ability to think kicks back in. "You wanted me to get closer to her, didn't you?"

His father studies him for long seconds. "You did that because I asked you to keep an eye on her?"

"Why else would I kiss a Dead Born?"

The anger slowly dissipates from Oren's face. "You surprise me, son."

There's that word again. *Son.* "I was raised to fight for what I believe in." He doesn't add it was his mother who always encouraged that.

"I'm glad to hear that," says Oren. He glances around as if checking nothing's moved and River's glad Flora's computer was already turned off. "Although I don't want to find either of you in LaB alone or outside of work hours."

River nods. "Sorry, I should've thought it through. It won't happen again." With a straight spine, he walks past his father. "I'd best get to bed."

He's almost at the door when his father speaks. "River."

He stops, not turning around but glancing over his shoulder. "Yes?"

"Keep your heart separate and your mind focused on what's important." There's a pause and River thinks he's finished. "Or this won't end well."

The softly spoken words pierce straight through River's chest, like well-aimed daggers. Were they said by a concerned father?

Or an unfeeling leader...

He leaves quickly, feeling guilty for even thinking that question, and takes the elevator back to his floor. He's not surprised to find Echo waiting outside his door.

She pushes away from the wall. "Did you tell him it was all part of getting close to me?"

He nods, surprised she thought of it, too. In fact, probably before they'd even kissed. Which means it was nothing more than a decoy to her. "From what I can tell, he believed it."

She grins. "We make a good team, River."

He doesn't answer that. The kiss has complicated everything. It felt like so much more, and yet, it was little more than a ploy to Echo. She's probably kissed that Chase guy a hundred times like that. It reminds him he's not sure whether he can trust her. In fact, it was easier when they were determined enemies rather than fragile allies.

Echo's smile fades a little and her eyes narrow as she looks at him. "It'll hold us in good stead in the Dead Zone."

She's checking whether they're still going. Or rather, whether he intends on taking her with him.

Unfortunately, despite the complications and strange truce they've forged, he needs Echo to navigate the unknown that is the Dead Zone.

"We'll go back to our rooms, lie low for a bit and pack," he says. "Meet me in mine in an hour."

Echo nods, her smile flaring before disappearing altogether. She slips into her room, leaving River alone. He draws in a steadying breath, but it doesn't help.

Excitement and nervousness curdle in his gut, making him a little nauseous.

He's going to the Dead Zone.

CHAPTER
SEVENTEEN
ECHO

The hard floor in the hallway outside River's door makes for an uncomfortable seat.

He'd said to wait an hour before they leave for the Dead Zone so they can pack. Which would be fine apart from two things. Firstly, she doesn't have any possessions to pack. And secondly, she doesn't trust him not to leave without her. Not after the way he'd tried to sneak into the LaB alone.

When River went back to his room, she'd slipped out and slumped down the wall in the dimly lit hallway to keep watch. Nobody is getting in or out of his room without her knowing about it. She wouldn't put it past him to try to leave without her.

Her eyelids droop and she shakes her head to force them wide open. She can't fall asleep now. That would defeat the whole purpose of sitting on these hard tiles in the middle of the night.

She hates that she's going back to the Dead Zone when she'd sworn she wouldn't. But there's no way she can let River go on his own. The Dead Borns will eat him alive. Almost literally, given how hungry they are. Plus, she *really* wants that password.

With Echo by his side, not only can she keep him safe, but they can get this whole crazy mission over a lot faster. They'll track down Flora, find out what this impossible password is, and get back to the Green Zone. Maybe they can even do it fast enough that Oren won't notice them missing. Although, that may be wishful thinking.

There's a soft thud in River's room that she assumes is him settling his bag down in front of the door. How much stuff has he packed? Perhaps he's bringing a stash of food, not realizing humans can run for quite some time on an empty stomach, or that he'll make himself a target. It's the water bottles at the exit to the Sting that they should think about taking with them.

She smiles, realizing she's the mentor now. River is about to step on her turf. There's just as much she can teach him as he's taught her. A flush rises to her cheeks as she remembers what else they taught each other in the LaB just now. Things that have nothing to do with computers or passwords or secrets, and everything to do with...

Her fingers flutter to her lips. That kiss was supposed to be a cover up. An excuse to explain why they were sneaking around the LaB when they shouldn't have been. And it had been exactly that because it had worked like a charm.

Except it had also been a whole lot more because it had been her first kiss. Exactly the kiss she'd dreamed of sharing with Chase when she was confirmed a Vulnerable, yet it had been with River. Which wouldn't necessarily be a problem if it weren't for the fact it had felt so good.

Lust. That's the word she's looking for. Because surely that kiss had nothing to do with love? She's only just met River. Unlike Chase who she's known her whole life. Maybe all kissing feels like that? It's not like she has any other experience to compare it to.

She imagines kissing Reed or Tuff or Clover, and shudders at the thought. No, it had felt like that because of the person attached to the lips she'd been kissing.

Like it or not, she's attracted to River. Which is highly inconvenient for a number of reasons, including that it's obvious he doesn't feel the same way.

She stands up and stretches her legs, needing to shift this dangerous thought pattern.

She's in love with Chase. *Well, maybe.* No, she is. *Definitely!* Then why had she turned away from his kiss in the orchard? And why had she enjoyed kissing River so much? Is it possible the reason she was never able to describe her feelings for Chase was because it was nothing more than a friendship that she wished would morph into something more? Because, like it or not, there's nothing indescribable about how she'd felt kissing River. It was downright beautiful.

"Urgh," she says out loud. She really doesn't have time for this. They need to get moving. Surely, it's been more than an hour?

She knocks softly on River's door and waits. When she gets no response, she tries again a little louder. Hopefully Clover doesn't hear her and come running down the hallway, ready to fight for River's attention. Although, if Clover's kissed River, Echo can now understand why she's so keen. He's very good at it...

Hang on. Has Clover kissed River?

"Urgh," she says again, knowing this is none of her business.

She knocks a third time. "River? It's time to go."

There's still no response so she tries the handle and pushes the door open. There are no locks in the Green Zone. Everyone is *so* trustworthy. How ironic, especially since they have passwords on their computers.

The bag on the other side of the door stops it from opening and she pushes harder, trying to shift it out of the way.

"River?" she whispers. "It's me. I can't get in."

The door moves a fraction more, just enough for her to slide her small frame through the gap. Blinking in the bright light of the room, she looks down and gasps to see it isn't River's bag blocking the door.

It's River.

He's sprawled on the floor in an awkward position, unmoving. His eyes are closed and his skin is as pale as his crumpled white shirt.

She quickly closes the door and squats beside him, slapping him gently on his cheek.

"River! Wake up! Can you hear me?"

He moans softly and relief washes through her to realize he's not dead.

"River. Come on. It's time to wake up." She rolls him onto his back and it's obvious there's no waking him. He's not just asleep. He's *asleep*. Maybe even unconscious. Has someone drugged him? But nobody had come into his room since he went in there. She'd have seen them. She didn't leave his door, not even for a second. Unless there's someone in here who's waiting for her to leave before they make their escape?

Standing, she does a quick inspection of the room, pulling back the blanket on his bed, opening his closet and checking the bathroom.

"Who's in here?" she asks, trying to keep her voice from shaking. "Clover, is it you?"

It quickly becomes obvious there's nobody else here. The room is far too small to hide anyone. Whoever drugged River, they must have done it after she left the LaB but before he returned here. She remembers a story her father told her once about a girl in the forest who ate a poison apple that sent her into a deep sleep. Had Oren done something similar to River? Had he somehow found out about their plans to leave and is trying to stop them? But that's impossible. They'd only decided to leave moments before they'd been discovered together. Oren wouldn't have had time to hatch any such plans.

She rubs at her eyes, feeling a little sleepy herself, which is in no way going to help River. She has to keep her wits about her.

"Come on, River. Wake up. Please, wake up." She sits on the floor beside him and puts a hand on his face, stroking her thumb down his cheek. She'd thought it was his green eyes that made him so handsome but given he's just as appealing with them firmly closed, she might have to think again. Dammit, this guy really is very good looking. And even more so now that she knows what it feels like to press her lips against his own.

"Who did this to you?" she asks, determined not to leave his side until he wakes. She won't let anyone cause him more harm on her watch. Enough damage has been done to him already.

Letting out a wide yawn, she decides it won't hurt to lie down beside him while she figures this out. Because her head feels so...fluffy right now. She smiles at the word fluffy, imagining her head stuffed with the soft pillows that sit on her bed made from clouds.

Her eyes close, then spring open as icy realization slides through her. She's not sleepy because she's tired. She's been drugged, too! There's no way under normal circumstances, she'd be considering taking a nap right now. Not when River's relying on her to keep him safe.

She tries to sit up, but her body is made from lead. Tucking herself into River's side is the best she can do.

"River." Her voice is a slurred whisper so she tries again. "Ribba."

Okay, so that was even worse.

Fighting sleep, she lifts her head and smiles at this small victory only to realize her head is actually still firmly resting on the tiles.

"No!" She's not even sure this time the word makes it past her lips.

The darkness is dragging her under, leaving her with only one remaining hope...

That eventually she's going to wake up.

EIGHTEEN

RIVER

R iver's eyes flutter open, the music flowing around his room feeling far too loud and obtrusive. He squints against the bright light, groggy and confused.

There was somewhere he was supposed to be...

He sits up so fast his head swims, the swirling feeling shooting straight down to his gut. Gripping his temples, he looks around. What's he doing in his bed? He was supposed to go to the Dead Zone!

But according to the clock above the door, it's morning. The music playing is the same alarm he's heard all his life. He's woken up to another day in the Green Zone.

Yet, he has no recollection of falling asleep.

His last memory was pacing his room, impatiently counting down the minutes until Echo was supposed to come.

But she didn't.

He must've fallen asleep, exhausted after the day, and she didn't bother to wake him.

"Good morning, Green Zone," Daphne's voice filters into

the room. "We hope you slept well. It's time to wake up and contribute to your colony. Be in peace."

Pushing to his feet, he grips his head even tighter. His mouth feels like dirt. Sometimes he wakes up feeling like this, but it's never been this bad. How could he have slept so heavily that he didn't go after his sister?

Discovering he's still dressed from yesterday, River stumbles out of his room and thumps his fist on Echo's door.

The room that used to be Flora's.

There's no answer, so he knocks again, this time even louder.

Still no answer.

Feeling stupid for believing he could trust Echo, he enters the room. If she's not here, he'll go looking for her in the LaB. She needs to know whatever fragile friendship they'd been forging is gone.

He stops inside the room, surprised to find Echo still in bed, seemingly asleep. In the short time he's known her, she's always been up the moment the music starts. It suggested she has a strong work ethic.

Grunting, he shoves that thought from his mind. Naïve, trusting River needs to take a hike.

"Echo," he snaps. "Wake up."

She doesn't stir, so he takes a step closer. He doesn't want to have her jumping out of her skin, but patience isn't something he has right now. "Echo!"

Despite the loud, sharp way he says her name, all she does is stir. "River?" she asks thickly.

"You thought I wouldn't say anything, didn't you?" Because he doesn't create ripples. Doesn't rock the boat.

He hasn't even told his father that Echo met with someone from the Dead Zone.

Well, all that's going to change.

Echo pushes up, shoving her dark hair out of her face. "What?" She blinks, looking around. "What are you..." She inhales sharply, leaping to her feet. "River! Are you okay?"

"No, I'm not. I'm angry." And hurt. Like the fool he is, he thought Echo might help him. As if she cared.

Echo frowns, looking down at herself and running her hands over her nightshirt. "What the..."

"I fell asleep, and you never bothered to wake me," he says through gritted teeth. "Because you lied. You never intended for us to go to the Dead Zone."

Her gaze snaps to his. "What? I did go to your room." Her eyes widen. "And you were out, cold, on the floor."

"I'm tired of your lies, Echo."

"I'm telling you the truth!" She looks around the room, as if the answers are lurking somewhere. "I tried to wake you, and then I...I fell asleep, too."

"Except I woke up in my bed and you, yours," he snaps. Her story isn't even a plausible one.

Echo presses her fingertips to her temples as she frowns. "I know. It doesn't make sense. Someone must've moved us, to make it look like it never happened."

River snorts. "Really? That's the best you've got?" He takes a step closer. "Are you so used to lying that it doesn't even occur to you to tell the truth?"

She narrows her eyes at him, not backing down. "I *am* telling the truth. I went to get you. We were drugged somehow. Then whoever did it returned me to my room, so it looked like it never happened."

The fact she's clinging to such a ludicrous story only hurts more. River focuses on the anger simmering in his veins, finding that far more preferable. "You didn't want to go to the Dead Zone. Because you're too busy trying to undermine the Green Zone to leave."

"Because something very wrong is going on here. Your precious Green Zone is built on the misery of others!"

He draws back, the anger flaring even brighter. "I knew you'd start spitting out your twisted version of the truth eventually."

Echo crosses her arms, unapologetic as always. She winces in surprise and quickly unwinds them. Pulling her up her sleeve she scans the inside of her arm.

And gasps.

"There! There's your proof," she cries triumphantly as she points to a tiny puncture wound on the inside of her elbow. "Someone took a sample last night!"

River stares at the small red dot, his eyebrows slowly climbing down. Surely not...

He shakes his head as he takes another step back. He's more naïve than he thought. "For all I know, you gave blood yesterday and now you're twisting the truth to support your crazy story."

"Check your own arm, then," says Echo, looking frustrated yet stubborn. "I bet you have one, too."

River almost refuses, not wanting to give her craziness credence. And what if there is a mark...

Although, this is his chance to prove the Green Zone isn't the evil colony Echo's so determined it is. He yanks his sleeve up, exposing his inner arm.

Echo draws in a sharp breath as she stares. Her eyes widen.

River's stomach ties into a painful knot. There can't be...

He glances down, relief a soothing flood when he sees his arm is unmarked. Blemish free. There's no puncture wound to give fuel to Echo's traitorous theories.

"Anything else you want to make up while I'm here? Like maybe they did tests on us? That we're nothing more than secret lab rats?"

Echo clenches her jaw but doesn't respond
"I didn't think so."

River storms out and back into his room. With furious movements, he undresses and steps into the shower. He can't believe that even for a split second he entertained her wild idea. A small part of him actually thought he might see something on his arm.

He keeps his shower short and punishingly hot. He's determined to find his father and tell him everything. River's loyalty is to the Green Zone, and no one else.

Stepping out, he quickly dries himself off, wondering where Oren might be. His best bet is the LaB, where his office is, going over today's announcements with Daphne. Which means he needs to get there before Echo.

River's just placed his foot on a stool to dry off his leg when he stills. His gut clenches, pushing his breath out in a whoosh.

He reaches down with a trembling finger to touch what's caught his attention. And not let go.

There, on the side of his foot, is a small, red dot.

A puncture wound the size of a needle.

He rubs at it, noting it's tender. And it's not wiping away.

I bet you have one, too.

Echo was right. But that would suggest the rest of her story is true...

Dressing as fast as he can, River exits his room, practically running to the elevator. None of this makes sense.

The truth feels like it's constantly shifting. Moving. Morphing.

It's time to pin it down.

He bursts out of the elevator, sucking in hard breaths as if he just ran all the way up here, and almost crashes into a trolley laden with produce.

"Whoa," says Reed, maneuvering it away. "Where's the swarm?"

"I need to talk to my father."

"Sure, he's in his office," Reed says, his eyebrows hiking up. "Although he's—"

River doesn't wait for him to finish. His father's always busy. He has been all his life.

He reaches the door and is about to knock when it opens. Oren's brow crinkles. "River."

"I need to talk to you."

Oren glances over his shoulder at Reed. "Now's not a good time—"

"It's important."

Except his father doesn't step back. "Can it wait until later? I have morning announcements to get to."

River blinks. His father can't be a few minutes late to convey the messages to Daphne so she can record them?

"It has to do with Echo," he says in a low voice.

Oren's face tightens with impatience. "Look, I know it's taking some time, but I can see she's trying. She'll settle in soon. You no longer need to keep an eye on her. It'll be fine."

"It's not." Everything is as far from fine as it can be. "She's—"

"River," his father snaps. He lets out a breath, unwinding his shoulders. "Vernon's dead."

He reels back. "He can't be!" Vern's Immune.

"His alcoholism compromised his immunity," says Oren. "It's a lesson for all of us. But this will unsettle people. I need to make a formal announcement before the rumors start. And the people need to see me going about business as usual."

River steps back, still trying to process his father's words. "Of course."

"And like I said, you no longer need to keep an eye on Echo." With a last glare, his father strides away.

River watches him, his mind blank and spinning all at once.

Vern's dead. No one's died of a bee sting in the Green Zone as far as he knows. No matter what they ate or drank.

Although he's never known anyone to drink as much as Vern does.

Did.

Vern will never stumble through the Sting carrying his bottle of kasi, meeting people's scorn with a smile and a salute. He'll never regale River with stories of his mother. He's gone.

River steps back into the main room of the LaB, frowning.

"You heard?" Reed asks from where he is beside his computer, the trolley of produce to his left.

"How could he be dead?" River knows it's a stupid question, but he still can't comprehend it.

"That's a long, technical answer I don't want to bore you with. In short, it's like Oren would've said—the kasi compromised his immunity."

River glances at Flora's computer. Was it only last night that he and Echo were trying to get into her files? He frowns even deeper. That was when they—he—decided to go to the Dead Zone to get some answers.

To find his twin.

"Would Flora have understood the answer?" he asks.

Reed blinks in surprise. "Ah, I'm not sure. Why do you ask?"

River steps closer to her computer. "Why did Flora have a folder with a password no one knows, Reed?"

He shifts a little as he pulls up a smile. "I have no idea. Maybe she had a list of all the guys she was crushing on."

Flora never mentioned anything like that. River takes another step. "I need some answers, Reed."

It almost feels like everyone is skirting around him, hoping he'll back off.

Reed frowns. "Look, River, I know you miss your sister, but—"

"We're twins, and I'm Immune and she's not," he grinds out, determination solidifying in his gut. Now Vern's dead. And there's a mysterious puncture mark on his foot. "Doesn't that seem odd to you?"

Before Reed can answer, the doors to the LaB open and Echo rushes in. "So sorry, it's been one of those mornings."

She stops in her tracks when she finds Reed's not alone. Her brow slams down as she doesn't quite meet River's gaze. "Shouldn't you be in Eden? With Clover?"

"I just had a quick word with Oren," he snaps back.

Echo's eyes narrow as she glares at him, not saying anything. Tension fills the air, stretching River's nerves taught. He never got a chance to tell his father anything. In fact, he's no longer required to keep an eye on her.

Their time together is over.

He tells himself he's glad. Despite everything, there's a chance there could be some merit in her theories. River's world is imploding, and she's pulling the trigger.

Reed clears his throat. "Echo, could you take this trolley of produce to the seventh floor for freeze drying, please?"

She turns to him, pulling up a blazing smile. "Sure. Anything for the colony," she says sweetly.

Taking the trolley, she wheels it to the elevator. She looks at him only once the doors are sliding shut. Her dark eyes are full of anger, but also something else.

Disappointment.

Possibly hurt.

River turns away. She was using him. She wants to destroy his whole world.

And that's all that's important to her.

He pins Reed with a glare. "What did Flora know that I don't?"

Reed sighs. "Look, the genetic code for immunity is complicated. Anomalies happen all the time—"

"Enough!" This time, River shouts the word. He's tired of not knowing.

Too many things aren't making sense. And he can no longer respond to Echo's insinuations with conviction.

Reed stiffens just as the doors to the Restricted Area slide open and Tuff steps out. He glances between the two, obviously realizing he just interrupted something. He stills, looking like he's not sure what to do next as his gaze drops to the floor.

River lets out a pent-up breath. "What did she not tell me, Reed?" he says, far quieter. Almost pleading.

Reed's jaw tenses as he pushes to his feet. "I. Don't. Know," he grinds out. "Why don't you ask Tuff? He spent more time with her than I did." Throwing his hands up, he stalks out of the LaB.

Another thing River didn't know. Flora never mentioned Tuff. He picks up the keyboard from a nearby computer and hurls it across the room. It crashes into the wall and shatters, pieces flying everywhere. Tuff doesn't even flinch, simply remains where he is, staring at the floor.

River regrets the action even before the keyboard hits the ground. The silence in the LaB weighs heavily as he walks over to collect the pieces. He squats down, picking up a small square. The letter D.

For despair.

Or dejected.

And downright defeated.

What does he do now? "Flora's missing," he whispers. "Am I supposed to just let that go?"

There's a sharp inhale across the room, so soft that River almost doesn't hear it. He glances over at Tuff, wondering if he said too much. He's not supposed to know about Flora.

The older man avoids making eye contact as he walks to a bench and sits down, pulling over a notepad and pen. Acting as if he's the only one in the room, he starts scrawling on the page.

River sighs. Like Reed said, even if Tuff realizes what he just said is significant, he won't be telling anyone.

He picks up the shattered pieces of the keyboard and places them on the bench. He's expected to go to Eden and work like a good member of the colony. Maybe that's what he should've done all along. He makes his way to the door, his body heavy and his heart heavier.

River's just reached it when a single word splinters the air. "Here."

He spins around, shocked. *Tuff just spoke!*

The older man is standing at the bench, holding out a piece of paper he's torn from the notepad, his lips tightly closed.

River takes a step forward, then stops. "What is it?" he asks cautiously.

Tuff doesn't answer. Instead, he sits the piece of paper on the bench, spins on his heel, and disappears into the Restricted Area. The one place where River can't follow.

Frowning, he walks to the bench and picks up the strange note Tuff left. It's a picture of some sort, with regularly spaced lines intersecting over the top.

No, it's a map. With gridlines, just like the Green Zone has.

River looks more closely. The Betadome is to the west. He's about to flip the page around—the Betadome has always been on the east of the Green Zone—when he stills. Tuff has marked true north. The map isn't of his colony.

It's a crude sketch of the Dead Zone.

With an X close to the far edge.

River's gaze shoots to the door of the Restricted Zone. Does Tuff know where Flora might be? Reed just said they spent a lot of time together here in the LaB.

And contrary to what everyone believes, Tuff can talk.

River tucks the piece of paper in his pocket, a new emotion marching up his spine.

Determination.

It's time to get some answers.

Tonight, he goes to the Dead Zone.

Alone.

CHAPTER
NINETEEN

ECHO

Echo pushes the trolley of produce that Reed had asked her to take to the Processing Center for freeze drying. The wheels have a faint squeak to them and this obvious sign that not everything functions perfectly in the Green Zone makes her smile.

She maneuvers her way into the elevator and her finger hovers over the button for the basement. Then she frowns, remembering how rude River was to her just now and presses the button to the residential floor instead.

The Green Zone doesn't need all this food. Most of it looks like herbs, which would go a long way to adding flavor and nutrition to the watery stews of the Dead Zone. The whole idea of freeze drying is an insult to her colony. It's an admission that the Green Borns have a surplus. And while saving things for a rainy day isn't always a bad idea, when she pictures her father's skin riddled with bruises from the scurge, then it's just plain wrong.

She'll hide these herbs in her room and take them to the orchard at dusk with whatever else she can manage to scavenge. The Dead Zone needs nutrients now, not on some mythical day in the distant future. Providing food was literally the only task Chase gave her. It will also give her a chance to check the tree hollow to see if he's left her further instructions. Helping Chase seems far preferable right now to doing anything to help Reed or River.

The elevator hums and Echo's aware her body no longer reacts to the sudden movement as it takes off. Humans have the ability to adjust quickly to new surroundings. It's one of the reasons the species has continued to exist after so many years. Although, then again, it's also one of the reasons humans are now in so much danger.

The doors slide open and Echo jolts to see Daphne smiling at her.

"Hello, Echo." She steps into the elevator and eyes the trolley. "What are you doing all the way up here?"

"Reed wants me to take these to the Processing Center," Echo says quickly, returning Daphne's megawatt smile, hoping it's enough to disguise the way her breathing has increased. "Except I've forgotten what floor he said it was on."

"That would be the basement." Daphne firmly presses the correct button, her perfectly manicured fingertip glinting in the light.

Echo grips the trolley, reminding herself that Daphne can't read her thoughts. She doesn't know what Echo had been planning. "Thanks. Lucky I ran into you. Otherwise I'd have had to play Sting Roulette."

"Are you settling in well?" Daphne asks, expertly changing the subject. "It's a big honor for you to be chosen to work in the LaB."

"Technically, I wasn't chosen," says Echo, reminding Daphne of the random nature of her allocation.

"Of course." Something changes in Daphne's perfect

expression and she blinks it away. "Sorry. Poor choice of words."

Echo doubts the woman who selects the words to announce the most important messages to the colony would be guilty of such a thing, but she holds her tongue. Just another thing to add to the list of things that make no sense around here.

"The LaB's fine," Echo says in answer to her question. "Reed's been keeping me very busy, as you can see here." She glances down at the trolley.

Daphne nods her approval as the doors to the seventh floor slide open. "This is my stop."

"Be in peace," says Echo, trying to get in first for once.

"Be in peace." Daphne steps out and gives Echo a little wave.

The doors close again and Echo lets out a breath, wondering how she would have explained herself had she been caught going into her room with the trolley. That wasn't such a wise idea. If she's going to help Chase and get the Dead Zone any kind of food, she needs to be more careful.

She waits as the elevator takes her to the basement, watching as the view from the glass wall turns from green to solid brown as it slips beneath the surface of the earth. She wheels the trolley out and looks around the brightly lit foyer. This glaring white hexagonal space is just as spartan as all other the foyers in this building, aside from the customary water bottles sitting on a cart outside the main doors. She glances around as she picks up a bottle and takes a long swig of cool liquid. That's another thing she's adapted to since she's been here—the sterile taste of clean water. It almost seems normal now.

Draining the bottle, she places it on the lower shelf. Then taking a few bunches of herbs from her trolley, she stashes them behind the line of empty bottles. Glancing around again, she stands and smooths out the fabric of her trousers and wheels her trolley confidently into the Processing Center.

The large space she finds herself in is in direct contrast to the spartan foyer. Tables are piled high with produce, some of which may even have been picked by her own hands at Harvest Day. There are pumpkins, sprouts, apricots, cherries, beans, lemons and so many more. Other tables are laden with herbs just like the ones she's delivering now. She blinks at the yellows, and oranges, and reds and greens, her eyes not used to this assault of color after spending so long inside the Sting. There's enough food here to fill every belly in both the colonies two or three times over. It's as obscene as it is impressive. This colony might not be perfect, but they sure know how to guarantee their survival.

She straightens her back, wondering how she's going to convince the Green Borns to share what they have with the Dead Zone. Kindness exists here in this very building. She's witnessed it with her own eyes. The people here aren't the selfish species she'd expected them to be. They're just naive, set in their ways, and used to following orders—as color blind as the very bees they worship. There has to be a way to change that.

Stepping forward, she heads toward the tables. Workers in white aprons are lined up, chopping and slicing and placing food onto trays that are then being collected by another worker who's inserting them into slots in a machine that lines the back wall.

"Ah, these must be from the LaB," says a man, going to Echo and putting his hands on her trolley.

She reluctantly lets go as she nods. "Reed asked me to bring them to you."

"Rose!" the man calls to one of the females at the workbench. "The delivery from the LaB is here."

Rose's brows shoot up and she hurries over to take the trolley, smiling at Echo. "Tell Reed I'll take good care of this batch."

Echo nods, wondering what's so special about these herbs given the masses of food already here.

"Be in peace." The man nods at Echo to dismiss her and bends over the trolley, saying something to Rose in a hushed voice.

"Be in peace," says Echo. When the man doesn't so much as glance up at her response, she takes the opportunity to pick up a small sack of cherries and hold it against her chest as she turns away. This is exactly the kind of food Chase was talking about.

"Excuse me!" Rose's voice rings out across the Processing Center. "The girl from the LaB. Wait!"

Echo freezes as a sick feeling winds its way from her stomach and clenches around her heart. Daphne had bought her excuse in the elevator but explaining away the sack of food she was about to walk out with may prove a little more difficult.

She turns her head, keeping her body angled away. "Yes?"

"I don't know your name," Rose says.

"Echo." Her voice comes out as a squeak, so she tries again. "My name's Echo."

"Be in peace, Echo." Rose smiles as she turns back to the trolley.

"Be in peace." Echo scurries out the door, collects the herbs she'd left on the water cart, and with her arms completely full she presses the button to the elevator several times, hoping that will make it come faster. She's got to get out of here!

The doors spring open moments later and she scurries in,

relieved Daphne isn't in there waiting for her. Deciding she can't risk going back to the residential floor again, she hits the button for the ground floor. If she's going to take this food to the orchard, then she needs to do it now. What she's holding could feed a starving family for a week. Images of skinny children with dirt-stained faces lugging buckets of muddy water back from the creek plague her mind. They deserve this food just as much as the privileged children of the Green Zone. Possibly even more.

Echo clutches her haul, heart pounding and sweat beading on her forehead. Getting this food to the orchard is a bold plan, and she knows it. But she's in too deep now. She has to see it through. And besides, after the night she'd just had—being both drugged and having blood taken against her will, only to be accused by River of twisting the truth—this is about the only thing that's going to make her feel better. The food she's taken is only a drop in the ocean of what they have here.

The elevator grinds to a halt at the ground floor and Echo's heart sinks as she sees someone, convinced Daphne is about to bust her once more. Or even worse, River. He's the one person who won't accept any of her excuses.

But the doors open fully to reveal a man she's never seen before. He gets into the elevator and nods politely at Echo, seeming more interested in looking out the glass panel at the view across the Green Zone than he is in her.

She draws in a slow breath, surprised the thumping of her heart isn't causing the food she's holding to leap out of her arms. If she acts like nothing is wrong, it won't even occur to this man that she might be doing anything that strays from the rules. She's just another obedient member of this colony going about their business.

"Nice day, isn't it?" she says, stepping out of the elevator and cringing at how obvious she's being at trying to not be obvious.

"Every day's a nice day," the man replies, still deep in thought. "We are blessed."

"We are." Echo smiles, even though he's not looking at her, hoping that her friendly exterior will reach her voice.

"Hey!" the man calls after her, pressing a button to stop the doors from closing.

Dammit. She knew it was too good to be true. She freezes, just like she had in the Processing Center when Rose had called her back. Although she doubts very much this man is interested in learning her name.

"You dropped this." He holds out a bunch of leafy stalks that must've fallen out of her arms in her haste.

"Thanks," she says, hoping her cheeks aren't burning as brightly on the outside as they are on the inside.

The man puts the bunch on top of her pile of food and pats it down safely. "Be in peace."

"Be in peace," she replies, turning and heading to the airlock.

As soon as she's out in the fresh air, she draws in several deep breaths. Maybe it's not too late to back out of this whole crazy idea. She can return these herbs to the Processing Center and give back the cherries while she's there. Rose is about as suspicious of her as the man in the elevator.

'The scurge is growing stronger in me,' Nola's voice hisses from the recesses of her mind. *'I can feel it.'*

She pictures her old friend sitting in her beat-up chair as yet another tooth falls from her bleeding gums. It's enough to send Echo dashing toward the nearest pod. This plan might be crazy, and it might not be a permanent solution to all the disparity between the colonies, but it will have to do for now. It's all she has.

Remembering the coordinates for the orchard from last time, she types them into the keypad, hoping she has the letters and numbers around the right way. This time there's no announcement from Daphne, which is a relief. Echo's already had more than enough of her.

The pod zooms off and she restacks the food to make sure she doesn't drop any again. She thinks she can recognize rosemary amongst the herbs from the LaB but she's not really sure what that bunch of green herbs she'd dropped are. They don't smell especially appetizing. But they must have some kind of nutritional value. It's better than eating dirt.

She's at the orchard in minutes and climbs out, glad she'd recalled the coordinates correctly. Walking calmly, she remembers the man from the elevator and how little attention he'd paid her. It's not in these people's nature to be suspicious of anyone's motives. They're all working for the good of the colony. None of them are aware in the slightest that there's one amongst them who's different. One who wants to shake their hive so hard that all the honey falls out.

Echo marches down one of the long rows of vegetable seedlings, the weight of the food in her arms feeling like a trophy. People nod and smile as she walks past and she keeps her head high, having no idea what excuse to use if anyone questions her. The crops are being replanted after Harvest Day, all the abundance that was there only days before having been stripped bare. It makes her feel even more justified in what she's doing. Chase will have no hope of finding anything to eat from this particular field if he comes on one of his midnight runs. He needs what she's bringing him. Her people are counting on it.

It's only when she reaches the shadows of the trees in the orchard that she turns and scans the fields to see if anyone is watching her.

And there he is.

River.

Head slowly shaking his disapproval, River plants one hand on his hip, his other holding a bunch of something green. She must've dropped those strange-smelling stalks again.

They lock eyes and their kiss from only the night before burns at her lips. She's never known anyone to stir up such a vortex of feelings inside her. He's one of the people here who's shown her that love and kindness exist. Yet he's also one who's proven to her how little they're prepared to change. She knows there's goodness behind those complicated green eyes. His unwavering loyalty to his sister proves that. But how can she get him to trust her?

She sighs, accepting that she can't. Because he won't, especially not now that he's seen her sneaking out food. She can expect about as much of River's trust as she had food back home.

Walking further into the trees, Echo knows he'll follow to speak his mind, and she doesn't particularly want to hear it. No doubt, it will only confuse her even more.

She sets down the food behind the tree trunk and shoves her hand into the hollow to feel for a message from Chase. Disappointment stings her to find it empty.

River doesn't trust her. And Chase doesn't need her. And that makes her feel more alone than she ever has. Becoming an Immune has left her an outcast. She most definitely doesn't fit in here, but she's no longer sure she'd fit in back home either. Not after everything she's learned. The two colonies aren't painted in blocks of green and black like she'd always believed. They're a kaleidoscope of colors and shades, with just as many similarities as they have contrasts. But if she can see that, why can't anyone else?

"What do you think you're doing?" River asks.

She ignores him.

"I said, what do you think you're doing?" he asks again.

"It's called *sharing*." She stands and flicks her dark plait over her shoulder as she crosses her arms. "You should try it sometime."

"Did you take all that from the LaB?" He points at the pile of food, steam practically shooting out of his ears.

"Just the herbs," she says. "The cherries are from the Processing Center. But seriously, River, have you been in there? I've never seen so much food in my life."

He draws in a deep breath and she notices a slight wheeze. Hopefully he's not going to have another breathing episode like he had in the cornfield. She really isn't in the mood to save his life again.

"Why did you follow me?" she asks when he doesn't say anything. "You don't trust me, do you?"

"I wanted to be wrong about you," he says on a sigh. "That's why. But I can see now that I was right. You're doing something just as stupid and selfish as I'd expect you to do."

"Sharing isn't selfish," she points out. "If I were selfish, I'd keep all this food for myself."

"You don't get it, do you?" His green eyes are cold, far from the simmering pools she'd seen in the dim light of the LaB. "They're not herbs. Reed preserves endangered species of plants for our future. They're used to make medicines. The Processing Center has a special freezer for the things Reed sends them."

"Oh." Echo remembers the way Rose had made a fuss of the trolley she'd brought her, promising to take good care of what was on it. "I thought—"

"No, Echo. You didn't think." River glares as he waves the green stalks at her that she'd dropped. "This is serpentwood. Notoriously difficult to grow, almost extinct, yet one of our most powerful medicinal plants. It's one of the key ingredients in adrenacure. And you treated it like it meant nothing at all. We need this. What use would it be in the Dead Zone? For all you know, some of this stuff might be toxic. You could have killed someone."

"I...I didn't..." She bites down on her lip, guilt adding to all her feelings of anguish. She'd acted impulsively and the consequences could have been devastating. "I didn't know."

He groans, seeming more frustrated than angry now. "All you had to do was ask."

"That's not fair." She throws out her hands. "I've done nothing but ask questions since I arrived here. But nobody gives me any answers."

"That's because you're asking all the wrong questions," he points out. "You need to learn how to listen more than you talk."

"And maybe you need to think more than you listen." She's aware she's pouting but can't seem to pull her face back into a neutral expression.

"What does that even mean?" River's breathing is getting worse out here. He needs to get back to his sterile building with its antiseptic air and long held views of the way the world is supposed to function. Except she's not ready to let him go just yet.

"It means that you need to think for yourself," she says. "Instead of blindly accepting what you're told. We were drugged last night, River. I was in your room and you were unconscious on the floor. Why won't you believe me?"

Ignoring her question, he picks up the plants she'd taken from the LaB, leaving the cherries behind. "Oren told me I'm no longer your mentor. You're free to make your own mistakes from now on."

She clenches her fists, wondering what's behind this decision. Has Oren decided he can trust her, even though River so clearly doesn't? Or had River asked to be released from the duties he seemed to hate so much?

"But what if I still need a mentor?" she asks, not ready to end their strange relationship. She may not fit in here, but the reality is that River is all she has.

"I'm sure Daphne will be only too happy to help," he snaps.

She swallows, realizing that while she hasn't given up on him just yet, he's most certainly given up on her.

"We still need to find Flora," she says, hoping that his sister's name will help bring back the softer side to this guy she knows is there. "We can leave right now if you like."

He shakes his head. "*We* are not doing anything. I just told you I'm not your mentor anymore."

River stalks off, leaving Echo with her sack of cherries and a feeling of dread pooling in her stomach.

She steps into the sunshine and watches him leave, wishing she could run after him and shake some sense into him. Can't he see how much stronger they'd both be if they chose to work together instead of alone? He needs Echo just as much as she needs him, even if she can't tell the difference between herbs and endangered plant species.

Walking back to the tree, she sticks her hand into the empty hollow again, checking to see if she missed anything.

Her heart leaps, this time in pure joy. Tucked underneath some bark is a piece of tightly folded paper.

With shaking hands, she unfolds the note and smooths it out on her leg.

She gasps at the three words, scrawled in Chase's hurried handwriting.

Flora is ded.

TWENTY

RIVER

Although it's still dark when River arrives at the Betadome, the faintest hint of dawn is lighting the horizon, brushing it with pale amber. He stops by the green door, catching his breath. It's a little later than he'd intended, but not too late.

Everyone in the Green Zone is still asleep, the entire colony silent in a way he's never seen.

But daylight will be here soon, lighting his path as he makes his way through the Dead Zone.

So he can find Flora.

River glances over his shoulder, conscious of how loud the air wheezing in and out of his lungs must sound. It's because he ran most of the way here, not wanting to use a pod in the early hours of the morning. Not only would it be conspicuous, but someone could track him. He just hadn't expected it to get him so out of breath. He leans back and expands his chest as his shoulders heave up and down. He just needs a second to get a little more air in. It's making his head swim.

The sound of a bird announcing the approaching day has

him straightening. He'll have to catch his breath on the other side of the Betadome. He has to be gone before anyone in the colony is up.

Including Echo.

Just thinking about the girl puts his teeth on edge. He's never met anyone so stubborn. So smart, yet so incredibly short-sighted. So...unsettling. Creating some distance between them, quite literally, is the right thing to do right now. Catching her stealing food to sneak to the Dead Zone helped reinforce his decision to leave. They're too different for anything between them to work.

Although there's still an uncomfortable band around his chest, River determinedly steps into the Betadome. Despite the fact all that separated him was wire mesh, the buzzing of the bees seems louder the moment he's inside. The sweet smell of honey hangs heavily in the air, feeling viscous in his lungs. His wheeze becomes more of a rasp, sawing up and down his throat.

Undeterred, River focuses straight ahead. A few yards and he'll be at the black door, and Flora is somewhere on the other side. The sun crests as he takes his first step, golden fingers of light reaching out to caress the porous bubble he's in and he blinks. Dew sparkles on the tips of leaves. The reds and yellows and pinks and blues of the blossoms absorb and reflect the dawn radiance. Shadows appear, stretching across lush grass, only there because the growing light allows them to be.

Viridescent, as his twin would say. What River would do to hear her say it again. To whisper the word with her.

His stride extends as his determination sinks deeper in his gut. This is what the Green Zone is protecting. The Betadome is a crucible. Holding the future of the planet. Of mankind. As an Immune, he has a responsibility to ensure it survives.

The moment his pace picks up, so does the humming. It

increases in volume, rising in pitch. It has his heart rate doing the same. Remembering where he is, that he's surrounded by insects who are just as deadly as they are essential, River adjusts his gait. His mother's words float through his mind. Smooth. Slow. Silent.

The moment he relaxes, the buzzing eases. Several bees still hover around as if they're investigating. Waiting to make sure he's not a threat. River's conscious of his labored breathing more than ever—he might be smooth and slow, but he's far from silent. The knowledge that Vern was Immune and yet he died anyway seems to tighten his lungs even more.

But he continues on. Nothing is stopping him from finding Flora.

The black door ahead blurs and swims. Blinking rapidly, River's forced to stop. He bends over, his hand on his knees as he tries to get enough air into his shrinking lungs. It's happening again. Just like in the cornfield.

Although he's no longer moving, the number of bees above multiplies. He knows he needs to be quiet, but he also needs oxygen like he never has before. And his throat is so tight. His chest is collapsing. Panic claws at his consciousness.

Echo's face floats before his narrowing vision. "Breathe, River. In, out."

He focuses on doing just that. In. Out. He remembers the feeling of her hands on his cheeks, her steady gaze becoming his anchor.

In.

Out.

The sound continues to agitate the bees, but River tunes it out. Smooth. Slow. If he can't be silent, he needs to get out of the Betadome. Although his feet feel molded from lead, he places one in front of the other, trudging forward.

Echo's voice encourages him. "That's it. One breath at a time. One step at a time."

Black fills his vision, and for brief, painful seconds, River thinks it didn't work. Oblivion is coming for him. Who knows how long before anyone finds him. Whether crumpling to the ground will be the final movement that triggers the bees.

How many stings can an Immune withstand? It only took one with Vernon.

River reaches out blindly, relief coursing through him when his hand hits something solid and flat. The door. The black he saw was the door.

Leaning against it, he presses the pad to open it. A blast of smoky air engulfs him as he walks through, preventing the bees from exiting and protecting the Vulnerables in the Dead Zone. He finds himself in an airlock, just like the entrance to the Sting, and he stumbles through the second door the moment he can.

His feet kick up dust as he shuffles forward. Then stops.

River slowly straightens, the shock of his surroundings seeming to cure his breathing almost instantly. The Dead Zone stretches out before him, no longer a colony obscured by the wire of the Betadome or blurred by distance.

He's now in it.

And it's far more desolate, infinitely bleaker than he ever imagined.

The sun creeps over the Betadome, bathing the Dead Zone in harsh light and River almost gasps. Barren soil stretches as far as he can see, the only thing fracturing it are derelict huts. Some stand alone, forlorn and faded, others are grouped together, as if they're leaning against each other for support. Morning light beats down on everything. There's no vegetation to soften it. To moderate its ferocity. To cast cooling shadows.

River swallows as he straightens. The Dead Zone was

called this for a reason. What's more, humans are the ones who created it, purely so they could survive. By excluding bees and killing any who are foolish enough to find a way through the netting, the Vulnerables are ensuring their survival.

Blinking, River does another slow scan. But at what price? There would be some grasses, probably wheat and corn. Anything that's pollinated by wind. But without vegetation, some shred of biodiversity, the land is nothing but a shriveled, sunken remnant of what it's supposed to be.

And Flora's in here, somewhere.

His heart constricts, then shudders. Flora's soul would've withered the moment she saw this place.

Clenching his jaw, River pulls out the map Tuff gave him. From what he can tell, Flora's somewhere on the other side of this decaying colony. His finger traces what looks like a waterway, curving not far from the X. He has no idea what he's going to do when he finds her, only that he needs to. He can't continue to live in the Green Zone, knowing she's here, dying along with everything else.

Tucking the map back in his pocket, he sets off. Once he's reunited with her, everything will fall into place. They'll figure out what happens next.

A woman exits the first hut as he approaches it, her hand flying to her throat when she sees him. He smiles, wanting to reassure he means no harm, but the motion dies as he gets closer.

The woman's hair is dirty and limp, her face sunken and gray. But that's not what has his stomach turning. The back of her hand is covered in sores. Some are scabbed over, but others are still exposed and weeping. They extend up her arm, mottling and bruising the skin, disappearing beneath the rag that is her dress.

River's steps falter and she sneers at him, exposing fleshy

gums with more gaps than teeth. Instinctively, he recoils. He's read about the scurge, but he never imagined it looked...like that.

Mentally shaking himself, he resumes his approach. The woman's eyes widen and she darts away, disappearing among the huts ahead. River frowns, although he knows he shouldn't be surprised. He glances down at his white suit. It's very obvious he's not from around here.

He just needs a chance to explain why he's here. They'll see there's nothing to be scared of. That he doesn't mean any harm.

River's reached the first cluster of huts when more people appear. They emerge from doorways and shift away from walls, their skin almost blending with the grimy surroundings. River stops, pulling up a smile again as whispers swirl around.

"Green Born."

"Immune."

"Greedy, selfish bastards."

The last has him stiffening, but he maintains his smile. The Green Zone is most definitely not greedy or selfish. He raises his hands to show they're empty. "Be in peace."

A man steps forward, scowling. "What'd you say?"

"Be in peace," repeats River, a little louder but just as gently.

The man's nostrils flare as his lip curls, revealing bruised and bleeding gums. "You think you can come here and tell us what to do?"

River blinks, registering the animosity that's climbing up each and every face. "Of course not—"

The man stalks closer and River finds himself instinctively moving backward. He bumps into something and just as he realizes that it's another person, he's shoved forward. He stumbles and he falls to his knees. Before he can right himself, a foot slams into his face.

The force has his head snapping up and his body jack-knifing to the side as he groans in pain. He lands on his hip, his hands splayed on the dusty ground. "Wait, you don't understand—"

"No!" roars the man, fury shaking his frail body. "You don't understand, Green Born. You don't get to come here with your clean clothes and clear skin and full stomach, talking about peace." The man spits and a fat globule of blood lands beside River. "Take off your clothes."

River's gaze darts up. "I'm looking for my sister. Her name's—"

The man roughly shoves his foot in River's chest. "I'm looking for justice. Now take them off before they get any dirtier."

The Vulnerables contract around the man, their eyes filled with everything from hostility through to hatred. Both men and women, a mix of ages, but the older they are, the more sore-riddled and emaciated they are. They're all dying.

And River's a picture of health. Of everything they don't have.

He's a fool. Echo was right. He shouldn't have come here alone.

"Please," he rasps, his jaw aching from the strike. "I—"

The next blow is dealt with the back of the man's hand. A cheer rises from the crowd as blood explodes from River's nose, gushing into his mouth.

"Get them off! Before he gets his precious Immune blood on 'em," someone screams.

The crowd surges and River lifts his arms instinctively, even though he knows it won't help. He may be healthier and stronger, but there are at least a dozen of them. And they're alive with fury.

It's clear they don't just want his clothes. They want him dead.

River catches a glance of the woman he first saw when he arrived a few feet away. She looks sad. A little disgusted. Maybe horrified. But all she does is turn her head away.

She doesn't care if he dies.

The next thought stuns him.

Just like he never cared whether she or any of the other Dead Borns died.

A hand painfully grabs his hair. Others claw at his arms and chest. One of his shoes is yanked off. River stops struggling, no longer fighting whatever's happening here. He's not sure he has a right to.

"Get away!" shouts a voice. A voice River recognizes.

Echo pushes her way through the crowd, coming to stand in front of River as she shoves away grasping hands and flailing feet. "Move back!"

Most of the people do, seemingly just as surprised as River to see her here. She plants her hands on her hips, becoming a human shield as she glares at them. "I said, get back."

The circle grows a little but the man steps forward. "He came in here thinking he could ask for stuff," he growls. "Like they ain't taken enough already."

"My guess is you didn't give him a chance to talk, Trid," says Echo archly.

"We don't wanna hear what those greedy bastards have to say!" someone calls from the crowd.

The others shout their agreement and the crowd swells again, closing in. River quickly scrambles to his feet, wiping the blood caking his upper lip. "Echo," he says in a low voice, although he's not sure what he's trying to communicate.

She shouldn't be here, ready to fight her own people. Putting herself in danger.

Because of him.

But she ignores him, keeping her gaze steady on the man— Trid. "So you attacked him?" she demands. "The first Green Born to show an interest in the Dead Zone, and this is how you treat him?"

Trid frowns as several people shift their weight.

"River's realized this—" she waves her arms to encompass the dirt and decay— "isn't okay. He came here to learn about how we're forced to live."

He can't help the flush that climbs up his cheeks as wide-eyed gazes fall on him, one by one.

"River's different," continues Echo, her voice more subdued. "He cares. He wants to figure out a way to stop the suffering and injustice."

More shuffling feet and unblinking eyes and River has to work to hold their gazes. Shame is scorching him from the inside out.

Trid crosses his arms. "You bring any food?"

Echo stealing and hiding the food in the orchard is suddenly making sense. River opens his mouth, not sure what to say, when Echo speaks first.

"And cause a riot?" she snorts. "We're not here to see more people needlessly die."

Trid grunts in agreement. He slides a glance at River. "You had no idea what it was like here, did ya?"

He shakes his head. "No, I didn't," he says honestly.

Trid grunts again but doesn't say anything. Silence weaves through the dusty air and River shifts uncomfortably. Echo saved him from the crowd, but now things are just as unknown.

Will they believe her? And what will it mean for River if they do?

The crowd parts and a guy not much older than River appears. "Here's your shoe," he mutters, throwing it at his feet.

It bounces in the dirt, stirring up the dust. River looks down at his exposed foot. The bones don't jut out of thin, bruised skin, each groove and bump starkly visible. Unlike every foot he's surrounded by...

He pulls off the other shoe and, picking up the first, throws it to the guy. "You have them."

The guy snatches them, glances at River, then runs off.

"Get the word out," Echo says to the others. "A Green Born is here to see the Dead Zone. It's time for them to learn the truth."

The crowd disperses, people glancing at each other and murmuring among themselves. River's frozen to the spot.

He's willing to admit that he came here naively. That life in the Dead Zone is nothing like he imagined.

But now the Dead Borns are expecting something from him. Something he's not sure he has to give. He's the son of Oren, the leader of the Green Zone!

Echo turns to him, an eyebrow raised but he speaks before she gets a chance.

"Echo, what the hell have you done?"

CHAPTER
TWENTY-ONE

ECHO

E cho tries not to smile as she watches River limping beside her in his bare feet.

"What?" he asks, sounding annoyed.

"Nothing." This time she can't help but smile. "It's just that you thought I was impulsive when I got to the Green Zone, and what's the first thing you do when you get here? Give your shoes away. What were you thinking?"

"I was thinking that guy needed them more than me." River winces as he steps on a sharp stone.

"Well, I'm not sure it was such a great idea," she says. "I mean, it was noble, but a little stupid."

Echo pauses to slip out of her shoes. She lifts one foot to show River the tough skin on her sole. "We all grow up barefoot around here. You've spent your life on those smooth tiles inside the Sting. Trust me, that guy *did not* need your shoes more than you."

She tears the white fabric at the back of her shoes to turn them into sandals, enjoying the feeling of being the expert.

River is on her turf now. She's the mentor. And it's about time he started listening to her.

She holds the newly fashioned shoes out to him.

"No, I couldn't." He waves a hand in protest. "They'll be too small anyway."

Echo rolls her eyes. "When I got to the Green Zone, I listened to you. Now it's your turn. Put the shoes on."

"You didn't always listen to me," he points out.

"Seriously, I don't want them. I'd rather go barefoot." She throws her shoes onto the ground and steps away.

River sighs as he picks them up and slips them on.

Now her smile's impossible to hide. They look ridiculous on his large feet.

"You're laughing at me?" He marches on at a far greater pace, despite the strange gait he's forced to adopt to keep her shoes from slipping off.

She follows, the familiar feeling of the dirt under her feet an ironic comfort. It's odd coming home wearing the white clothing of the Green Zone, like this external change in her appearance is an indicator of her having also changed on the inside. Which undoubtedly, she has. But connecting with the earth like this reminds her who she is—*who she really is.*

A Dead Born. And it makes her feel strangely proud.

"This way." River points to a road that leads to the dirty creek where they fetch their water. "We need to go there."

"What are you not telling me?" She puts a hand on his arm to stop him. "How do you know what's down that way to know you need to go there?"

He shuffles his shoddily-clod feet and looks down.

"I see." Echo jams her hands on her hips. "So, I save your life back there, and you still don't trust me? I suppose you're upset I followed you."

"We've been following each other everywhere!" River's

gaze snaps up, the dazzling green of his irises a contrast to their bleak surroundings. "I'm upset because you told them I came here to stop all the suffering and injustice. I'm here to find Flora. That's it. And you know it."

She crosses her arms tightly. "What I know is that I really misjudged you. Here I was thinking you had a kind heart and it seems you're just as selfish as the rest of them."

He throws out his hands. "How is finding my sister selfish? Sitting back in the Green Zone and forgetting her would be selfish."

Echo lets out a long breath, wondering how she can possibly break the news to River that his twin is dead. He came here for nothing. It's too late for him to save his sister, but there are hundreds of other people's sisters he can save instead.

"River..." She unwinds her arms, struggling to find her words. "We need to find Chase before we look for Flora."

That way, at least he can get the full story. Surely, it has to hurt less if he can find out what happened to her, rather than just hearing the heartbreaking outcome.

River shakes his head and points back down the road to the creek. "You can go and find your boyfriend if you like, but I'm going that way."

"River..." she tries again. "I don't know what you think's down that way, but I can guarantee you it won't be Flora. Let's find Chase first."

He shakes his head. "I told you, I'm going that way."

She groans at the stalemate they've reached. He knows full well she won't let him go anywhere alone. Not unless she wants to find him naked and dead in the creek, which she most certainly does not. But he doesn't understand. They have to talk to Chase before they go wherever it is he's convinced Flora is hiding.

River takes a few steps and a rail-thin woman dressed in a torn blue dress steps out in front of him, forcing him to stop. She has a bundle of rags clutched to her chest and tears streak jagged trails down her dirt-stained cheeks.

"Excuse me," says River politely as he steps to the side. "I need to pass. Be in peace."

The woman steps in front of him once more, opening the bundle of rags to reveal what's inside.

River gasps. Or perhaps it's a choked cry. Whatever it is, the strangled noise has Echo dashing to his side, letting out a moan of her own as she sees the small baby in the woman's arms. The young child's skin is gray and it's lying so still there can be no doubt it hasn't drawn breath for quite some time.

"I couldn't make enough milk to feed my daughter." The woman's voice is as lifeless as the baby she's holding. "She starved because I couldn't feed her."

"What about your rations?" River asks, clearly distressed. "We give you rations to keep you healthy."

Three young children dash forward, hugging their frail mother's legs. The tallest of them reaches up to stroke the cheek of their dead sibling.

"Mama made us eat her share," the child sobs. "We didn't want to. I swear we didn't. But we were so hungry."

River opens his mouth as if to reply, but just like Echo only moments before, he can't seem to find the words.

A man with a bent back stumbles over and pokes River on the arm. "Got anything for us to eat? Nothing too hard, mind you." He grins widely at River to reveal his missing teeth and bleeding gums. "Chewing ain't my specialty these days. But what I wouldn't give for a juicy peach. Had one of them when I was a boy. Never forgotten it."

River stares at the man with wide eyes, words still escaping him as more people approach, not wanting to miss their chance to plead their case.

"Okay, everyone!" Echo holds up her hand. "Please give our guest some space. There's a lot for him to take in."

The people edge back slowly and Echo slips her hand into River's, both to comfort him and to make sure he doesn't try to leave her side again. He clutches her like she's a lifeline.

"I didn't know," he whispers. "I had no idea."

She squeezes his hand. "There was plenty I didn't know about your colony either."

The crowd of people continue to retreat and Echo spots Jupiter amongst them. The last time she'd seen Jupiter they were getting a shot of adrenacure in the Betadome before being directed out through the black door.

"Jupiter!" she calls. "Can we talk to you?"

Jupiter ambles over, eyes darting around as they walk.

"You're Immune," they say, staring at Echo like she's an alien. "Congratulations."

"Thanks," she says automatically.

"Why are you back here?" Jupiter asks. "Nobody comes back here."

"I'm not nobody." Echo grins. "I came back to help. We both did."

Jupiter runs a hand through their short dark hair. "What can you possibly do for us?"

"I don't know," Echo says, giving the most honest answer she can. "Have you seen Chase? I need to talk to him."

"He's at your house." Jupiter's expression darkens. "I'm sorry to have to tell you, but your dad..."

"Died," Echo says, sparing Jupiter the pain of having to say it. "I know."

Jupiter nods, still not smiling. River tightens his grip on

Echo, now giving the comfort instead of being on the receiving end.

"You seem different," Echo says to Jupiter, remembering how positive and helpful they'd been at the Confirmation, reassuring Avid and leading them all into the Betadome. "Are you okay?"

Jupiter shrugs. "Things feel different now. No more hope, I suppose."

A lead weight settles in Echo's stomach, reminding her exactly why she came back here. It wasn't just to protect River. It was because things have to change. She can't sit on her hands knowing her entire colony is living without one of life's most important treasures—hope.

"I remember you in the Betadome," says River. "You were brave."

"So was your sister." Jupiter nods. "I'm sorry about what happened to her."

Echo's eyes flare as she urgently tries to tell Jupiter not to say more.

"Thanks," says River, clearly thinking they're talking about Flora's fate as a Vulnerable, not her recent death.

"What's Chase doing at my house?" asks Echo, changing the subject.

"He took the new Green Born Vulnerables there," says Jupiter. "They had nowhere else to go and he said you wouldn't mind."

Echo nods as she automatically strokes the locket around her neck. Her dad would be happy to know their home has become a sanctuary of sorts. Chase did well. She waits for the familiar electricity to thrum through her veins at the thought of Chase but is left with all her senses dulled.

"It really was a shame about your sister, though," says Jupiter, looking back to River. "I liked her."

"Liked?" River frowns. "What do you mean *liked*?"

"Before she disappeared." Echo pulls on River's hand, stepping in the direction of her house. "That's what you meant, isn't it, Jupiter?"

Jupiter looks confused, then realization crosses their eyes and they fall silent.

"Thanks, Jupiter," says Echo, leading a dazed River a few more steps. "I might see you later."

She manages to drag River down the length of the street and almost to the door of her house before he stops to speak again.

"Flora's dead, isn't she?" he asks quietly as his eyes spill over with tears.

Echo nods, reaching for his other hand. But he breaks their hold, stepping back from both Echo and the news she's confirming.

"No," he says, as he begins to shake. "No."

"I'm sorry, River." She closes the gap between them, but he doesn't want any part of her. "It's true."

"Why didn't you tell me?" Anger flashes through his grief.

"I didn't get the chance." She winces, hearing how pathetic her words sound. "And I don't know any of the details. That's why I wanted to find Chase. So he could tell you."

"You thought I'd rather hear that kind of news from your... boyfriend?" He practically spits out that last word.

"Firstly, he's not my boyfriend," she says, wondering why it feels so important to make that clear. "And secondly, I thought you didn't trust me. Why would you want to hear that from me?"

He blinks back his tears as he holds his spine straight. "I do trust you, Echo. You challenge me, that's all."

"I really am sorry," she says, remembering how much it

had hurt to learn her father had died and wishing she could comfort River in the same way he'd comforted her.

"I want to talk to Chase. I want to know what happened." River pulls back his shoulders and continues toward the door of the small house she'd shared with her father.

Echo's heart breaks at the sight of him standing so tall when his whole world has just shattered into sharp-edged fragments. And he trusts her. She just *challenges him*. That's welcome news. Because as she watches him now, she knows she trusts him too.

She follows River, restraining herself from putting her hand on his back, the gesture so hard to resist it has her admitting she likes this guy. She wants to mold herself to him and take away all his pain.

Before she can decide how much of a problem this is, Chase opens the door and now she's looking at the two most important men in her life. And she has no idea which one of them she likes more.

Chase. Her known-him-forever-guy. The one she loved at first sight. The one who kept secrets even though she gave him her heart. The guy she longed to kiss yet turned her cheek when she had the chance.

And River. Her known-him-for-five-minutes-guy. The one who annoyed her at first sight. The one who lets down his walls the more she lets down hers. The guy she fake kissed, not expecting it to burn her through to her soul.

"Echo," says Chase, ignoring River standing directly in front of him. "What are you doing here?"

"That's a long story," she says. "But first, River has some questions for you."

Chase shifts his gaze to River, and Echo sees something in his eyes she hasn't seen before—jealousy. And it doesn't suit him one bit.

"What did you animals do to my sister?" River leaps at Chase and grabs him by the front of his shirt, all the grief that had built up inside him exploding.

Chase expertly raises and flicks his arms to break River's hold. In seconds he has the same grip on River, pinning him against the doorframe.

And now the two most important men in Echo's life are glaring at each other, their mutual hatred of what they stand for seeping out of their pores in a cloud of rage. River may be fueled by anger, but Chase is far more skilled at combat. There's no question who will win this fight.

"Stop that!" Echo squeezes herself between them, her back to River as she beats on Chase's chest, pushing him forward. "If you want to hurt him, you'll have to hurt me first."

Chase lets go and walks into Echo's house muttering words she's certain River never heard growing up in the Sting.

"I know you're upset," she hisses at River. "But that's not the way to handle it."

"I don't like that guy." River smooths down his shirt. "He killed Flora. I know it."

Echo sighs. "He didn't. And if you could keep your cool for just a moment, maybe we can find out what happened. Can you do that?"

River nods, although the purple color staining his cheeks doesn't exactly look like he's calmed down just yet.

Echo leads him into the small home she'd shared with her father to see Chase sitting on the mat she used to sleep on. There's a blonde girl by his side and several more Green Born Vulnerables scattered around the room, their white clothing now stained brown.

The room looks different. The figurines that used to sit on her shelf are missing, but the yellow plastic flower is still there. She looks for more signs of her former life, quickly realizing the room doesn't *look* different. It feels different. Because her father isn't here. He was the reason this place had felt like home. Without him, it's just four walls and a leaking roof.

"Cascade!" River says to the blonde beside Chase. "Clover's been so worried about you."

The girl rolls her eyes, and Echo can clearly see the strong resemblance she has to the sister who's always draping herself over River—except this younger version seems to prefer Chase.

"I'm sure Clover has other distractions," says Cascade dryly. "Although, I can't imagine she'd be happy with you being here. I thought you two would be all cozied up by now."

"What happened to Flora?" River asks, directing his question at Cascade.

"She was stung by a bee," says Chase, answering for her. "Without any adrenacure, there wasn't much we could do for her."

"How is that even possible?" sneers River. "You have a net to keep them out."

Echo puts a steadying hand on his arm. "They get through sometimes. We've asked for adrenacure shots but have always been told there isn't enough to spare."

River's eyes widen. "But that's—"

"Unfair," says Chase. "I'm glad we can agree on something. Although, it's a shame it took your sister's death for you to realize it."

"Chase," Echo warns. "He's just had upsetting news."

"Oh, poor River," Cascade says sarcastically, immediately looking at Chase for approval.

He drapes an arm around her, his eyes flickering to Echo to see if she notices. She physically recoils at how low he's stooping. She hadn't made him jealous on purpose. Why would he intentionally try to cause her pain?

"We should go," she says to River. "We got what we came for."

River doesn't need any further encouragement and marches out the door.

"We'll talk later," she says to Chase, her loyalties still torn despite the childish way he's behaving.

Echo follows River, pleased to see he's waiting for her outside.

"What do you see in that guy?" he asks, throwing out his hands.

She shakes her head. "He's not usually like that. And he really isn't my boyfriend."

River grunts as he reaches into his pocket, produces a piece of paper and hands it to Echo.

She unfolds it to find a crudely drawn map of the Dead Zone. A large X has been placed at the edge next to the creek. Now it makes sense why he'd wanted to go there.

"Take me to the X," he says. "Please."

"Who gave you this?" she asks.

He swallows, not seeming to want to answer. "Tuff."

"What?" Of all the names she'd expected he might say, that wasn't one of them.

River nods. "He knew Flora."

"He talked to you?" She shakes her head. "I knew he could talk!"

"Not exactly," says River. "He just gave me this map. It's where Flora was. Or maybe even where she still is."

"Chase wouldn't have lied about her death," she says gently. "He may have acted like an ass back there, but he wouldn't make something like that up. I know him, River. If he says Flora's dead, then she's dead. You can't hold out false hope like this."

She winces at her own words, remembering how she'd

225

reacted to Jupiter's loss of hope. Maybe it's not such a bad thing for River to believe the impossible, even if she doesn't. If hope is all River has then perhaps it's better not to extinguish that.

Somebody clears their throat behind them and Echo spins around.

One of the Green Born Vulnerables has followed them outside. She's short and thin, looking deceptively younger than her seventeen years. Her eyes are full of sadness and Echo's heart breaks to know she won't last much longer out here.

"Lily," says River. "What's wrong?"

"Don't trust Chase," she whispers. "You're right. Flora's alive."

CHAPTER
TWENTY-TWO
RIVER

The creek that River's standing beside mirrors the rest of the Dead Zone. Dirty. Sick. Weak. It trickles listlessly, the water almost the same color as the dirt it's carved through. And yet, a woman is squatting a few yards away, filling a clay jar with it.

River looks away, only to come face to face with another Dead Born. Just as dirty and sick and weak.

He wishes he could close his eyes, pretend he's back in the Sting, because no matter where he looks, there's another person watching him. Waiting.

Dirty.

Sick.

Weak.

It feels like every Vulnerable has come out to see him. To show their missing teeth or sore-riddled skin or the stones that they use to record their dead, sometimes scratching out nothing but a line to mark a loved-one's existence because that's all there's room for.

But River keeps his eyes open, meeting their gazes. In some

ways, because hiding from what's going on in the Dead Zone has contributed to what he's seeing.

And in part, because he refuses to believe Flora's dead.

He scans every face, accepting the painful discomfort that comes with being so close to abject poverty, hoping it's her. Is she still wearing her white suit like the others? Her dark hair would no longer be shiny, her skin would be dirt-stained, her feet would be bare, but he'd recognize her in an instant. She's his twin.

And he doesn't care what Echo says about that guy, Chase. River doesn't trust him. Even Lily said Flora's alive.

But every set of eyes that blink back at him aren't Flora's. Just people desperate to be seen. To be acknowledged.

And for the injustice to stop.

Which River has no idea what to do with.

Yes, the Green Zone is rich. Yes, they have no idea what hardships are being endured on the other side of the Betadome.

But these people are Vulnerable. The walking dead even before the scurge. And compromising the Green Zone is a death sentence for the rest of humanity.

"That's the place," says Echo quietly.

River turns to find her pointing at a shack at the edge of the colony that overlooks the sickly creek. She's holding the map he gave her, the X Tuff marked clearly visible. "I wonder if it's Tuff's house. Before he was found to be an Immune."

That would mean Flora and Tuff were friends. That he told her to come here if she was Vulnerable. Something she never mentioned.

He frowns. Hopefully he'll get some answers shortly.

River determinedly walks toward the house. Where Flora is.

She has to be.

"River," says Echo, rushing to catch up to him. "You need to be prepared—"

"You said Chase wouldn't lie about Flora's death, and yet Lily says otherwise. What else has he lied to you about, Echo?"

She scowls and he expects one of her snappy remarks. "I know, okay? You're not the only one dealing with some revelations right now."

That stops River. He turns to face Echo, shuffling a little in her too-small shoes. He glances over his shoulder at the house they're not far from. "It seems the people we care about have been keeping secrets."

Echo bites her lip. "It does."

Which leaves both of them floundering in a strange limbo neither of them knew existed—technically belonging to one Zone, somehow not quite fitting into either, and indelibly connected to both.

"Truce?" he asks quietly. Maybe they're not the enemies they assumed they were.

Echo looks up at him, her dark eyes swimming with turbulent emotion. Her lips dance in the ghost of a smile. "Truce."

They nod simultaneously, even though River's not entirely sure what they just agreed to. Or whether it's even possible. All he knows is that Echo is the closest thing he has to a friend right now.

They make their way to the house silently, the crowd back at the creek murmuring among themselves. They're probably wondering why they're going to this particular house. River almost feels guilty that he came here expressly for his own needs. If it weren't for losing his twin, he wouldn't be here, seeing all of this.

They've just reached the door made of pieces of timber held together with what looks like clay the same color as the rest of the Dead Zone when it opens. A man steps out, smiling widely to show dark gums and missing teeth. "Welcome, River! What took you so long?"

River stops in his tracks. "You were expecting me?" Does Flora know he's coming?

"Of course. Everyone in the Dead Zone has been waiting to see who you'd visit first." He arches a scraggly brow as he leans in a little closer. "And I must say, I'm not surprised it was my house you chose."

River tries to rein in his disappointment. It's clear everyone knows who he is. This man just wants to put his suffering on display, like all the others.

"I just wanted to ask—"

But the man doesn't let him finish. "Goodness, where are my manners? My name's Ruff." He waves for them to enter. "Come, come. Have something to eat. To drink."

Echo looks at River in surprise, although he's not sure why. They follow the man inside, finding a young woman sitting at the table in the center of the room. A plate sits beside her tightly clenched hands, a brown cloth over it.

"This is my daughter, Navy," Ruff says proudly. He leans into River again, and this time, the smell of his rotting mouth is unmistakable. "She still has all her teeth."

River smiles politely even though his stomach is flip-flopping. "I'm glad for her."

Ruff beams, indicating for River to take a seat. When Echo goes to sit beside him, Ruff quickly slips between them, his head bobbing as he points at the chair beside his daughter. Feeling increasingly uncomfortable, River does as he's told, finding Navy on one side and Ruff on the other. Echo takes the seat across from him, looking both cautious and amused.

"Ruff," starts River. "I'm here because—"

"We're one of the richest families in the Dead Zone," Ruff

finishes proudly. "It's perfectly understandable that you'd want to stay in comfort considering where you've come from."

River blinks. The floor beneath his feet is dirt. The walls are coated in clay. And the chair he's sitting on doesn't feel like it can take his weight. He clears his throat. "That's wonderful, but I believe someone I know could be here—"

Ruff grins even wider as he winks. "Navy does have quite the reputation." He nudges his daughter and she yanks up a smile, revealing that she does, indeed, have all her teeth.

River clenches his jaw. He glances around the room they're in, noting there's a single door at the rear. Probably leading to a bedroom. Could Flora be in there?

Ruff claps his hands twice. "Let's eat."

Navy, who still hasn't said a word, pulls the dirty piece of material off in a flourish. Sitting on a dented metal plate are two pieces of flatbread, a pale piece of corn and what looks like a slice of pumpkin. Although River hasn't eaten all day, the last thing he wants to do is take these people's meager rations.

He shakes his head. "Thank you, but I'm fine. I just want to know—"

Ruff frowns for the first time since they arrived. River quickly realizes he can't afford to offend this man, but Echo leans forward before he can speak.

"Is it just you and your daughter, Ruff?"

The man relaxes a little. "My wife died along with my son during his birth. I've raised Navy all on my own." He lifts his chin. "There's nothing I won't do for her."

Echo nods in understanding. "You're obviously very proud of her. And she's clearly quite healthy."

Ruff beams again, his gapped smile a stark contrast to that of his daughter's. River takes in a slow breath. He needs to take Echo's lead. Get to know this family before he asks about Flora.

Echo angles her head, curiosity filling her features. "How is it you have so many rations then, for a household of two?"

Ruff's smile slips a little. "We're very careful."

"We're all careful in the Dead Zone," agrees Echo. "It's just that Navy's doing so well..."

River stills. He doesn't see what Echo does—the plate before him is meager, what he thought would be a portion of rations. Navy looks like a Green Born might, just dirtier.

But clearly, something's amiss. If Ruff stockpiles rations, then Navy shouldn't...have all her teeth.

Echo smiles as she waves her hand, as if what she just said doesn't matter. "You look like someone I know, Ruff. A guy in the Green Zone. His name's Tuff."

River realizes she's right. It's there in the sprightly sprigs of hair and wide jaw.

"That's because he's my brother." Ruff puffs out his chest.

"Of course," says Echo, her eyebrows ever so slightly hiked. "Ruff and Tuff. Do you have another brother called Buff by any chance?"

Ruff shakes his head, not seeming to get the joke. "I'm directly related to an Immune. Which means Navy also is."

River turns back to their host. "Tuff gave me a map to your house."

Ruff is beaming once more. "I knew he'd take care of us." He nudges Navy, who stands and brings the plate to River. "Please, take it all."

"I couldn't," says River, lifting his hands and shaking his head.

"You must," says Ruff, his voice hiking. "It's a gift."

"You don't understand. I'm just here looking for someone. Flora."

Ruff frowns. "I don't know a Flora."

"Please," says River again. "Tuff sent her here. If you've seen her—"

Ruff pushes to his feet. "Tuff sent you here so I could take care of my daughter. He loved his niece like his own."

"No. There's been a misunderstanding. Flora came here."

"I haven't seen no Green Born called Flora," snaps Ruff.

River draws in a sharp breath. "Are you sure? She's shorter than me, the same dark hair and green eyes—"

"No, no one like that!" Ruff steps around to stand beside his daughter. "Now, you going to take it, or what?"

"I'm not hungry, thank you," says River through gritted teeth. Even if he was starving, he wouldn't take these people's food.

Echo's now looking at the table, shoulders hunched. "You don't understand, River. Navy is part of the package."

River reels back in horror. The man's offering him his daughter?

Navy smiles as she takes a cautious step forward, the plate she's holding trembling ever so slightly. Yet she holds his gaze. She looks hopeful just as much as terrified.

"You can't," gasps River. "You said you loved her."

Ruff's lip curls, exposing a black gap. "I do. I'd do anything to make sure she survives."

A fresh wave of nausea ricochets through River. Entering the Dead Zone has meant a storm of them, constantly hitting him. He shakes his head. "But this is wrong," he chokes. Navy isn't a commodity. She's a person.

"You think you're too good for my girl?" snarls Ruff. "That just cause you're Immune you're better somchow? That you should get more food, more chances, more everything, while she rots and dies?"

River takes a stumbling step back, surprised to find Echo now beside him. "No, I don't think that—"

"Then take my daughter as yours. She can make your time here memorable." Ruff opens his hands, a pleading note winding its way through his words. "Then you could send back some rations every now and again. So she stays healthy."

River's eyes leap from Ruff and his desperate, angry eyes, to Navy with her scared but resigned features, to the poverty surrounding this awful offer. The poverty that gave rise to it.

Finally, he looks to Echo, who's watching him carefully. Compassionately. "I can't," he whispers, not entirely sure what he's referring to.

The offer of a young woman's body in exchange for rations.

Accepting that Flora hasn't been seen.

Being here.

Echo turns to Ruff. "You may not see it now, but it's a good thing that River's the sort of person who would never take you up on your offer."

She takes his hand and tugs him out of the shack, then keeps walking back into the village. It's only once they're several houses deep that River stops. "Where are we going?"

He doesn't want to see anyone else. Find out how far people will go to help those they love.

Echo tugs him again, walking on with determination. "We need somewhere to lie low for a little bit. While we figure out what we do next."

River lets her lead him, progressively feeling more and more numb.

Because maybe Chase was telling the truth. Flora never reached the address Tuff gave her.

Maybe his twin is dead.

TWENTY-THREE

ECHO

Echo stops outside Nola's hut and draws in a deep breath. "Here," she says. "We can hide here while we work out what to do next."

"Whose house is this?" River seems uncertain. "It's tiny."

"All homes here are tiny," she points out, seeing nothing different about Nola's hut from anyone else's.

"Or maybe ours are just large." He shrugs off this comment like it means nothing. But it does. It's proof he's starting to see the world through different eyes.

Echo knocks on the small door.

"Nola!" she calls. "It's Echo."

There's the sound of something falling over inside, clearly audible through the thin walls.

"Nola!" Echo calls again. "Can I come in?"

"Echo's an Immune," Nola shouts back, her voice muffled from the netting that's no doubt wrapped around her face. "And I'm not an idiot. Go away, whoever you are."

"Nola, it's me," she insists. "It's Echo. I came back."

"Nobody comes back." Nola's voice is quieter. More serious and tainted with concern. "Unless you were Forgotten."

"I wasn't Forgotten," she says. "I just came back. Please, let us in and we can talk about it."

"Us?" Nola's clearly as sharp as ever. "Who's with you?"

"My friend." Echo looks across at River. Her friend. It feels nice to have made a truce and be able to say those words out loud. Right now, it seems like he might be her only friend. Because she's still got no idea what to think about Chase.

"How do I know it's you?" Nola asks.

Echo smiles. Still sharp. But also still suspicious.

"Right now, you're sitting in your armchair," says Echo. "It's dark green. Made from fabric that was once soft but has worn down to the threads. It has a tear in the seat and the left armrest wobbles when you lean on it to stand up. Which, I might add, is not very often."

Nola scoffs and Echo can well imagine the unimpressed look on her face. "Anybody could know what my chair looks like. I found it on the street."

"You told me before I went to the Betadome that there were only three possible outcomes," Echo continues. "One, I'd be a Vulnerable and return directly here. Two, I'd be an Immune and eat oranges and pumpkin for breakfast. And three, I'll be killed."

"I said oranges for breakfast, and pumpkin for dinner," Nola corrects. "Nobody eats pumpkin for breakfast."

Echo rolls her eyes and River smiles.

"Maybe this isn't a good idea?" he whispers.

She holds up a hand, asking him to give her a minute.

"If I had some pumpkin, would you eat it for breakfast?" Echo pulls out a piece of pumpkin from her sleeve, having swiped it at Ruff's house when he'd been busy making his unsavory proposition to River. It's a little worse for wear, but still the best thing anyone around here would have eaten in a long time. "Nola, let me in and I'll give you a nice juicy piece of pumpkin."

River's eyes widen as she holds it out, but he says nothing. His days of judging her actions seem to be over. Besides, it's obvious that anyone who lives in this falling-down hut needs the sustenance more than Tuff's awful brother.

"Okay, you can come in," says Nola, making it clear that while she's sharp and suspicious, she's also starving. "But first, you tell me your friend's name. I don't like strangers."

"River," says Echo, wondering how his name could possibly matter.

Nola makes a strangled sound. "Oren's son."

"You know him?" Echo looks to River for confirmation, finding him shrugging.

"All Green Borns know Oren's children," says Nola. "And he can't come in here."

"Well, I can't leave him out here," Echo protests. "He's being swamped with people asking him to save them."

"Then stay out there with him," huffs Nola. "Because he's not coming in here. I don't need you."

"You're so frustrating, Nola!" Echo kicks at the ground. "I'm just trying to help you."

River leans forward to speak quietly. "I'll be okay. You go in there and give her the food. She needs to eat. We'll find somewhere else to go when you're finished."

Echo squats at the small door to Nola's home, looking up at River. "Are you sure?"

He nods, his face full of concern. It's no wonder Reed described him as kind-hearted. She couldn't see it at the time, because she didn't know him. But here he is, having risked everything to find his sister, and willing her to leave him alone out here so a stranger can have something to eat.

"You know something?" she says, as she forces the door open and pushes aside the rags.

"What?" River shrugs.

"You're actually a pretty good guy." She shoots him a smile and turns before she can see his reaction. Passing through Nola's door, she closes it behind her, wishing she was the sort of person who could sneak River in here anyway. But Nola has so little say in her life, Echo can't possibly take away any of the power she has left.

"You didn't let him in, did you?" Nola calls as Echo parts the curtain in the doorway.

"It's just me," says Echo, trying to hide her shock at how emaciated Nola has become in the short time she's been gone. Even in the dim light, she can see how thin she's gotten. "Here's your breakfast."

Nola unwinds the netting she has looped around her face and shoves the cooked pumpkin into her mouth. It's gone in a matter of seconds.

"Have you been eating at all?" Echo asks, leaning forward to touch her on her bruised arm. "Has Chase been bringing you food?"

"Don't worry about me." Nola waves her hand to shoo her back. "I'm fine."

"Has Chase been bringing you food?" she asks again.

"I told you not to worry about me." Nola glares at her with bloodshot eyes as she avoids her question. "I'm fine."

There's a noise outside that has Echo's head snapping up.

"You okay, River?" she calls.

"I'm fine," he shouts back.

"Seems you're both fine." Echo crosses her arms, trying to

ignore the stale stench in the room. "I'm not needed around here."

Nola hauls herself out of her chair. "Don't be daft. We all need you. You're just what the world's been waiting for. Now are you going to help me wash, or what?"

Echo guides her to her washbowl and out of her dress. "I didn't bring any water."

"Got plenty here." Nola dips her washrag into the cloudy water and rubs her bruised body with it.

"What did you mean I'm what the world's been waiting for?" Echo asks gently.

Nola considers this question for a moment. "I was wrong about the possible outcomes of your Confirmation," she says. "There was a fourth option. You came back. Not a Vulnerable, and not Forgotten. You just came back. Nobody's done that before. You're special. Oren won't like that."

"What do you know about Oren?" Echo takes Nola's bedpan and opens the large hatch in the back wall, shifts aside the curtain and tips out the contents. "Are you afraid of him?"

Nola grunts as she slams the washrag back in the bowl and reaches for a slightly less filthy dress to put on. "Oren doesn't scare me. Pretty sure he's the one who's scared of me."

"Why is he scared of you?" Echo looks at this woman, no more than bruised skin and bone, and thinks of the powerful leader of the Green Zone. Could he possibly be scared of Nola?

"I know things." Nola dresses and limps back to her chair, sitting in it proudly like she's a queen on her throne.

"Do you know where Flora is?" Echo asks, knowing this is the longest shot in the world but it's the one question River came here to ask.

Nola's nostrils flare as her eyebrows shoot up. "Oren's daughter. Why would I know where she is?"

"She's a Vulnerable," says Echo. "And she's gone missing. Nobody knows where she is."

"Well, she's not hiding in my chair." Nola rubs at the armrests. "Why don't you ask her mother?"

"Her mother's dead." Echo leans forward. "Did you know her?"

"Nobody knew her." Nola's eyes glass over. "Not well, anyway. But I know she never trusted Oren. And nor should you."

"Is that why you won't let his son in?" Echo frowns.

"Sons are always like their fathers." Nola shakes her head.

"Not this one," says Echo. "River's different. He's...good."

"Go and find Flora." Nola waves her away once more. "Stop wasting your time with an old woman like me. You've seen I'm alive, now go. Go! Find this girl you're looking for. Make sure she's okay if it's so important to you."

"Echo!" River calls from the other side of the thin walls. "Echo, can you come out please?"

Not liking the anxious tone to River's voice, Echo touches Nola on the arm.

"I have to go," she says. "Please, eat something. And get out of that chair every now and then."

"Echo!" River calls again.

"Go," says Nola.

"I'll be back," Echo promises as something tugs at her, telling her she needs to continue this conversation.

Nola wraps the netting back over her face, either shutting Echo out, or exhausted from finally having stood up from her chair and needing to sleep.

Echo pushes through the curtain and scrambles out of the small house, blinking in the harsh daylight.

River is pressed up against the side of Nola's hut. He's breathing heavily as he looks from side to side.

"There are so many of them," he says.

Echo turns to see a swarm of Dead Borns marching down the small road from both directions. Some of them look healthy enough, but many are riddled with the scurge. If she had to guess, she'd say most of them haven't left their house in weeks. Women, men and children lean on each other as they walk, their desperate eyes fixed on one thing only.

River.

CHAPTER
TWENTY-FOUR

RIVER

River looks from Echo to the people progressively coming closer. If he could climb up onto the roof of the tiny shack, he would. But there's no way it'll hold his weight. That leaves him plastered against the side, his heart hammering so hard he's pretty sure he can feel it against the rough wall behind him.

He's surrounded by pain and suffering. By people carrying in their eyes the knowledge they're dying.

And they're looking at him like he's some sort of savior.

Except he's anything but that. He just came here to find his sister.

Echo grabs his arm and yanks him closer. "Quick, come in here." She shoves him down and through the small door to the hut.

"But—"

"You want to stay out here?" she demands.

"Please, do you have any food?" a woman cries somewhere behind them.

River quickly crawls through the half-door, Echo right

behind him, even though he's not exactly welcome. He finds himself in a small, gloomy space, a curtain obscuring the rest of the shack.

"Echo? What's going on?" comes the croaky older voice he heard earlier.

"It's okay, Nola. I just had to bring River in because he's kinda popular right now."

"You what?" screeches the woman.

Echo looks at River, concern crinkling her brow. She cracks open the curtains. "It's okay, he's a friend—"

"No, no, no! He can't come in here!"

The panic in the old woman's voice is unmistakable and River stills. It's clear he's the source of that fear, and that's the last thing he wants. Although going outside doesn't seem very palatable right now...

Echo rushes through. "Nola, there's nothing to be scared of. River's—"

Nola screeches, and River peeks through the curtains, seeing a frail woman tucked back into an equally frail-looking recliner. Her head is wrapped in swathes of netting, while she throws her arms out as if she's being attacked. "Get him out of here! Get him out of here!" she screeches.

Echo glances at River as he steps more fully through, no doubt thinking of the mass of people outside, waiting for him. Her head snaps to the other side of the hut, although it's too gloomy for River to know what she's looking at.

"This way," she says urgently.

She once more grabs his hand and yanks him across the small space. It turns out it's not the safe haven she'd hoped it would be.

They pass Nola and the old woman shrinks even further into her chair. "Stay away," she wails, her clawed hands waving in the air. "Stay away!"

River does as he's told, turning away and walking faster, wincing at the fear in her voice. Maybe it's because he's male? Or Green Born? Or Oren's son? Or would she be like this with anyone who entered her tightly closed hut?

Echo pulls him to the opposite wall where she opens a large hatch. "Quick, through here."

He wrinkles his nose at the smell, but Nola's next scream has him leaping to get away from the chaos one woman is creating. He's more than willing to face the other Vulnerables rather than this. He feels like he's killing her and he's only been in here for a minute.

The moment he's through, River tucks himself into a ball, knowing hard ground is waiting for him on the other side. He lands with a grunt, his shoulders making contact first, and he registers the soil's damp. He rolls, trying to propel himself now that he realizes exactly what gets thrown out that hatch.

He gets to his feet, grimacing. A quick check shows only his right shoulder has damp soil clinging to it. His stomach revolts at knowing where that moisture came from.

From the woman who just freaked out in a way he's never seen before because he was in her hut.

There's a shuffling sound and River realizes Echo's coming through the hatch in the same way he did. He leaps forward, catching her before she hits the ground. Stepping back, he quickly lowers her to her feet, making sure she's steady before he releases her.

Except, Echo's hands on his upper arms remain where they are. She smiles up at him. "Thanks."

He flushes, the memory of their kiss blossoming in his mind. "Sure." He clears his throat, conscious his own hands are still around her waist.

This truce between them has...confused things. He'd

normally step away. But now he can't help but admit he doesn't want to.

The hatch slams shut behind Echo. "And stay out!" screams Nola.

They grin at each other. They just jumped into a toilet puddle to do that. They're lucky the soil is so dry most of the moisture was quickly wicked away.

"It's not personal," Echo says quietly. "She never lets anyone in apart from me. Now I know why."

"We'll wait for them," says a voice on the other side of the hut, having no doubt heard Nola's screams. "They gotta come out eventually."

Echo slips her hand into River's. "Come on," she whispers. "We need to find somewhere else to lie low. Hopefully, Chase can think of a place."

River scowls at the mention of the guy. Chase isn't someone he wants help from. He lied to Echo. And it was clear that putting his arm around Cascade was all for Echo's benefit. The guy is a manipulator.

And he's the one trying to convince River that Flora's dead.

But River doesn't have a choice. Echo's right. He's the outsider now. The clueless intruder who everyone wants a piece of. He needs to follow her lead.

Echo guides him through the maze that is the Dead Born colony, holding his hand the whole time as they run. The huts become a blur of brown and more brown, the alleys turning and twisting until River has no idea which direction they're running.

Echo finally slows down, panting. "We're almost there."

River looks around, seeing the Betadome in the distance. And beyond that, the Sting. They seem a world away, which he supposes they are. The divide between the Dead Zone and Green Zone is far greater than he ever imagined. He never could've conceived such differences could exist so close to each other. As neighbors. Somehow, it makes the riches of the Green Zone all the more glaring. And the poverty of the Dead Zone all the more...wrong.

River startles at the thought. He's beginning to sound like Echo, and he's not sure what that means.

"This way—"

He turns to find out why Echo didn't finish her sentence, instantly alert and half-expecting a crowd of Dead Borns to be descending on them. But the alley ahead is empty. Apart from one person.

Chase.

And he's running in the opposite direction to where they're standing.

Echo frowns but doesn't call out.

"What's wrong?" asks River.

She chews her lip, watching as Chase disappears. "He didn't see me. Us, I mean. He was too focused on something."

Echo doesn't want to voice it, but she suspects Chase is up to something. This time, it's River who grabs her hand. "Let's see where he's going."

There's the briefest hesitation, but then she breaks into a run, taking River with her. They race to the end of the alley, glancing around the edge of an awkwardly leaning hut. Chase is already darting around another corner.

Whatever he's after, he's in a hurry.

River and Echo follow, increasing their speed so they can catch up. At the next turn, they find Chase is only about halfway down. They also discover why.

He's running after someone, in the same way they're running after him. A young woman or a girl. River narrows his eyes as he realizes there's something different about the girl. It's her clothes.

She's wearing a suit from the Green Zone! It's dirty and stained, but definitely a suit, just like his. He gasps and almost trips as he registers the short, dark hair.

Chase is running after Flora!

River breaks into a sprint, moving the fastest he ever has in his life. Just as he suspected, Chase lied! Lily was telling the truth! His twin is alive!

"River," Echo calls from behind him.

"It's Flora!" he tells her, not slowing down. "And she's trying to get away from him!"

Chase looks over his shoulder at the shouts, his eyes widening when he sees River and Echo barreling toward him. He faces forward again, his shoulders hunching as if he intends on getting to Flora first.

There's no way River's going to let that happen.

"Flora!" he shouts. "It's me, River!"

But she darts down a narrow lane, not even glancing over her shoulder. She must be too scared. Or thinks someone is trying to trick her.

River comes around the corner only a second after Chase. They both duck as a stack of decaying boxes come tumbling down on them, pulled over by Flora. River slams his arm through one as it comes at his head and it smashes into splinters, as fragile and decayed as everything else in the Dead Zone. A quick glance over his shoulder shows Echo's just behind, now leaping over the tumbling crates.

River keeps running, his heart thundering against his ribs, conscious he's catching up to Flora. If only she'd turn around, she'd see there's no danger.

She'd see it's her brother.

Flora takes a sharp left and River skids around the corner after her. He comes to a stop when he sees what she does. The alley is a dead end.

"Flora," he pants. "It's me—"

She spins around, breathing frantically, her terrified eyes darting around as Chase and Echo arrive.

River freezes, all the energy draining from his body as he sees her face. His breath disintegrates. His heart stops.

It's not Flora.

The trembling girl is a Dead Born.

Chase strides past him and grabs the girl by the arm. "Where did you get these clothes?" he demands.

"I...I found them, I swear!" cries the girl, cowering. "My mama said to sell them, but I've never had something with no holes. It even covers all of my back."

Chase shakes her. "Tell me the truth!"

The girl cowers, covering her head with her hands. The one that was so similar to River's sister.

But isn't.

"I'm telling the truth, I swear it on my mama's life. I found the clothes half-buried next to a deserted hut!"

Echo joins Chase, her face somber as she takes the other girl's arm. "I believe her, Chase. Look at her, she's too scared to lie." Her dark gaze lifts to River's, her face tight. The weight of what her words mean tug at the edge of her mouth.

River takes a step back. Then another.

The girl is wearing Flora's suit. There's no way his sister would've given up her last link to the Green Zone. Not willingly.

His heart fractures, the same pain from Confirmation slicing through him as he accepts he's lost Flora all over again.

TWENTY-FIVE

ECHO

E cho watches the scared girl run from the alley. All she'd wanted was clothes without holes in them, and instead had earned herself a whole lot of trouble.

She switches her gaze to River. All he'd wanted was to find his sister. And the realization that isn't going to happen is crushing him. His shoulders are hunched and his face is etched with pain.

"I told you she was dead," snaps Chase, lacking any of the empathy Echo's feeling.

"Then why were you chasing her?" asks River, straightening his spine.

"I thought another one of your kind had come here." Chase points his chin in the direction of the Green Zone. "You seem to be multiplying lately."

"We're all the same kind," says Echo, wanting Chase to see things the way she's started to. "We just live diff—"

"We're not the same." Chase scowls. "What's happened to you, Echo? Open your eyes."

"My eyes are open." Echo crosses her arms, not used to this

kind of aggression from Chase. "And I've seen a whole lot more than you could ever imagine."

"He's manipulating you." Chase points a finger directly at River. "And I don't like it. Flora said he..."

River's head snaps up at his sister's name. Except Chase doesn't seem keen on finishing his sentence.

"What did Flora say about me?" River's voice is choked, his need to know what his twin said seeming to overpower his pain.

"Nothing." Chase takes a step back. "She said nothing."

Echo's heart aches, remembering the agony she'd felt when she'd learned of her father's death and knowing River must certainly be feeling the same. "Tell him what she said, Chase. He needs to know."

Chase turns his dark eyes to her. The same eyes she used to get lost in, as she yearned to trail her fingertips down his face. He shakes his head. It's a small movement—almost impercep- tible—more like a warning than a response. Her well-honed instinct to trust him screams at her to listen. But she can't.

"What did Flora say about River?" she asks again.

"You sure you want to know?" Chase looks almost sympa- thetically at River.

"Tell me," he says through gritted teeth.

"She said you were naïve." Chase keeps his voice impassive. "That you'd do whatever your father told you to do. She said you were weak."

River reels back like Chase just punched him. "She didn't say that. You're a liar."

Echo puts a hand on River's back. He's trembling, although now it seems driven by rage rather than grief.

"Well, you wanted to know," says Chase, leaving Echo feeling torn as she struggles to decide what to believe.

Chase hadn't wanted to tell River what he just did. He'd

warned her to leave it alone. Which makes her think Flora must have said those awful words.

But one look at River has her unable to reconcile those words with the sister he's described. Which makes her think Flora couldn't possibly have said them.

In either case, perhaps it doesn't matter. Because one thing is certain—she's dead, having taken all her words with her.

"I'm going back to the house." Chase shifts his focus to Echo. "Come with me."

Every muscle in River's back tenses, but he remains silent.

"We can't," she says.

"I meant you," Chase clarifies. "Let this Green Born go back to the people he loves so much. You were right—you belong here. With me."

There's a softness in Chase's eyes. The exact kind she'd been seeking from him for so long. But now that she has it, she knows without any doubt she no longer wants it.

"I don't know where I belong." She shakes her head slowly. "But I do know it's not with you. I'm sorry, Chase."

"You're choosing him?" Chase tilts his head toward River, his eyes wide.

"I'm choosing me, actually." She plants both hands on her hips, not liking the idea of being forced to make a choice. In time, her heart will tell her exactly which way it wants to go. All she knows for now is that River was there for her when the loss of her father caused her world to fall apart. She can't possibly abandon him now.

"Fine." Chase stalks off down the alley, running from her like he always does when times get tough.

She knows she should feel sadness at what just passed between them but comes up empty. Perhaps that's sad in itself given how much Chase had once meant to her.

"Flora didn't say that," whispers River, still trying to process what he'd just been told. "I know she didn't."

Echo looks at her broken friend and it's now that her heart aches as it floods with his pain. She wraps her arms around his shoulders. It's like hugging a tree trunk, his spine is so stiff. She holds her embrace, trying to urge him to fold into her, but he remains frozen.

"She would never say that," he insists.

"I know," she says, even though she has no idea what the mysterious Flora may or may not have said. "I know."

River crumples, like her agreement was all he needed to give into his grief. He bends forward, his entire body softening as he puts his arms around her waist and accepts her comfort. He's taller than her, but somehow they fit together and she's reminded of their kiss—not because this moment is in any way romantic but because of the surprising depth of feeling that lies behind it.

She presses herself closer to him and realizes she already made her choice. This is exactly where she's meant to be right now. And exactly who she's meant to be with. The world had just been spinning too fast for her to see it.

"I'm taking you back home," she says, gently pulling away to look at him. "We need to slow down and make a better plan. Flora's not here, and it's not safe for you to stay."

River hesitates, a battle raging behind the depths of his green eyes. Then he gives in to her and nods.

With one arm wrapped around him, she leads him down a narrow side alley, taking him the back way towards the Beta-dome. It's late afternoon and the sun is already low in the sky, dragging down all their hopes of finding River's twin along with its golden rays of light.

They walk back past the rear of Nola's house, this time not stopping to go in.

"Is Nola going to be okay?" River asks, always thinking of someone other than himself. "She seemed pretty shaken up."

Echo smiles, not wanting to add to River's worries. "You know what? I think we might have saved her."

"How do you figure that?"

"She was going to sit in that chair until she starved to death," says Echo. "But with a crowd of people lining up outside her front door, something tells me she's no longer going to have that luxury. What we did could be just what she needed to get moving."

"But the scurge will kill her eventually, won't it?" River looks ahead as he walks. "It's what took your father."

Echo swallows, unable to deny this. "It will. But at least now Nola will go out fighting. That counts for a lot here."

"That's the bit I can't get over." River takes Echo's arm from his waist and holds her hand, stroking her skin with his thumb. "Dead Borns have to fight for everything. I didn't realize just how hard life was. Maybe Flora was right. I am naïve."

Echo sees a group of people ahead and steers River down an alternative route. "I thought we established Flora never said that?"

"But what if she did?" he asks. "Because I *was* naïve. And I *did* do everything Oren told me to. And if that doesn't make me weak, I don't know what does."

Echo pauses her footsteps. "You're not weak, River. You were shielded. That's all. A weak person wouldn't have lifted that shield and risked their life to see what was behind it."

River nods, although it's clear he's not ready to believe her.

They emerge from the end of the laneway into the open, dusty expanse of land that leads to the Betadome. The netted hexagonal cage looks ominous at this time of day as it casts a long shadow across the earth. Echo thinks of her Confirmation and the whirlwind of feelings she'd had trapped inside her as she'd walked this same path. All she'd wanted to do was be returned back to her life here.

And now, here she stands holding the hand of a Green Born as she contemplates a very different kind of life. One where she lives neither here nor there but changes it for everyone.

"Stop." River pulls her back into the shadow of the laneway.

"What's wrong?" she asks. "We have to go back. There's nothing left for us to do here for now."

River shakes his head, pressing a finger to his lips.

She squints into the dying light and sees what has his attention.

A familiar figure is walking away from the Betadome into the Dead Zone.

"Tuff," Echo breathes, as she watches him walk with some difficulty due to the heavy sack he carries on his back. He's wearing clothes that seem to have been stitched together from hessian. Clearly, he doesn't want to attract the same kind of attention that she and River had. "What's he doing here?"

River pulls the crumpled map from his pocket and taps his finger on the X as he raises his eyebrows in a question.

Echo nods, agreeing that's likely where Tuff is headed. He's bringing his brother food. It was no wonder he had so much more than anyone else.

"We have to follow him," says River, daring to raise his voice a little now that Tuff is some distance away.

"Why?" Echo throws out her hands, not seeing the point. "We know what he's doing."

"I want to see for myself," says River. "Then I want to talk to him. Find out why he gave me this map if it meant nothing."

"You can do that back in the Green Zone," says Echo. "The

longer we're missing, the more of your father's questions you'll need to answer."

"Or maybe the more questions he'll need to answer from me." River pulls back his shoulders. "Echo, we've come this far. I just want to see what he's up to."

"Fine." Echo sighs, seeing how important this is to him. And at least the idea of doing something practical has sparked him up. Further proof that he's anything but weak. There's no way she'd have been able to do any of this the night she'd learned of her father's death.

She takes River's hand once more and they follow Tuff at a safe distance, the growing darkness acting as their cloak.

As expected, Tuff walks directly to the creek, not glancing once behind him to see if he's being followed. Perhaps he's trying not to look suspicious. Or, more likely, he's done this so many times he feels secure.

He follows the creek and makes his way to his brother's house. There's a glow inside the falling down hut that can only be coming from a candle. Another luxury item out here. Most other families are forced to go to sleep with the sun, then rise with it.

Echo and River tuck themselves behind a large rock as they watch Tuff knock gently on the door.

There are some muffled words, then the door opens and Tuff steps inside.

"Come on." Echo and River dash up to the hut and squat underneath the large window that faces the creek. There are curtains hanging with a gap at the bottom where the fabric has frayed, and they peer through.

Echo sees Tuff place the sack on the table and sit down. Ruff makes a grab for the sack and pulls out the items with greedy hands. It's food from Harvest Day. More rations than anyone in the Dead Zone would see in a month.

"Navy!" calls Ruff. "Girl! Get down here. Time to eat!"

Navy appears in the room, looking as excited to see her uncle as she had been to see them earlier.

"Say thank you," Ruff instructs.

Navy bends stiffly and kisses Tuff on the cheek. Ruff had told them his brother loves this girl like his own, although if this is true it seems he's not very good at showing it. He sits completely still in his chair.

"It's all I could get," Tuff says to his brother. "I'll bring more when I can."

River and Echo look at each other with raised brows to hear Tuff speak. His voice is deep and gravelly—exactly as she imagined it would be.

"Excellent," says Ruff. "We need more. Especially now."

"Where is she?" Tuff asks, glancing around.

"Girl!" Ruff shouts. "Girl!"

Echo's brow pulls together. Why is he shouting for Navy when she's clearly standing right there?

"Come out and see your friend, Girl!" calls Ruff. "Don't be rude."

River draws in a sharp breath and Echo slips her hand into the crook of his arm as they wait to see who this girl might be.

A shadow emerges at the back of the hut and someone steps forward.

Now it's Echo's turn to gasp as she clutches River's arm.

Echo only saw Flora once, back in the Betadome, but there's no question that she's looking at the same girl.

Flora is most certainly alive.

CHAPTER
TWENTY-SIX
RIVER

River shoots to his feet, his heart beating hard against his ribs, demanding he get inside that hut.

Flora's alive!

And she's only a few feet away!

He powers through the door and it slams against the opposite wall. His entrance means everyone turns to him in shock.

Ruff and Tuff.

Navy.

And Flora. His sister. His twin.

Her hand flies to her mouth, her green eyes wide and luminous. "River," she whispers.

He covers the short distance across the hut and scoops her up, holding her tighter than he ever has before. "I knew you weren't dead. I just knew it."

She grips him back, burying her head in his shoulder in a way that's so familiar, it hurts. "What are you doing here?" she asks, her voice small.

River pulls back, gazing at her dear, sweet face. For long hours, he thought he'd never see it again. "Looking for you."

She glances at him quizzically. "The River I knew would never have done that."

He smiles crookedly. "A lot's happened in a short space of time." He glances over his shoulder, noting the way Echo's watching them closely. "And yet, it's kinda a long story."

Echo grins. "Tell me about it."

Impossibly, his heart swells some more.

There's a scuffle to his right, and River sees Ruff quickly grabbing the food Tuff had brought and shoving it back in the sack. "My daughter needs this more than you do," he snarls. He hoists the sack with one hand and grabs Navy's hand with the other. "Come on, we got to hide this stuff."

He drags his daughter through the door to the second room and slams it shut.

Flora rolls her eyes. "Gee, I wonder where he's going to put it," she whispers.

River chuckles, surprised when Tuff does the same. He looks over to find the older man looking at Flora, his face soft in a way he's never seen before. His harsh, weary lines are completely gone. River's not too sure what to make of that.

Feeling a little protective, he pulls her over to the table and sits down, drawing the chair across from him closer.

Flora sits down. "How did you know I was here?"

"Actually, we were here earlier." To think they almost went back to the Green Zone, assuming she was dead. The thought is like a sledgehammer to the gut. "We saw Tuff and followed him back. He's the one who gave me a map marked with this house back in the Green Zone."

"He was going to look for you, no matter what," mutters Tuff as he pushes his chair back a little. "It would only make more trouble for you if he turned the Dead Zone upside down first."

"What's she doing here?" Flora glances at Echo. "Someone obviously wanted to visit home."

"I left without her," says River. He smiles at Echo. "She followed me."

And saved him. More than once.

A sense of peace winds around his heart. There's no tightness in his chest. For the first time since Confirmation, it feels like things might be okay.

He reaches over and takes Flora's hand. "When you weren't here earlier, I thought Chase was telling the truth. That you were dead."

Flora's hand twitches in his. "He told you I'm dead?" She frowns. "I don't know why he'd say that."

River glances at Echo. "He was obviously trying to keep us apart."

Echo's lips thin but she doesn't say anything. He wonders for a moment whether she meant it—that she doesn't want anything to do with Chase anymore. Hopefully, this is more evidence she made the right choice. There's something about Chase that sets River's teeth on edge.

"I'm sure that's not why he did it," Flora says with a smile. "Chase has a good heart. He really helped me when I first arrived. He's the one who gave me clothes so I could get rid of the suit." Her lashes flutter. "Green Borns are treated differently here."

"Yeah, I've learned that," says River. He shuffles a little closer. "That's why I think you should come back with me."

Echo gasps as Flora's mouth goes slack. Even Tuff shifts a little, his chair scraping back another inch. Flora shakes her head. "I can't go back, River."

Now that he's said the words, River realizes this is why he came here. He's not okay with Flora being in the Dead Zone.

It's not okay for anyone to be here, but until he figures that out, the least he can do is end the suffering for his twin.

He holds her hand tightly, wanting to reassure her. "I know it's against the rules. But we'll find a way, I promise. I can't leave you here."

But Flora's shaking her head. "No, you don't understand," she says, as if she just read his thoughts. "I don't *want* to go back."

"What?" He's so surprised that he sits back, releasing her hand.

"You've seen it, or you wouldn't be here. The Green Zone isn't what it seems." Her face tenses, looking almost angry. "Our father isn't who he says he is."

Echo leans forward. "This has got to do with those files on your computer. The password protected ones."

Flora looks from Echo to River, startled. "You've been trying to get into my files?"

"It's one of the reasons we're here," says Echo. "To get the password."

His sister gazes at River steadily. "You know what it is."

River frowns. He tried everything he could think of.

"I used the one word I share with my twin brother. One that no one else would think of."

He grins as he realizes what it is. They say it simultaneously, like they have so many times before.

"Viridescent."

Echo snorts softly. "I never would've spelled that right."

River chuckles. In part, because the password feels so obvious, now. In part, because Flora chose a word that honors their deep connection. In part because Echo's right, she'd never have spelled that correctly.

But then he sobers. "What's on there, Flora?"

What has she learned that now means she doesn't want to return to her home?

His sister stills in her chair, her gaze steady on his, yet somehow unreadable. The realization shocks him. He'd always thought he knew Flora as well as he knew himself.

Then again, nothing's been certain since Confirmation. Everything's been upside down.

And he's done things he never thought he would. Sitting here, in Ruff's hut in the Dead Zone, is a testament to that.

"Do you really want to know, River?" Flora turns suddenly, grabbing one of the wooden cups on the table and passing it to him. "Here, have a drink."

Although he's not sure why it's important he do so in the middle of their conversation, he does as he's asked. Bracing himself for the taste of dirt and death, he takes a small sip of the Dead Zone's water.

Frowns.

Then takes a larger mouthful.

"It tastes...good." Clean in a way he didn't know water could taste.

"That's because all you're drinking is water." Flora nods knowingly but doesn't elaborate. "And have you ever wondered why no one can be inside the Sting on Harvest Day?"

River's about to say it's so they can all partake in the joy of harvesting, but he stops himself.

That's the automatic answer.

The unquestioned one.

The same mindset that assumed the water in the Dead Zone would taste worse than the Green Zone.

River looks across at Echo as he tries to understand what's going on. She looks surprised and unsurprised, all at once.

He leans forward. "What are you trying to tell me, Flora?"

Except she looks away. "You know what? Forget it, River.

Go back to the Green Zone, your home, and forget you saw me. Forget I told you any of this."

"I could never do that." It would mean all of this...pain had been for nothing.

"Well, you need to," she says, suddenly fierce. "I'm never going back, and you don't want this, not deep down."

River shoots to his feet. "I'm here, aren't I?"

Flora shakes her head. "You have a future in the Green Zone. Find a girl to pledge yourself to. Work hard. Be in peace like every other Green Born."

Despite Flora painting everything he always imagined for himself, he knows it was nothing more than a dream. What's more, it was a dream that could never have come true. It was built on assumptions and lies. It never had a foundation.

And although he's not sure what he wants, he knows he doesn't want that.

"No," he says to Flora. "I'm not going to do that."

His twin looks back at him, her green eyes even more unreadable than before. "I know you think you've changed, River, but have you? Really?"

She's wrong. He has changed. But she can't see that. Nor can he tell what she thinks of the distance she's creating between them, which scares him the most.

"Don't you see?" Flora asks, her voice pained. "Things aren't meant to change in the Green Zone. And you're a part of that."

Tuff comes to his feet and moves to stand beside Flora, placing a hand on her shoulder. She looks up at him, nodding in thanks. Because he's supporting her. He understands what's going on.

And River isn't doing either.

He takes a faltering step backward. The divide between the

Dead Zone and the Green Zone now exists between himself and his twin.

"Just leave, River. You can't fix this. We're too different now." Her face is cold. More like that of a stranger than the twin he's spent his life standing beside.

He looks to Echo, the heart that was healing breaking all over again. "Let's get back."

She nods solemnly and comes to his side. She even takes his hand, a silent show he's not as alone as he's feeling.

They exit the hut and Flora doesn't call him back. Of all the things the Confirmation took from him, he didn't think it would be this.

The twin bond he'd always assumed was unbreakable.

They're several huts away before Echo speaks. "You're not giving up, are you?"

"No," he says grimly. "Never."

It's time to go back to the Green Zone.

It's time for answers.

CHAPTER

TWENTY-SEVEN

ECHO

E cho walks toward the LaB, rehearsing the cover story she'd worked out with River. There's no doubt their absence will have been noticed.

It had been late by the time they'd crept into the Sting and reluctantly parted, agreeing it would be best to return to their own rooms and pretend everything was normal.

She'd slept soundly, the rollercoaster of her long day catching up with her. She doubts River got much rest at all after their shock discovery of Flora, then being outright rejected by her. The pain on his face at her betrayal had been even worse than when he'd thought she was dead.

"Oh," says Reed, feigning shock from behind his desk when she appears. "You decided to turn up today, did you?"

Echo nods, deciding not to offer him any explanation. "What are we working on?"

"We?" He laughs quietly. "I'm working on extracting plant DNA. You're going to talk to Oren."

"That's funny, is it?" She cocks an eyebrow at him.

"Echo." He leans back in his chair and crosses his arms.

"I've been patient with you. Really, I have. But you can't just disappear for an entire day and expect not to have to explain yourself. In this colony, we work together. Everyone does their bit. We don't just please ourselves like you're clearly used to doing where you came from."

The fine hairs on the nape of her neck bristle as she draws in a slow breath. Her brief trip home had been a stark reminder of just how false this perception is. But without Reed seeing it for himself, how can she ever hope to help him understand?

River bursts into the LaB, looking just as exhausted as she expected. He has circles under his eyes and his dark hair is mussed. It's kind of adorable and she has to stop herself from going to him and slipping an arm around his waist.

"Someone slept well," says Reed, amused yet again.

"I'm told Oren wants to see us," River says, not seeming to want to explain himself to Reed, either.

Reed points with his chin toward Oren's office. "He's in there."

River catches Echo's eye and they give each other a small nod. They have a plan. They know exactly what they need to say. Oren won't be happy, but with any luck, he also won't be too upset.

They walk to the opaque glass wall and River knocks on the door to his father's spacious office.

"Come in peace," Oren softly calls.

River opens the door and Echo follows him through. Oren doesn't look up from his computer, so they sit opposite the desk and wait.

Echo studies this well put together enigma of a man. How is it possible his genetic code created half the incredible guy seated beside her? There's a slight physical resemblance in their same piercing green eyes, but Oren's graying hair and beard set him apart. Is this what River will look like in time?

Not if he joins Echo in blowing the two colonies apart and forming a new way for everyone to live. Nobody will have the luxury of preening themselves to perfection like that if they succeed. They'll be far too busy doing actual work to secure the survival of the species to be worried about anything superficial.

After what feels like several eternities, Oren decides to acknowledge them.

"Would you like to tell me where you were yesterday?" he asks, cutting directly to the point.

"It was my fault," says Echo. "I asked River to take me to the orchard. There was some fruit up high that was missed on Harvest Day and it didn't feel right to leave it for the birds. I wanted to pick it to add to the Dead Zone rations."

After much debate, this was the story they'd settled on. Oren would never believe Echo was entirely innocent. She was best to confess to something that wouldn't warrant too much of a punishment.

"Is this the truth?" Oren looks at his son.

River nods. "We filled a basket and took it to the Processing Center to add to the rations."

"Who took it from you?" Oren asks. "Was it Rose?"

"No." Echo says this a bit more forcefully than she intended, not wanting to bring Rose into this after how kind she'd been to her during their brief meeting. "It was a man."

"And this task took all day?" Oren rubs at his chin.

Echo glances at River, her heart rate picking up as she realizes Oren's not buying any of their story. Perhaps coming up with an alibi in the middle of the night after an emotionally exhausting day wasn't the best idea.

"We fell asleep," says River. "In the orchard. It was such a beautiful day and we sat down to rest. The next thing we knew it was night."

"Let me get this straight." Oren stands and walks to his window, staring out across the Green Zone. The orchard can be seen in the far distance. "You took a pod to the orchard in the morning. Is that right?"

River and Echo nod.

"Then you picked fruit from high up in the trees and filled a basket?"

"That's right," says River, eagerly.

"And then you fell asleep." Oren continues to survey his vast green colony. "And when you woke, it was nighttime, so you put the basket in a pod and came straight back to the Sting to take it to the Processing Center."

River begins to nod but his movement is cut short by Oren's raised voice.

"A Processing Center that's not open at night!" Oren switches his gaze from the window directly to his son.

River swallows and looks across at Echo as Oren takes his seat once more. He turns his screen around so that it's facing them and presses some keys on his computer.

The screen comes to life with footage of the foyer of the Sting. It's empty, void of both people and daylight. The clock in the corner of the screen indicates it's early morning. River can clearly be seen walking through the foyer and heading outside.

"You have cameras?" River's jaw falls. "But that's—"

"My right," finishes Oren. "As your leader. Now, please, continue watching. We haven't reached the good part yet."

The camera switches to one positioned outside the Sting and River can be seen getting into a pod.

Alone.

Which blows the first part of their story. Had they gone to the orchard, they'd most certainly have left together.

The next piece of footage shows River exiting the pod. Not at the orchard but the Betadome. He can be seen walking inside, his shoulders hunched and taking care to look behind him before he disappears through the green door.

And there goes the second part of their story.

The timer ticks by in the corner of the screen. A full minute passes before Echo appears. She slips through the same door, moving swiftly, almost looking like a shadow in the dim light of dawn.

The screen flickers and goes dark. Oren turns it back to face him, then rests his elbows on his desk, lacing his long fingertips together as he waits for their response.

Echo remains silent, knowing there are no words to explain their way out of this.

River clears his throat. "We just—"

"Were. Not. Thinking!" Oren roars. "That was dangerous!"

Echo flinches to hear Oren raise his voice. No matter how upset she's seen him in the past, he's always maintained a cool composure.

Oren stands and leans over his desk until his face is only inches from River's.

"Never do that again!" he booms. "Do you understand me?"

River nods. "Yes, Oren."

"Father," he sneers. "I am your father, and you will refer to me as such from now on."

"Sorry, Father." River blinks at the man he seems to both revere and fear.

Echo slouches in her chair, wishing she could become invisible. This isn't going like they planned. And Oren's not finished with them yet.

"What did you do in there all day?" he asks, taking his seat and shaking his head.

Echo's jaw drops open a little. If he's asking that, then he doesn't have cameras in the Betadome. Which would seem odd given he clearly has them everywhere else.

"I asked you a question." Oren's voice is strained.

"It was the honey I wanted," says Echo quickly. "Not fruit. I wanted honey for the Dead Zone. We didn't go to the orchard. We went to the Betadome."

This doesn't seem to placate the once composed leader who fixes his angry gaze on her. "You could have killed my son. You know how many bees are in there."

"But he's an Immune," she squeaks, hating that she feels so intimidated. "We both are."

"So was Vernon," snaps Oren. "And look what happened to him."

Echo swallows, wondering if he'd be more or less furious if they told him the full truth, but knowing it's not worth the risk.

"We're sorry, F-father," says River, practically choking on this new name he's being made to use. "It won't happen again."

"That's right." Oren looks at his son, his expression softening momentarily. "It won't."

Echo stands, keen to get out of here. "If you don't mind excusing us, we have to—"

"I do mind." Oren stares at her, fire burning in his eyes. "I'm not finished with you yet. Did you know that I asked my son to stay away from you?"

"He tried," she says, slumping back into the chair. "I was the one who followed him. You saw that on your footage. It was me."

"For once we agree on something." Oren smiles and it sends shivers down her spine. "Which is why I'm choosing you a new role at the Sting. You no longer work in the LaB."

Echo's chest tightens. This is the worst case scenario. How

is she supposed to get into Flora's files and gain access to the Restricted Area if she's no longer in the LaB?

"But Reed—" she begins.

"Reed is fine." Oren bangs a fist on his desk. "You will report into the Processing Center immediately. They could use an extra pair of hands with another Harvest Day coming up soon. And, clearly, you've already made some new friends there."

"Oren," says River, shifting a little closer to Echo in his chair. "I mean, Father. I'm really not sure any of this is necessary."

"Which brings me to you." Oren turns to his son. "I've thought long and hard all night about what to do with you."

Somehow, this seems an even more frightening concept. Oren had allowed his only daughter to be sent to the Dead Zone to face certain death. What evil plan might he have in mind for his son?

"Your actions have shown you in a new light, River. You have more spirit than I realized. I'm putting you second in charge," says Oren. "It's time you stepped up in your leadership of this colony."

River gasps, seeming as shocked by this as Echo is. Although, it's a genius move to get him on Oren's side. Instead of punishing him, Oren is giving River everything he ever wanted. He must've dreamed of this moment as a boy, imagining himself taking over from his father and leading his people into a secure future.

Except Oren doesn't realize how much River knows. He can't possibly accept after what he learned yesterday on the other side of that net. This isn't a colony anyone would want to lead once their eyes were opened to the truth of it.

She grips the arms of her chair and waits for River to throw his father's offer back in his face.

"But Father," he says, breaking into a wide smile. "Do you really think I'm worthy?"

Instead of seeming horrified at the thought of being a figurehead to such a selfish colony, River's exuding an air of... sheer and utter joy.

Bile rises in the back of Echo's throat. Of course, he's worthy! River's worth a thousand Orens. Has this evil man really raised him with such low self-esteem that with one simple offer he can erase everything River just learned about the world?

"I think you'll do an excellent job," says Oren. "You'll be working right by my side. The colony will see that we're united."

Right. So that's what's happening here. Oren is worried about how River's recent rebellious behavior might reflect on him personally. This decision has absolutely nothing to do with River and everything to do with Oren.

Oren turns to Echo and nods. "Be in peace," he says, dismissing her.

She looks at River only to find he's turned away, deflecting her gaze.

"Oh. And Echo, your room has been moved to the twelfth floor," Oren adds. "You'll be much happier there with your new friends."

"Great," Echo mutters through gritted teeth as she stands, wondering how she's ever going to get access to River again.

"I've moved someone else into Flora's room," says Oren. "Someone a lot more appropriate for my son to associate himself with."

"Who?" River asks, seeming annoyingly eager for the answer.

"The girl you've been pledged to, of course." Oren leans back in his chair and chuckles. "She's known about this for a while now. I wanted you to come to this decision naturally, but you seem to be a slow learner in that department. You needed a little push."

"Clover," breathes River, still avoiding Echo's eye, which is just as well as Echo's finding it hard to look at anyone right now. Of all people, it had to be Clover! She can't bear the thought of River being pledged to that self-righteous shiny specimen of a Green Born.

Oren smiles. "That's right. Clover's a pretty girl, isn't she? Loyal, too. Works hard for her colony."

Echo turns and leaves before she can witness River agreeing to this latest request of his father. She's already heard more than enough.

It seems what she'd told Chase about having chosen herself was right. She just hadn't known it at the time.

She pulls back her shoulders, trying to give the appearance of being stronger than the crumpled mess she feels. Absolutely everything has fallen apart.

Which means it's time to make a new plan.

And this time she's going to have to work alone.

CHAPTER
TWENTY-EIGHT
RIVER

Echo leaves and the guilt burrows deeper into River's bones. It takes everything he has to stay in his seat and not go after her. He never meant for her to be hurt by all of this. That's the last thing he wants. It's just that he never expected this to be an outcome of everything they've learned together.

If they hadn't run away, River wouldn't be sitting here, having his dream life offered to him by his smiling father.

Ignoring the guilt, no matter how jagged and painful it is, River shuffles forward on his seat. "What do you need me to do?" He makes sure he sounds eager. Excited. There's no room for anything else right now.

Oren's smile grows. "We're going to make the Green Zone even greater, son. Together."

Images of dirty, decrepit huts, of starving, sick bodies, of pleading, pitiful eyes rise in River's mind, each one more painful and piercing than the last. But he shuts them away, along with the complicated, confusing feelings he has for Echo, knowing he can't dwell on them right now.

River nods. "That's all I ever wanted," he says, knowing he's speaking the truth.

He's spent his life wanting his father to be looking at him just like he is now. Wanting to serve the Green Zone.

His father nods approvingly. "I know you'll make me proud." He leans forward, steepling his fingers. "There's another Harvest Day coming up. I'd like you to coordinate it."

River can't help his eyes widening. "Of course. Anything for the Green Zone."

"You're going to be busy," his father warns. "This is the corn harvest—grain moisture is almost at its peak. The cornfield will need to be divided into quadrants, Green Borns allocated, the husking of the cobs themselves coordinated, then ensuring they get to the Processing Center."

Where Echo is now allocated. River's going to have little chance to see her or talk to her over the coming days. His father's obviously planned that.

His hands clench in his lap. It's probably for the best.

River straightens his spine. "I promise I'll work hard."

"I'll mentor you closely as you learn the processes. This will be much better suited to you than Eden. You're a thinker, River. I didn't realize that about you."

Who would've thought spending time with Echo would've led to his father noticing him like this? That the slightest show of rebelling would have Oren drawing him in closer.

River pulls up a smile, his mind reeling. "I look forward to it."

His father leans down and pulls something from a drawer. He slides a small, white electronic square across the desk. "It's a pager. If I need you, I'll call."

Meaning River's now at his beck and call. His father's really serious about this. "Sure. Thanks."

There's a knock on the door and his father glances at his screen. "It's time for announcements. Come in," he calls out.

Daphne enters, at first surprised to see River there, but then smiling warmly. "Be in peace."

"Be in peace," he murmurs back.

"We have wonderful news today, Daphne," his father says, throwing his arms out wide. "River's officially training to be my successor."

The words hit River like a sonic boom. For long seconds, his breath disintegrates. His head fills with white noise. His throat clogs with a thousand words he can't say.

He desperately wishes this wasn't so hard.

"That's wonderful news, River. You'll be great," Daphne assures, possibly noticing that he's looking a little ill.

He pushes to his feet, having to consciously lock the muscles of his legs. "Thank you. It's an honor to serve the Green Zone." He glances at his father. "I'll go review the corn estimates while you're doing this."

"See? Already picking up the mantle." His father smiles, an unfamiliar glint in his eyes. "And I suspect there's someone who's excited to talk to you."

Daphne beams. "Clover's a very special girl. Beautiful, too."

River exits before he blanches. How did he not see that others had plans for his future, too? Was his father intending this all along, and it was so obvious, everyone could see? Then again, hadn't River wanted the Green Zone to mold him to what it needed?

Voices trail after him as the door to his father's office closes.

"We'll have to get the wording right," says his father.

"Such exciting times," agrees Daphne.

Quickly walking out, River avoids Reed's gaze. In the elevator, he still keeps his eyes down, not wanting to see his reflection. He starts a mantra in his head.

I'm excited. My dreams have come true. It's everything I've ever wanted.

He's so focused on repeating those words, he discovers he's outside his room rather than having gone to Eden. He slips inside, glad for the brief reprieve. He needs a few minutes before he faces Clover.

The girl he's pledged to.

"Hello, River."

He stops as the door slides closed behind him. He won't be getting a break. Clover's sitting on his bed, waiting for him.

She pushes to her feet. "I came by first thing as I wanted to talk, but you'd already left."

"I...met with my father."

She steps a little closer. "And?"

"I'm going to be working with him. Training to be his second in charge."

"Great! It's what you've always wanted," says Clover, beaming, although there's something in the way she's looking at him that tells him she already knew about this.

"Yeah, it really is." He shifts his weight. "Clover—"

But she takes another step forward, stopping in front of him. "Look, I know you've been having a rough time since Flora left." She presses a hand to his chest. "Things have been... confusing. But it's all falling into place now. And I'm going to be here, helping in any way I can."

He smiles, seeing why others think so highly of her. She's sweet and passionate and a true believer in the Green Zone. "Thanks." She's actually a great match for Oren's son.

She leans in, her lashes fluttering as she looks up at him. "I would be honored to be pledged to you, River. It's *my* dream come true."

His pulse stutters, trips, and tumbles. He has no idea what to say to that.

Clover smiles, not seeming to need a response. "We'll be good together. You'll see."

She pushes up on her toes, bringing her lips an inch away from his, then hovering. "I want you to want this, too," she breathes, her breath warm against his face.

River hesitates, not pulling away, but not claiming the small span between them. Kissing Clover will seal this deal. His father's right-hand man. Clover's partner. The future leader of the Green Zone.

I'm sorry, Echo.

River presses his lips to Clover's and she melts against him. Her arms slip around his shoulders, pulling him down, deepening the kiss as she sighs. River rests his hands on her hips as his fingers tighten. Clover is soft and supple, her lips are warm and welcoming. It's certainly not *unpleasant.*

But it's also not the flames that scorched him when he and Echo kissed.

There's a whoosh, a change in pressure as the door opens, then a gasp.

River yanks away, recognizing the voice even as he desperately wishes he's wrong.

"Wow, you work quick," snarls Echo, and River's not sure who the barb is aimed at.

Clover's arms slip down, coming to rest on River's chest. "Hello, Echo," she says, cheeks flushed a pretty pink. "Did you come here to congratulate us?"

Echo looks away, disgust twisting her features. "For being mindless drones? I don't think so."

River steps back from Clover. "Echo and I need to talk. Do you mind?"

She hesitates, but then nods, her confident smile back. "I'll see you later. We can talk about our pledging ceremony."

He nods even though it feels like his neck is going to snap and Clover steps around him, giving Echo a wide berth as she slips through the door.

"Ever the good girl, aren't you Clover?" sneers Echo. "Always doing what you're told."

Clover doesn't answer, simply glances at River over her shoulder and leaves.

Echo clenches her hands. It's clear she's angry. Hurt. And she has every right to be. "I came back because I was sure you wouldn't want this. Only to find you...face sucking Clover!"

"Did you forget who I am?" he asks, even as he hates himself. He resists the urge to glance around, confirming whether his father has cameras here, too. Instead, he glares at Echo. "Of course I was going to be my father's successor!"

"Are you doing this because you think you'll have an in? Because you don't—"

"This is what I want, Echo," he says, stopping the conversation from going there. "It's what I've always wanted."

Echo blinks, as if she hadn't expected to hear those words. Or for them to hurt as much as they do. "It didn't take much, did it?"

"Everything I've ever wanted?" he shoots back.

She steps back to the door, and it slides open. "No. The promise of mindless comfort for the rest of your life."

She stalks out, spine stiff and head held high. River lets the door close, shutting off the image of her walking away, taking his words with her.

Leaving hers behind.

He leans his head against the cool, white surface. His stomach feels like it's full of acid. His chest feels like it's being corroded from the inside out. He hates that Echo has become collateral damage.

A beeping sounds in his pocket and he realizes his father's summoning him. He pulls out the pager and presses it, leaving his room and heading to the elevator. At least he's over the worst of it. Inside, he connects with his mantra.

I'm excited. My dreams have come true. It's everything I've ever wanted.

His father is still sitting behind his desk as River enters his office. He takes a seat. "Yes, Father?"

"We're going to go and collect a few corn cobs so we can test moisture levels. While we're there, we'll take some soil samples so we can see what's needed to get it optimized in preparation for the next crop. On the way back, we'll check the nitrogen has been increased at the compost piles in preparation for the husks."

River nods. "Of course." He gets ready to stand again. "Maybe we could stop off and confirm how far away the barley harvest will be."

"Yes, good thinking." His father remains where he is. "But first, I have something I need to ask you."

River slowly returns his weight to the chair. "Yes?"

"It's about Echo. And whether she's a threat."

River steels himself. He knew this was coming. That there would be one more gauntlet to run. One more task. The ultimate test of his faithfulness to the Green Zone.

He was just hoping it wouldn't have to be today, let alone now.

"I need to know," his father says in a low voice, his gaze intense. "What really happened in the Betadome?"

CHAPTER
TWENTY-NINE

ECHO

Echo slips out of her new room on the twelfth floor, pleased she's no longer anywhere near that mindless drone called River. It's been three days since she walked in on him sucking Clover's face and she still can't shake the traitorous image from her mind.

"Asshole," she mutters as she surveys the dimly lit corridor. She'd thought River was different, not someone who could be bought off by anything—even if the *anything* is everything he ever wanted. Surely, his wants had changed after spending a day in the Dead Zone?

As much as she hates to admit it, it's been lonely without River to annoy her. And her work in the Processing Center has been mind-numbingly boring, which hasn't been in any way helpful to distract her from the aching pain he left in her heart. She still can't understand how he could do that to her. Maybe he wasn't the guy she thought he was. But she'd been so sure...

Echo walks quietly down the row of closed doors that seal the Green Borns into their hexagonal shaped bedrooms.

They're all asleep, their dreams waiting to be interrupted by the gentle music of the Sting. If she's timed her exit correctly, that should be happening any moment now. All she has to do is...

There.

Music fills her ears and within minutes, Daphne's voice floats through the speakers. Doors begin to open and the corridor buzzes with excitement for another Harvest Day. It's just the cover she needs. Oren's cameras will be filled with a blur of movement, making it far harder for him to detect her. That is, if he's even looking for her.

She reaches the elevator and presses the button to go up. While she waits, she keeps her face angled down, hiding in plain sight amongst the sea of keen Green Borns, all ready to work hard and contribute to their colony. They're all just as noble as they are ignorant.

The elevator doors slide open and her heart hammers now that she's actually carrying out her plan. She just needs to keep her cool. And hope for the same kind of luck they had in the Betadome when the cameras weren't working. She's certain Tuff had something to do with that, as his way to visit his brother without Oren knowing. But without access to the LaB, she hasn't been able to ask him. It's made her even more determined to get inside the Restricted Area.

And if not today, she doesn't know when.

The elevator is empty. Nobody is going up today, only down.

"You're going the wrong way," says a man as she steps into the empty space.

"I left my sample jars in the LaB," she replies quickly, doing her best to sound official. "We're testing this year's crop for parasites."

The man nods. "Sounds important."

"It is," she says as the elevator doors begin to close. "Be in peace."

"Be in peace," several people reply, not realizing how foolish their compliance with these senseless customs of the Green Zone makes them sound.

When Echo reaches the LaB, it's dark, the lights not having been turned on for the morning, and she leaves it that way, quickly crossing the room to Flora's computer.

She sits down and runs the word *viridescent* though her mind, trying for the millionth time to figure out how to spell it. She'd casually asked Rose if she knew, having found a way to work the word into their conversation as they'd been sorting a batch of celery stalks, but Rose hadn't even heard of the word let alone known how to spell it.

Turning on the computer, Echo calls on the memory of her father teaching her how to read. *Sound out the letters,* she hears him say. *One by one, make their sound, then join them all up.*

Surely, it can't be that hard? She knows all the sounds each letter makes.

Clicking on the locked file, she waits for the password box to pop up, then confidently types in the first letter.

V.

So, what's next?

I.

Feeling confident, she goes directly again.

R. I. D.

That has to be right so far. She sounds out what she has so far in her mind. *Virid.*

Now for the hard bit. How in the sweet land of vegetables does she spell *escent*?

E.S.E.N.T.

She hits return, just like Reed had shown her, only for the

computer to beep loudly. The dreaded triangle symbol bounces on the screen.

"Urgh." She starts again, typing quickly, deciding she knows what must be wrong. Some words have double letters, like *pass* or *buzz*.

V.I.R.I.D.E.S.S.E.N.T.

Beep!

Grimacing, she clenches her hands into fists and glances around the room half expecting Reed or Oren to come running in.

She tries again, knowing she's going to run out of time if she doesn't hurry up.

V.I.R.E.D.E.S.E.N.T.

Beep!

V.I.R.E.D.E.S.S.E.N.T.

Beep!

V.E.E.R.E.D.E.S.E.N.T.

Beep!

V.I.R.R.E.D.E.S.E.N.T.

Beep!

V.E.R.R.E.E.D.I.S.E.N.T.

Beep!

A bead of sweat trickles down Echo's forehead. This is even harder than she'd anticipated. She'd thought she'd get it in at least three tries.

She tries once more, using a new tactic.

V.I.R.I.D.E.Z.A.N.T.

Beep!

A shadow appears in the dim light and she leaps up from her chair, knowing it's too late. She's been caught out and it's sent her heart from hammering mode to an earthquake in her chest.

"Need some help?" The voice is unmistakably River's,

which sends both relief and panic surging through her veins. "I knew I'd find you here."

"It's you," she says, like he's committed a crime simply by being himself.

"Yes. And it's you," he says, coming closer so that his features take shape in the glow of the computer screen. If he weren't so handsome it really would be easier to hate this guy.

She swallows, wondering how long it's going to take Oren's right hand man to sound the alarm.

"Yeah, it's me," she whispers, disappointment flooding her.

River reaches out a hand and she flinches, unsure why she expects him to strike her when he's been nothing but gentle in her presence so far. He trails his fingertips down her cheek.

"It's always been you, Echo," he says.

"What does that mean?" she asks, forcing air into her lungs to steady her shaking limbs.

His fingertips slide from her face to the back of her head and he gently pulls her face closer to his.

She makes no move to resist him, even though her head is swimming with confusion. "I'm not like Clover."

"I know," he says, their faces now only an inch or two apart. "That must be why I like you so much."

"I don't understand." She grips the front of his shirt, wanting to both push him away and urge him closer. "You're pledged to her. You have everything you ever wanted. You said so yourself."

"I want you, Echo," he says. "Can't you see what I'm doing? My father wanted to know what we were doing in the Beta-dome. I told him we were telling the truth—that we fell asleep."

Hope ignites in her chest. Maybe he's not the traitor she thought he was. Or maybe he is, but it's not her he's betraying.

"What are you doing?" she asks, hating how much the

warmth of having him close is melting away all the loneliness of the past few days.

"I'm using my position to get the information we need." His voice is husky and it's doing strange things to her insides, and not just because he's telling her exactly what she wants to hear. "Things are going to change around here, even if Oren doesn't know it yet."

"And what else are you doing?" she asks, pushing up on her toes so their lips are only a breath apart.

He smiles, closes his eyes and extinguishes the gap between them.

Heat flares as their lips lock and all the passion of their first fake kiss ignites. It's undeniable that this kiss is every bit as real as the danger that surrounds them.

River moans softly as he deepens the kiss and she parts her mouth in response, sliding her hands up his chest to his shoulders.

The feel of his fingers tangling in her hair, the tip of his tongue meeting her own, the warmth of his breath lingering with hers, sends all her senses into meltdown.

This hadn't been what she'd walked in on between River and Clover, and she knows it. He's telling her the truth. What they have is different. Unique. It's a once in a lifetime kind of crazy chemistry that no amount of experiments in the LaB would ever be able to unlock.

She kisses him harder, wanting more of him. More than she can possibly have given the way the clock is continuing to tick, stealing away all possibility of taking this where she wishes it could go.

"Viridescent," she breathes, pulling back.

River's eyes open. "What did you say?" he murmurs.

"How do you spell it?" She bites down on her bottom lip as she waits for him to recover from that one heck of a kiss.

He presses his lips to her forehead then sits at the computer and begins to type. "V.I.R.I.D.E.S.C—"

"C?" Echo throws out her hands and huffs. "What the hell? How can there possibly be a C in there? I don't hear a C."

"Don't ask me." River shrugs. "E.N.T."

He presses the enter button and the computer remains silent for a beat. Echo holds her breath, certain her heart also misses a beat.

The screen fills with the contents of the secret file.

"River!" Echo puts a hand on his back then withdraws it, needing to keep a clear head. "You did it. We're in."

River scrolls through the file, looking for anything that mentions the Restricted Area. There are notes on all kinds of things. Formulas for who-knows-what and lists about what-the-heck-is-that. None of it seems to make any sense.

"The door code has to be in here somewhere," River says. "Why else would she password protect this file?"

Echo shrugs, having no idea how important any of the information they're looking at could be.

"Here!" He points at the screen and Echo leans forward and squints. At the end of one of the formulas is a long string of numbers with the letters RA beside them. "This has to be it." Grabbing a pencil, River scribbles down the jumble of numbers on a notepad and tears off the page.

"Hurry," says Echo, rushing toward the keypad at the door to the Restricted Area. They're so close now!

River's right behind her. "I'll read the code. You punch it in," he says, squinting in the dim light at his scrawl.

Echo readies her finger on the keypad. "Go."

He reads the number out slowly. "65118."

Determined to make up for the fact she didn't realize a C could sound like an S, Echo concentrates on getting the number right. As she hits the last digit, the door beeps twice and slides open.

Tucking the code into his pocket, River takes Echo's hand and squeezes. This is the moment they've worked toward. The answer to whatever it is that Oren's up to has to be hidden in here. Because Echo's certain that no matter how much Oren insists River's being groomed for his role, the Restricted Area hasn't been part of his induction.

They step inside a small holding area and the first thing Echo notices is the smell. It's artificial, just like the water she's been given no choice but to drink while in the Green Zone. But there's something else in the undertones, a smell that she's very familiar with from her days back home, tending to the sick.

It's the smell of fear.

The door slides closed behind them and Echo tightens her grip on River's hand. There's another door. Another threshold to step over. Maybe this was a mistake. Because whatever's going on there it's most definitely not good.

"We're doing this together," says River, urging her forward. It reminds her of the way Jupiter had encouraged Avid to step into the Betadome, unaware they were leading him not only to his death, but to the total devastation of any hope Jupiter had held in their heart.

But that only makes it even more important that Echo sees this through. She has to bring hope back to her people. Which means she has to find out what's going on.

River presses a green button at the next door and it whooshes open, filling the entrance with a golden glow.

Echo blinks as her eyes adjust and they take two steps forward, the door immediately closing behind them.

"What is this place?" Echo surveys the hexagonal room, unable to determine if the walls are golden or if it's just the glow of the soft light reflecting off them. It's such a contrast to the usual shiny white surfaces of the Sting. The tiled, yellow floor has a dark line that stretches from one side of the room to the other, dividing up the vast, empty space.

But it's the back wall that draws Echo's eyes directly to it. It glows and hums, giving the appearance that it's as alive as they are. There are dozens of bright yellow hexagonal shapes protruding from the wall, all coated in a white sticky substance that's dripping down the wall into a drain. Is that what's making the weird smell in here?

A bead of sweat runs down Echo's back and she notices how warm it is. There's something very wrong going on here. But what is it?

"I think I know where we are," River whispers, his eyes stretched wide in awe as he stares at the back wall. "This is the Hive."

Echo can't find her voice to answer. She's not sure what she'd expected to find in the Restricted Area, but this living wall wasn't it.

"We used to talk about this place when we were kids," says River. "Late at night, like a scary ghost story. I didn't think it was real. Nobody did..."

"River, what is it?" she asks, stepping impossibly closer to him as the smell of fear in the room grows to include her own. "What's the Hive?"

"The story is that there are people trapped inside," says River. "That the Forgotten aren't really sent to the Dead Zone. They're sent to the Hive to feed the Sovereign."

"What's the Sovereign?" Echo swallows, not sure she wants to know.

"A giant bee," says River. "A queen bee. She feeds off the blood of the humans trapped inside her hive."

Echo winces, having heard more than enough. "It's just a

story to stop you misbehaving. There's nobody here except us. And I can't see any giant bees."

A loud agonizing moan reverberates through the room, followed by another.

River lets go of Echo's hand and spins around. "Who's here?"

The moaning comes again.

"I've heard this sound before," says Echo. "When I was in the LaB. We have to find out what's going on."

"Echo, what if it's not just a story?" asks River, still scanning for the source of the awful sound. "What if there really are people trapped in here?"

He rushes toward the Hive and Echo follows, not keen on being left alone, even if by only a few feet.

River tugs at one of the honeycomb shapes, large enough to hold a human, but his hands get stuck as the slime separates and winds itself around his fingers. He manages to shake himself loose and gravity pulls long strings down into the drain.

"What is this stuff?" Echo grimaces, reaching out to poke the substance with a fingertip. It's warm and sticky and before she can withdraw her hand, it wraps itself around her with surprising speed and strength.

"Careful," says River, pulling her hand back and breaking the bond it has on her. "We don't want to get stuck."

She takes a step back, just as the sound of two beeps filter through the room.

"Someone's coming," says River. "That was the door. We have to hide!"

They scan the room, but the only thing here other than the hungry wall of slime is them.

"Over here!" River grabs Echo by the arm and hauls her across the room to a panel in the wall that she hadn't noticed.

The entrance door clicks as it begins to slide.

River slams his palm to the panel and it whooshes open. Before they can see what they're getting themselves into, they've launched themselves into the dark space that opens up before them and the door slides closed.

A bright light fills the room and Echo blinks as she takes in the fact they're somehow standing in Oren's office. She turns around to see the door they'd just come through looks like nothing more than an innocent panel in the wall.

"How did you know?" she asks River.

"Just a hunch," he says. "I've always looked at that panel from this side and wondered if Oren had his own secret entrance to the Restricted Area. Flora swore she saw him coming into his office from it once."

"Impressive." Echo takes a step away from the door, not wanting to accidentally open it again. "And fortunate."

"Flora also said something else..." River walks away from the door along the opaque glass wall. "She told me when she saw Oren coming through the door that this wall was actually a window and she got a glimpse of a room behind him with yellow lights."

Echo joins River at the wall. "Well, thankfully it's not a window, or we'd be in trouble right now. This glass is about as see-through as my head." She taps her temple then presses her fingertips to the glass.

The frosting on the glass instantly melts away and the window turns clear, giving them a full view of the Hive with Oren and Tuff standing only a few feet away from them.

Echo ducks behind Oren's desk, hoping she's fast enough. River is right beside her.

"Did they see us?" Echo whispers.

River peers out from behind the desk. "I don't think they

can see us. This wall is only see-through from this side. We're safe to come out."

"Are you sure?" Echo isn't keen to come out of hiding. She's not even sure she can stand, her legs are shaking so much.

"It's how Oren must keep an eye on us," says River, pointing in the direction of the LaB. It, too, is visible through what Echo had always believed was an opaque glass wall.

She rolls her eyes. First cameras, and now this. It seems privacy is as rare in the Sting as oranges are in the Dead Zone.

River stands and waves at Oren and Tuff, who pay him no attention. He waves more wildly, with both hands over his head.

"They can't see us," he says, putting out a hand to help Echo up. "They can't hear us either. This room must be soundproof."

She accepts his help and stands, pushing down a sick feeling in her stomach. Watching people without their knowledge doesn't feel right. But if it's good enough for Oren, maybe it's time he had some of his own medicine.

Oren nods at Tuff and they stand toward the back of the room and he presses one of the tiles on the wall. A thick glass screen slides up from the dark line that crosses the floor, separating the two men from the Hive.

"What are they doing?" Echo is glued to the scene before her, no longer caring about privacy. She has to see this.

When the screen is safely in place, a large hatch at the side of the room opens and a long metal leg protrudes.

"What the..." River gasps.

Then another leg pokes out. Bit by bit, a giant robotic queen bee emerges, complete with wings forged from black metal, a glowing circle on her back, and a sharp stinger on her silver abdomen. She turns her face toward Oren and Tuff, scanning them with two giant eyes while the smaller three keep watch on the Hive. Then she turns to look directly at Echo and River.

"She can see us," Echo breathes, stepping behind the desk once more but unable to tear her gaze away.

"It's the Sovereign," says River, frozen to the spot. "She's real."

The queen bee rears up on her back legs, exposing the underbelly of her thorax, then turns to the Hive. Her forelegs reach out to one of the hexagons and the slime drips away as if repelled by this giant beast. The robotic legs work on the cell, pulling it forward. It slides out, revealing a human-shaped form, cocooned in more of the sticky white slime.

"There are people in there." River's hand flies to his mouth. "The story is true."

The Sovereign gets to work, her forelegs tending to the body on the rack, stripping away the slime and letting it ooze to the floor.

"I think it's a man underneath all that," says Echo, squinting to get a better look. He seems familiar somehow. "Is he dead?"

The man sits up now that he's free of the slime and takes a swipe at the Sovereign, his expression frantic. He thrashes, his arms flailing, every sinew of his body in stark relief as if he's fighting for his life.

"That's Vernon!" River gasps. "Look! He's alive!"

The Sovereign's middle set of legs shoot out and flip Vernon over so he's lying on his stomach, his bare flesh exposed. He struggles and twists, but he's no match for six legs of steel. The Sovereign pins him as two robotic antennae inject right into the base of Vernon's spine. He lifts his head, his mouth open in a scream that can't be heard in Oren's sound-proof office, but it rings through Echo's head nonetheless.

"Vernon," River whimpers as he steps toward the door. "He never hurt anyone. We have to stop this."

Echo launches forward and grabs River's arm to stop him. "No! The best way we can help Vern is not to do anything rash."

"But the Sovereign's injecting him with something," says River, fighting against her. "It could be lethal."

Echo shakes her head. "I don't think she's injecting. She's taking something from him."

"Harvesting," says River, turning pale as he takes in what she's saying. "She's harvesting his spinal fluid."

"Harvest Day." Echo feels ill as the truth behind this term becomes clear. The people aren't sent outside just to pick fruit or work in the basement. They're being shielded from the screams that are shaking the Sting with sheer agony.

Harvest Day just became a whole lot more evil than she'd already thought.

The Sovereign's antennae disconnect from Vern's spine, leaving him limp and lifeless. Slime shoots from her forelegs, coating Vernon as she spins him like a spider would its prey, coating him in an oozing layer of gloop. When he's immobile once more, the robotic beast pushes the rack back into the wall, sealing Vernon off from the rest of the room.

Slime quickly reforms to cover the front of the hexagon while the Sovereign chooses her next victim.

Echo and River stand and watch in silent horror as twenty-seven people have their spinal fluid harvested, each one just as terrified and agonized as the last. Tears run down Echo's face as she grips River's hand.

This is the worst thing she's ever seen. Worse than the scurge. Worse than hungry babies dying from starvation. Worse than innocent people having lost all their hope. She'd thought the Dead Zone were the unfortunate and downtrodden, but now she sees that isn't true at all.

The Green Zone are the colony who are suffering the most. They're being raised to be naïve and obedient, and if they dare to think for themselves or act outside the norm, they're sent to the Hive to be harvested.

Finally, after what feels like at least a hundred years, the Sovereign's had her fill. She retreats back into her hatch and the glass screen lowers until it disappears into the floor.

"We have to do something," says River.

Oren steps forward, leaving Tuff alone in the golden glow at the rear of the room. But instead of turning toward the Hive, Oren walks to the glass wall of his office and stands facing it.

Echo instinctively takes a step back even though she knows he can't see them.

Oren reaches into his pocket, pulls out a square object, and presses a button.

Something in River's clothing beeps loudly, the sound bouncing around the room.

Oren looks directly at River, smiles broadly, then mouths two words.

Come here.

CHAPTER
THIRTY

RIVER

Somehow, River's veins have turned to ice, freezing him to the spot, and yet his pulse is a firestorm, blazing away his ability to understand the images now seared into his brain.

He can barely process what he and Echo just saw. The pain and terror Vernon and the others endured.

The Sovereign cruelly...harvesting them.

His father watching the whole thing, back straight and chin high.

River grips Echo's hand, using it as an anchor as he quells the feelings of horror, anguish and nausea. They have to figure out what to do next.

They've been caught.

His father takes an ominous step forward, and it feels like the thick glass between them could never be enough to protect them from his fury.

"Now!"

Although the room is soundproof, it's obvious Oren just screamed the word. It's there in the way his veins stand out in sharp relief on his forehead, the flush staining his skin a livid red, the tendons of his neck resembling cords stretched to snapping point. He slams his hand against the glass and the door slides open, exposing them.

Heralding the moment of truth.

The one Echo suspected all along.

River grips her hand and steps through, watching his father and Tuff closely. The shock is wearing off. And it's rapidly being replaced by his own sense of anger.

So many lies.

So much pain.

That's what the Green Zone, the very foundation of his life, has been built on.

It can't be too late to make it right...

River and Echo stay close to the wall as they leave the office, keeping as much distance as they can between themselves and Oren and Tuff.

Oren studies them carefully, like specimens, the anger now gone. Or maybe just locked in the walls of his frozen heart. River never knew this man. It makes him sick to think he's related to him. To know he was implicitly a part of all...this.

Oren takes a couple of steps back, returning to the center of the room. For a moment, River's relieved, but then he realizes it's a power move. He's showing them they're not a threat. He's also just placed himself in the one location he can easily corner them, no matter where they move.

As if Tuff knows this, he slips behind Oren, becoming his impassive shadow. River can't believe he's the same man who was sneaking food to his family in the Dead Zone. The whole time knowing what's happening here and turning a blind eye...

Oren's eyes narrow. "It seems your induction has been fast-tracked."

His father intended for him to be part of this someday? Acid burns in River's gut at the prospect that Oren thought that could be possible. That River's future had this woven into it.

"Release Vernon," snarls River. "Release them all."

Echo is a livewire of tension beside him. "How could you be so heartless?"

Oren shifts his weight subtly and River and Echo move instinctively, keeping what distance exists between them. It means they step subtly to the left, closer to the Hive, and further from the door, but it gives River an idea.

"Why?" he asks, knowing Echo's question lies at the heart of this all as he tugs her closer to his side. "Why would you do something so...cruel?"

Oren's lip curls in disgust. "Why would anyone? Because it's necessary."

"Nothing makes this remotely okay," snaps Echo.

River slides another inch to the left, keeping her close to his side. He feels her surprise as she registers the movement, but she follows him. She no doubt knows, just as he does, that they have limited options right now.

"Does the survival of the human species make it okay?" sneers Oren, clearly implying it's a rhetorical question.

River shakes his head. "What are you talking about? That's why we have Immunes and the Green Zone."

Oren crosses his arms, his face molding into the cold, hard aloofness River's known most of his life. "Not if no one's Immune."

The statement is like a battering ram through River's brain. Smashing everything he knew to be true. Oren's describing a reality he didn't know could exist.

"What do you mean?" asks Echo, clearly as stunned as River.

"Exactly that," spits Oren. "Immunity has been waning for

years until it no longer exists. I've been the one keeping us all alive."

"How?" River chokes.

"The water," breathes Echo, her eyes widening. "You've been supplementing the water."

The memory of the fresh, clear taste of the water in the Dead Zone rolls over River's senses. It hasn't tasted right since he returned.

"I always thought you were too clever for your own good," says Oren, glaring at Echo. "Yes, it's the water. It gifts people with immunity."

Fake immunity.

Meaning the Dead Borns and the Green Borns are the same. Equal. Yet, some have been selected to live in paradise, others in purgatory.

And Oren's doing the choosing. River glances at the wall of hexagonal cells, now only a few feet from him and Echo. "And they're the ones who provide it."

The nausea climbs further up River's throat. Immunity is being harvested, forcefully and painfully, from people like Vernon.

But some parts aren't making sense. Why are some people in the Confirmation declared Immune and others aren't? And how on earth did Echo make it through without drinking so much as a drop of their contaminated water?

"This is wrong," he says, tugging Echo a little further left. It's more important than ever that they escape. Others need to know. "You can't keep doing this."

"I can until I find the Sovereign," snaps Oren.

Echo stays close to River's side, seeming to realize the need to keep moving, but also keep Oren talking. They need answers, he needs to be distracted. "The what?" she asks, her voice tight.

"The Sovereign," he repeats. "She holds the key to immunity. She exists. We just need to find her."

"And how long will that take?" demands Echo. She startles as another question seems to hit her. "And what if you don't?"

Oren steps forward and River tugs Echo the same distance along the wall. The cells, the live, pulsing heart of this Hive are now behind them. Another half-revolution and they'll be close to the doors.

Their only escape.

"Don't you see, River?" asks Oren, his gaze steady on him and nowhere else. "We're doing this because we have to. To keep humankind alive until we can find the solution. Then *everyone* will be Immune."

"And how many people will die before that happens, Oren?" cries Echo. "Will you keep choosing who's worthy of immunity?"

Oren's gaze doesn't break, acting as if Echo's desperate questions aren't clinging to the air. "Now that you know, you have a choice to make, son." He straightens, a challenge hardening his eyes to flint. "Join me. Help me find the Sovereign and end all of this."

The decision doesn't need any thought. The answer is instantaneous. "Never," he vows. "I will never be a part of this."

Impossibly, Oren's face hardens more. It's now a mask frozen in fury. He growls out two words through colorless lips. "Now, Tuff."

The older man hesitates, the shutters over his eyes lifting for a brief second to reveal deeply tortured indecision.

With a growl of frustration, Oren steps past him.

It's only then that River realizes what his father was asking Tuff to do. It's heartless and cruel, even by Oren's standards.

And he was planning this from the moment he found them in here.

"No!" River shouts, breaking into a run.

Echo must realize it, too, because he doesn't have to pull her forward. She's already there. Already running.

But it's too late. Oren claps his hand on the same hexagonal tile he did before.

The glass wall explodes up, cleaving the room in two. Carving away their chance of escape.

Of surviving this.

River and Echo crash into the thick, clear partition, slamming it with their palms.

"Let us out, you monster!" screams Echo.

They both skitter back as the hatch in the wall begins to move. To open. To reveal what's been waiting for them.

The light glistens on metallic black as the queen bee crawls out once more. It bounces off the strange, glowing circle on her back. It curves over the body that's far bigger than them.

And it glints in the glittering lens of her eyes as she turns to face them. Her prey.

River and Echo stumble back, only stopping when they hit the slime-covered wall, quickly putting space between them and the sticky trap it now poses.

"Stop this, Oren!" River shouts. "You don't have to do it!"

His father steps to the side so he can see them as the Sovereign takes a step forward, the tips of her black legs clacking on the tiles. The moment River sees Oren's face, he knows demanding or pleading aren't going to make a difference. His shoulders are back, his chin up again. He's going to watch just like he did before.

But this time, there's a gleam in his father's eyes. He looks...excited.

He wants this.

"Why?" screams River, fear trying to swallow him whole.

Oren stalks forward, as if he wants to be as close as possible to watch their painful harvest. "Because you failed me as completely as your sister did. And your mother." His head angles slowly, his gaze falling squarely on Echo. "And you, Echo, may be the answer we've been looking for."

There's no chance to wonder what that means.

The Sovereign takes another clattering step closer, eclipsing anything but the view of her massive head. Glassy eyes. Twitching antennae. Mechanical jaws.

A pointed stinger that tap, tap, taps the ground, as if she's impatient.

Then, she leaps.

THE END

Ready for the next book in The Sovereign Code?

Check out Hive Mind now!

http://mybook.to/HiveMind

BOOK TWO - HIVE MIND
THE SOVEREIGN CODE

The hunt for the Sovereign has begun

Echo and River have blurred the line between Dead Born and Green Born, revealing the ultimate secret. They've discovered there's a way to save humanity. The Sovereign is the one who carries true immunity against the deadly superbees.

And now they must find her.

As the first Dead Born to have Immunity, Echo is the logical conclusion. Except countless have died in the search for the Sovereign. Because the one way to be sure is to be stung by a queen bee.

Only the true Sovereign will survive.

Lovers of the Hunger Games and Maze Runner, prepare to be blown away. The authors of the best-selling series, The Thaw Chronicles, have crafted another unique dystopian adventure full of romance, twists, and page-turning excitement.

Grab your copy now!
http://mybook.to/HiveMind

THE THAW CHRONICLES

Tamar Sloan and Heidi Catherine are the authors of the bestselling series, The Thaw Chronicles.

Get your free prequel now!
http://mybook.to/BurningThaw

WANT TO STAY IN TOUCH?

If you'd like to be the first for to hear all the news from Tamar and Heidi, be sure to sign up to our newsletter. Subscribers receive bonus content, early cover reveals and sneaky snippets of upcoming books. We'd love you to join us!

SIGN UP HERE:

https://sendfox.com/tamarandheidi

About the Authors

Tamar Sloan hasn't decided whether she's a psychologist who loves writing, or a writer with a lifelong fascination with psychology. She must have been someone pretty awesome in a previous life (past life regression indicated a Care Bear), because she gets to do both. When not reading, writing or working with teens, Tamar can be found with her husband and two children enjoying country life in their small slice of the Australian bush.

Heidi Catherine loves the way her books give her the opportunity to escape into worlds vastly different to her own life in the burbs. While she quite enjoys killing her characters (especially the awful ones), she promises she's far better behaved in real life. Other than writing and reading, Heidi's current obsessions include watching far too much reality TV with the excuse that it's research for her books.

MORE SERIES TO FALL IN LOVE WITH...

ALSO BY TAMAR SLOAN AND HEIDI CATHERINE

The Thaw Chronicles

ALSO BY TAMAR SLOAN

Keepers of the Grail

Keepers of the Light

Keepers of the Chalice

Keepers of the Excalibur

Zodiac Guardians

Descendants of the Gods

Prime Prophecy

ALSO BY HEIDI CATHERINE

The Kingdoms of Evernow

The Soulweaver

The Woman Who Didn't (written as HC Michaels)

The Girl Who Never (written as HC Michaels)